I0726802

THE HOUSEWIFE ASSASSIN'S GHOST PROTOCOL

JOSIE BROWN

A BOOK BY

SIGNAL PRESS

ONE OF MANY GREAT SIGNAL PRESS BOOKS

San Francisco, CA

Library of Congress Cataloging-in-Publication Data is available upon request

Cover Design by Andrew Brown, ClickTwiceDesign.com

Digital Formatting by Austin Brown, CheapEbookFormatting.com

Trade Paperback ISBN: 978-1-942052-55-5

Hardcover ISBN: 978-1-942052-56-2

V022319

can't wait to read the next in the series. Highly Recommended!"

"This was an addictive read–gritty but funny at the same time. I ended up reading it in just one evening and couldn't go to sleep until I knew what the outcome would be! It was action-packed and humorous from the start, and that continued throughout, I was pleased to discover that this is the first of a series and look forward to getting my hands on Book Two so I can see where life takes Donna and her family next!"

"The two halves of Donna's life make sense. As you follow her story, there's no point where you think of her as "Assassin Donna" vs. "Mummy Donna', her attitude to life is even throughout. I really like how well this is done. And as for Jack. I'll have one of those, please?"

Novels in The Housewife Assassin
Series

The Housewife Assassin's Handbook (Book 1)

The Housewife Assassin's Guide to Gracious Killing (Book 2)

The Housewife Assassin's Killer Christmas Tips (Book 3)

The Housewife Assassin's Relationship Survival Guide (Book 4)

The Housewife Assassin's Vacation to Die For (Book 5)

The Housewife Assassin's Recipes for Disaster (Book 6)

The Housewife Assassin's Hollywood Scream Play (Book 7)

The Housewife Assassin's Killer App (Book 8)

The Housewife Assassin's Hostage Hosting Tips (Book 9)

The Housewife Assassin's Garden of Deadly Delights (Book 10)

The Housewife Assassin's Tips for Weddings, Weapons, and Warfare (Book 11)

The Housewife Assassin's Husband Hunting Hints (Book 12)

The Housewife Assassin's Ghost Protocol (Book 13)

The Housewife Assassin's Terrorist TV Guide (Book 14)

The Housewife Assassin's Deadly Dossier (Book 15: The Series Prequel)

The Housewife Assassin's Greatest Hits (Book 16)

The Housewife Assassin's Fourth Estate Sale (Book 17)

The Housewife Assassin's Horrorscope (Book 18)

Drop Dead Gorgeous

Nobody wants to drop dead.

And yet, for some odd reason, the rest of us are all the more upset when someone young and gorgeous is "taken before her time."

"Why her?" we lament. "She had her whole life ahead of her!"

True that...

Guess not.

On the upside, she also avoided wrinkling and withering into a little old lady—not to mention having her spouse leave her for some young chippy.

She will not feel dismayed on birthdays by those who patronizingly proclaim, brightly if not sincerely, "You don't look a day over (fill in the blank) ha, ha! Everyone, let's give her a big hand..."

I purposely mix metaphors when I say "age before swine."

Should you have the choice to either flame out as a bright young thing, or age honestly and gracelessly, do yourself a favor: choose the latter.

Truth is, the longer they know you, the harder it is to forget you—and that's your true endgame, isn't it?

Dying young is SO overrated.

"Quit gawking." I don't have to move my sunglasses, let alone open my eyes, to chastise my husband, Jack.

"Why would you even assume I'm staring?" Hearing his deep chuckle, I suppress a grin. His question serves as a challenge.

Game on.

"We're on a beach in Biarritz," I remind him. "Of course you're staring at *someone*. Someone who is more than likely topless." With my eyes still closed, I point toward our left. "*C'est-là.*"

Jack shifts in his lounge chair so that he can lift the brim of my hat in order to stare down at me. "How the hell did you know?"

Before opening my eyes, I sigh, then remove my sunglasses and look left.

As I suspected, three comely *filles*, perhaps nineteen or twenty years old, lay on beach blankets a few yards away. One is on her back. Her naked breasts are already reddened by the glaring sun. Another is on her side. The plum of her comely backside, topped with a tramp stamp of entwined hearts and split by a thong, is pointed in our direction.

The third girl, a waifish gamine with white blond hair and a deep tan, is raised in a cobra pose on her beach blanket. Her naked breasts, now gravitationally erect, resemble over-inflated zeppelins flying in tandem.

Even our nineteen year-old cabana boy, Jean-Pierre, pauses the vigorous shaking of our mid-day martini in order to hear my answer.

In all honesty, I had a fifty-fifty chance that Jack was looking left as opposed to right. Luck of the draw. Not that I'll willingly admit it. "Simple deduction. You've been too quiet for much too long. At the same time you haven't turned a page in your book."

"It's *Moby Dick*. It takes at least an hour to fathom each damn paragraph."

"Liar. You were reading—and I use that term lightly—the latest swimsuit edition of *Sports Illustrated*." I glance in the direction of Jean-Pierre. "Admit I'm right, or else I'll ask our manservant to give me another massage."

"Busted," Jack's reluctant apology comes with a sly grin. "Sorry. Poor choice of words."

"I'll write it off to topless-of-mind awareness." I lower my shades so that he can see my wink.

"You know, you could cut me some slack." He too nods toward Jean-Pierre.

I don't mind that Jack thinks the kid has a crush on me. But I know it's because I'm a good tipper, so I shrug. "Done. I do concede, however, that prime beefcake trumps three cream puffs any day."

Up until now, Jean-Pierre has been ignoring the girls. French society's blasé attitude toward nudity has made him immune to their all too obvious attributes. But now that he's taken a better look at them, his face turns bright red—to my relief, not because I've embarrassed him.

"*Merde*! The one at the far end—she is Nicolette Beauchamp!"

"Who?" I ask.

"I am sorry." He shakes off his anger. "She is…an old friend of mine."

As red as his face just turned, I'm sure she is more than that to him still.

He answers my questioning eyes with a shrug. "A long time ago. We were merely *enfants*. In the meantime we've grown up, and apart." He shifts his gaze in her direction. His longing is all too obvious. "Her mother is Martine, a chambermaid here at the hotel. Should she see Nicolette sunbathing *sans un maillot de bain*, she will be—how do you say…livid? Our hotelier looks down his nose on any impertinence from the staff or their families. The guests…" He bites his lips. "Well, one may get the wrong idea, *n'est-ce pas*?"

I nod. "To put it mildly. I know I'd feel the same way if it were my daughter."

Jack picks up a pair of binoculars. "Looks like we have company."

He's right. Just beyond Nicolette yet another super-yacht is jockeying for position amongst the many that dot the calm turquoise waters just a few hundred feet from these golden shores. At four hundred or more feet in length and six bridges high, the ship could be mistaken for a small aircraft carrier, easily dwarfing the other behemoths around it. The bow of the lower bridge has been hollowed out, exposing a swimming pool surrounded by chaises and an outdoor bar.

Scrolled on the stern is its name—*Divide and Conquer*—and its homeport: Antibes.

Jean-Pierre frowns. I can barely make out what he mutters under his breath. However, the phrases *"brûle en l'enfer,"* *"fils de pute,"* and that classic standby, *"merde,"* are all recognizable.

I feel my brow arching. "I take it you know the yacht's owner."

"Oui, Madame. He is a very wealthy Saudi Arabian.'" His sneer comes with an eye roll. "He built that monstrosity over there." He points to a mansion on a cliff over a strip of beach on the right of us.

I shake my head in awe. "Interesting. And I thought that was just another hotel!" An honest mistake, considering that it is larger than any other structure flanking the beach.

"If only, Madame. The citizenry of our little town is… how do you say in English…'up in arms' because he has requisitioned the beach in front of it for his private use. He has an entourage of over a thousand friends and family."

"It looks as if his security detail is a third of it." Jack gazes at the empty wedge of beach sprawled under the rocky shoreline. A battalion of guards are lined up, perpendicular to the shoreline. If anyone attempts to go around them, they are shooed away with batons.

One of the girls—Thong—has also noticed the yacht. She nudges Nipples, who then sits up straight.

The tweet of a cell phone sends Nicolette rolling onto her back. She reaches for her beach bag and reads her text, then raises her sunglasses above her eyes in order to scrutinize the yacht's crew as they ready the onboard helicopter for their boss, a broad-shouldered man in a suit. The whirlwind caused by the helicopter's rotating rudders cause his keffiyeh to flap around his shoulders, but it doesn't deter him from texting on his cell phone.

Nicolette and he seem to tap off simultaneously. The reason for this becomes obvious when she waves at the copter as it hovers over her—and us—before alighting on the concrete deck adjacent to the cordoned-off sand.

She doesn't rise to greet him. Instead, she waits for one of his cronies to fetch her and her friends. Before sashaying off, she tosses on a tight T-shirt. Then she turns and smiles at Jean-Pierre.

He drops his head in defeat.

Nipples follows her. Thong, however, hesitates. She glances over at Jean-Pierre and blushes. Noting his scowl, she still blows him a kiss.

"She's quite beautiful," I point out.

"Gigi Marchand likes to pretend that she is in love with me," Jean-Pierre mutters. "Nicolette and the other girl—Suzette Caron—encourage it."

"And you don't want to play along?" Jack counters.

A ghost of a smile alights on Jean-Pierre's lips. Still, he shakes his head. "We all have our fantasies, eh?" His eyes are drawn to Nicolette and her lover.

So are everyone else's on the beach, for good reason. Their embrace is so erotic that heads of passersby seem to pivot a full three hundred and sixty degrees.

The man finally lets her go in order to lead her and her friends toward the helicopter.

"They aren't going into the grand villa?" I murmur to Jean-Pierre.

Jean-Pierre shakes his head adamantly. "He would not

want his mistress to run into his wife. The yacht is his domain solely. "

"What did you say his name was?" Jack asks.

Jean-Pierre mutters, "al-Sadah."

Jack turns toward me. His stare mirrors mine. Salem Rahmin al-Sadah was a recent titular head of the Quorum, a terrorist funding organization.

He is also recently dead—thanks to *moi*.

Trust me, I had good cause to take him out. He'd plotted to infiltrate an anti-terrorism summit hosted by the president of the United States, Lee Chiffray, in order to murder those in his region who seek peace.

He also tried to rape me on the eve of my wedding. I'd say I owed him a very long good-bye.

Salem could not have survived it. I know, because I watched him die.

Jack lays his hand on my arm. "Probably a brother, or a cousin. Remember, it's a big family."

I shiver, not because of any chill—after all, the sun shines overhead—but because it felt as if someone walked across my grave.

Or crawled out of one.

Just then, the helicopter takes off. It swoops low over us before arcing back over the water toward the yacht.

In its wake, my sunhat flies off, skipping over the sand before landing in the tide.

It floats downstream, toward al-Sadah's palace.

"Oh, hell," I mutter. "It was my favorite. Now it's ruined."

Jack laughs as he takes me by my wrists in order to lift

me off my chaise. "Don't worry. I'll buy you a new one—but not now. It's siesta time."

This is code for our afternoon delight. It is part of a daily ritual.

Our hotel was once a private villa. Its greatest feature is that it is small in comparison to the others along the beach, and that it has a handful of private cabanas staggered along the beach.

Ours juts out over the ocean. During high tide, when the waves slap against the pylons beneath our room, we feel as if we're floating out on the sea.

A large round bed is centered in the room, which is glassed in on three sides. Two face either end of the beach, while the third affords us a straight-on ocean view.

Wall-to-ceiling drapes give us complete privacy from the beach sides, if that is what we desire. We've yet to open them. Needless to say, we've been sleeping like newborns, partying like co-eds during Spring Break, and making love like the newlyweds we are.

So then, why do I feel as if our honeymoon is over?

"You're not here with me," Jack murmurs, despite the fact that I am nestled, naked, in the crook of his arm.

As usual, his intuition is spot on. My mind is a million miles away—in this case, the Beverly Wilshire on the day of my rendezvous with Salem Rahmin al-Sadah. My game plan was to retrieve intel secreted in his ring bearing the crest of the Quorum. His was to dominate me into sexual submission.

I got the ring. He got a bullet to the heart.

Now, I wonder: did Salem survive my kill shot? And, if so, how?

Under normal circumstances, post-coitus isn't the best time for post-op analysis. Still, Jack asked, so in for a dime, in for a dollar. "Hearing the name al-Sadah spooked me, I guess." I lift my head so that I can gauge his reaction to what I say next. "Jack, don't you find it strange that Salem's death was never made public? Why have we never heard a word about it?"

"Acme cleaned up behind us." Hearing the wariness in my tone, he adds, "Would it make you feel better if I called Ryan to confirm?"

"No, no—don't! I mean…well, we've been gone almost two weeks now, and we've held to our vow to stay away from work and home." By the time I've flipped over onto his chest, I've got a smile on my face. "I guess I'm a little bored…not to mention homesick."

Hearing this, his left brow almost hits the ceiling. "Oh, really? Despite having all of Hilldale on twenty-four hour surveillance?"

Okay, he's right. As far as my three children are concerned, I've not exactly gone dark. I'm monitoring Mary, Jeff, and Trisha's comings and goings, as well as those of our legal ward, Evan Martin.

"A parent can never be too diligent." Even to my own ears, my retort sounds a bit defensive. To make my point, I add, "Have you forgotten they're with Aunt Phyllis? It's akin to leaving the craziest inmate in charge of the asylum!"

Jack shrugs. "Granted, she's been lax about the amount

of TV they watch, and the number of video games they're allowed to play—"

"To say nothing about late bedtimes and the number of sleepovers she's allowed," I remind him. "Our home is now Hilldale's teen party central! And let's face it: she turns a blind eye to the obvious attraction between Mary and Evan. Since we've been gone, their flirting has become a full-court press."

"Donna, doll, you're jumping to all kinds of unfounded conclusions—"

"Unfounded?" It's my turn to hike a brow. "They've been sneaking off to the playhouse in the back. It's the only place on the property that doesn't have a webcam." Suddenly, I sit straight up in bed. "Oh, my God! There's a bed in there! Granted, it's only a twin—"

He pulls me back down into his arms. Gently, he puts a finger against my lips. "It's only natural that they feel empathy toward each other. They've both suffered public humiliations: parents who committed heinous crimes, as well as the personal tragedies of a parent's death. In Evan's case, both his father and mother. How many kids their age can say that?"

I flinch, knowing that my mother's fight with terminal breast cancer still haunts me. I was only eleven when she died.

Noting my reaction, Jack traces the curve of my face with his index finger. He has always been tender with me after lovemaking. But since his escape from Mexico, sadness deepens his already dark green eyes.

I concede with a nod. "You're right. I'm overreacting. I guess I'm antsy because I'm not use to just being...well, *happy."* I sigh. "I'm always waiting for the other shoe to drop."

Jack's kidnapping, on the night of our nuptials, almost killed us, and I mean that quite literally. While his sadistic captor pitted him in a series of death matches against other prisoners, I was at the beck and call of another of the Quorum's notorious leaders, Eric Weber.

Eric promised to release Jack if I followed through on a series of tasks that, when completed, would have marked me as a domestic terrorist. I did the tasks, but I had help. My team at Acme Industries shadowed my every move so that any intel I passed was black propaganda, and the kidnapping of an aeronautic scientist working on a top secret government project was extracted into WITSEC—the US Marshall's Witness Security Program.

Granted, there was one screw-up: my final mission was to exterminate my boss, Ryan Clancy.

Eric's directive was delivered at a time when I was naked, both in the Biblical sense and in the vernacular of our business—that is to say, I had no backup, and therefore no way to warn Ryan that I'd be gunning for him.

To save Jack, the hit had to take place.

So, yeah, I killed my boss and mentor.

As it turns out, Acme had my room bugged. Without my knowledge, Ryan's death was faked. I would say "all's well that ends well" except for the fact that despite jumping through all those hoops, I still almost lost Jack, both physically and emotionally.

Never again.

"I'll be damned if I'm going to spend the rest of our honeymoon reliving the worst day of our lives." If Jack's vow echoes my very thoughts, his actions speak louder than words. He kisses me: first, fiercely; but soon his actions become a drawn out achingly gentle game of touch and feel.

He's in it to win it.

He gains big points as his lips slide down my neck and between my breasts. There, he pauses for a moment. His eyes shifting to my right breast, then to the left, like a kid who has landed on a Candy Land game board and doesn't know which way to turn.

The left proves the luckier of the two.

His mouth seems to swallow it whole. Instinctively, I brace for the tingle due to come from the feel of his tongue on my nipple. Soon, I'm moaning from the pleasure of his touch. But in no time he has circled back down into the valley of my bosom and over to my right breast, licking my nipple until it too goes taut.

His lips meander. The stubble on his cheek tickles the slight swell of my belly. He takes my frenzied groan as the signal to quit teasing me.

He's right. It's time for the main event.

As Jack enters me, his body, cantilevered by his thick muscled arms, hovers over mine.

His eyes open wide in rapturous adoration. The late afternoon sun's rays, streaming through the undulating curtains, fan out behind his head, crowning him with a halo.

Am I imagining it? No. He is my protector.

The one true love of my life.

My angel.

His thrusts, steady and deep, fill my heart with joy. As Jack's ecstasy swells within me, all thoughts scatter from my mind, like crispy leaves whipped out of reach by a brisk autumn gale.

Finally, spent, he shudders as he collapses onto me.

We lay there for some time, chest to breast. His heart pulsates in tandem with mine.

As it should be.

Always.

If only.

A SCREAM WAKES US FROM OUR POST-COITAL SLUMBER.

The wailing doesn't stop, but only gets louder, more agitated. A moment later, voices are raised in raucous accusations.

The chorus of shouts also gets louder as time goes by.

Jack groans. Still, he unfurls his arms and legs from me in order to ease himself from our bed. His small nod to modesty is to open the curtain only partially, in order to view the ruckus.

It is evening. Right now the only light is coming off the super yachts. The glow, mirrored in still waters, casts long shadows on the man who still thrills me. It darkens his soulful eyes, heightens his cheekbones, and etches the sinews of his muscular physique. If his curls were alabaster instead of naturally dark brown, I'd swear he was a sculpture by Michelangelo.

My newly piqued lust quickly dissipates under the singsong blare of police sirens. I leap out of bed, too, scooping up a fallen robe and wrapping it around me before joining Jack at the window.

From what I can tell, a crowd has gathered on the beach a mere hundred yards from our terrace. Police officers seem to have taken control, shooing away the gawkers.

"A drowning?" I wonder out loud.

I've barely had time to take note of the action when we hear a rap on our door. I tie my robe tight around my middle while Jack slips into loose sweat pants and a T-shirt. When I see he's fully clothed, I open the door.

Two policemen face us. Jean-Pierre stands between them. He is wet and smeared with sand. Tears and fear brighten his red-rimmed eyes.

What the hell is going on?

"*Oui, les agents?*" Jack's nonchalance doesn't betray his own shock and awe.

As he asks, the nose of the older and bulkier of the two officers twitches. Perhaps he has noted our post-coital musk. "*Pardonnez-nous*, Monsieur and Madame Craig. May we have a moment of your time?" Switching to English is a courtesy proffered by most public servants along the French coastline, which is heavily trafficked by British and American tourists.

"But of course." Having lived in this country for many years, Jack's French is excellent, but for my benefit, he responds likewise. He leans forward in order to read the officer's nametag. Noting it, he nods. "How may we help you, Captain Duclos?"

The younger officer hides his smirk in a cough. Perhaps it has something to do with Jack's generous promotion for his partner, a mere beat cop.

"Jean-Pierre Gambon claims he has spent the last few hours here, with you. Can you confirm this?" Duclos's way to silence Jean-Pierre before he says anything is to clamp his hand so hard on our cabana boy's shoulder that he winces.

Jack looks to me, then to Jean-Pierre.

Jean-Pierre's eyes say it all: *Help me.*

Before Jack opens his mouth, I purr, "He gives wonderful massages, Captain. You should try one some time."

Duclos's response to my suggestion is a wary glare. "This is not a joking matter, Madame. Jean-Pierre was found on the beach, clinging to the body of a dead woman: Nicolette Beauchamp."

Jack's smile fades. "But—if she has drowned, why detain Jean-Pierre?"

Duclos shakes his head. "Drowned? *Non.* She was stran- gled. The coroner will soon determine the time of death." Duclos turns to me. "I ask you again, Madame: when exactly did you receive your massage?"

Jean-Pierre's mouth gapes open, but nothing comes out. His eyes implore me to save him.

To believe him.

For some reason, I do. When Jean-Pierre looked at Nico- lette, his eyes were filled with adoration. With love.

And, sadly, regret.

He has so much more to regret now.

"Jack's massage was first. It ran over an hour, didn't it, Jack?" I turn innocently to my husband.

His eyebrow arches. Still, he nods his head. "Yours was immediately afterward. And about the same amount of time." His tone leaves no room for doubt.

The younger officer takes a pad from his pocket and scribbles this down.

Duclos scowls. "Again, Monsieur, what time were these massages?"

"Well…" Jack looks skyward, as if searching his memory. "Jean-Pierre left only, say, a half hour before the sirens began."

"And only because I asked him to walk out onto the beach. I'd misplaced my sun hat. It's black, with a white band around the rim," I add. I tilt my head in Jean-Pierre's direction. "By the way, did you find it?"

Slowly, Jean-Pierre shakes his head. Still stunned, he says nothing.

Inspector Duclos is no idiot. He realizes his number one suspect has not just one alibi, but two. His grip loosens on Jean-Pierre. With a tip to the brim of his hat, he growls, "Good night, Madame and Monsieur."

"Wait! Officer, aren't you going to ask us what we might know about Nicolette's whereabouts?"

This stops Duclos in his tracks. "*Oui*, Madame. And what may that be?"

"Late this afternoon, the young lady was sunbathing beside us, along with two of her friends. When a humongous yacht dropped anchor, they ran over to the owner's helicopter and flew back to it with him—what is his name again? You know, the Middle-Eastern gentleman that owns the big pink monstrosity on the hill?"

The color drains from Duclos's face. "Salem al-Sadah?"

So, it is Salem after all.

But how could that be?

"Yes, that's the man," I assure him. "She welcomed him on the beach. Everyone around saw it. In fact, she was talking to him on his phone as his helicopter landed beside us. I remember this because I lost my hat because of it."

"I'm sure what my wife said can be verified by Mademoiselle Beauchamp's cell phone records," Jack adds. "Since Mr. al-Sadah may have been the last person to see her alive, why don't you start your investigation there?"

Duclos's lips pucker at this new information, and no wonder. If what Jean-Pierre said earlier—that the local police are paid to look the other way at al-Sadah's indiscretions—I assume he's not too eager to poke at that bear.

Well, too bad. It beats blaming an innocent man.

Finally, Duclos shrugs. "The gentleman is having a private party on his yacht, as we speak. A masked ball! But of course tomorrow morning we will inquire as to any such rendezvous."

"Mr. al-Sadah does not like to be bothered before noon," Duclos's partner reminds him. "In fact, the captain mentioned that the *Divide and Conquer* leaves port early in the morning."

His honesty earns him a scowl from Duclos.

"Seriously, you're just going to let him float away?" I taunt him. "You have a dead woman on your hands—for that matter, maybe more than one. Nicolette's friends accompanied her and al-Sadah. Have you questioned them? What will you do if two more bodies end up on the beach?"

"If you're implying that Mr. al-Sadah had anything to do with this tragedy, I assure you, Madame, nothing could be further from the truth."

Jack steps so close to Duclos that they are face to face. "You don't know if you don't ask."

Shame rises in a red blush on Duclos's face. Still, he says nothing.

"If you'll excuse us, now, it's the cocktail hour." Jack nods toward the suite's fully stocked bar. He takes out a twenty-euro note and sticks it in top left pocket of Duclos's jacket. "Thanks for returning our cabana boy. If we can think of anything else you may want to ignore, we'll be sure to give you a call."

I link one arm into Jean-Pierre's in order to draw him inside the room. The other arm firmly closes the door behind us.

"They thought I killed Nicolette. Don't they realize..." Jean-Pierre stares at the door as if he expects the long arm of the law to punch its way back in and pull him out.

"That you love her? A crime of passion always provides a possible suspect, Jean-Pierre. But you didn't kill her." Jack's tone insists that Jean-Pierre confirm this.

"*Mais non,* Monsieur! You must believe me!"

I pat his arm. "We do, Jean-Pierre. And since we are now your official alibi, you must tell us the truth about your whereabouts since we left you this afternoon, up until you were found with Nicolette on the beach."

He thinks for a moment. "The concierge told me there had been a request I retrieve the suitcase for another guest from his room and take it to the luggage room. The man was checking out soon. When I took the bag from him, I mentioned I was also the hotel's masseur. He asked that I accommodate him after dropping off the bag. Of course, I did."

"Then this guest could contradict us as to your where-abouts," I point out.

"No! He has...what I mean to say is..." He runs his fingers through his thick curly blond hair. "He will be... discreet. He has too much to lose."

"I see."

Jean-Pierre shakes his head. "It is not what you think at all! You see, he too does not want others to know he is here. He is spying on his wife, who is here with her lover." He shrugs. "Then again, he was here with his lover."

"How very French," I murmur.

"Not at all," Jean-Pierre replies. "From his accent, he could be Austrian."

The joke is on me, I guess. "What is the man's name?"

"Smith. John Smith."

"An old Austrian moniker if I ever heard one." Jack shakes his head. "How did you end up on the beach beside the body?"

"After Monsieur Smith's massage, his lover requested one as well. In the meantime, he went for a walk on the beach. When he returned he realized he'd taken off his sunglasses while watching the sunset. Because they were running late to catch their flight, he asked me to retrieve them. I found them a few meters from where Nicolette lay." He takes the glasses out of his pocket and holds them up. "I would have mentioned them to the police, but while I was being questioned, I noticed their limousine drive off." He hesitates then adds, "It was an imposition to use your names, but I had no choice! You can see this, *oui*?"

"*Oui*," I mutter. "How convenient that his glasses were practically in the exact spot as Nicolette's body."

Jean-Pierre's eyes open wide. "Do you believe he had anything to do with her death?"

"It is an obvious coincidence," Jack concedes. "Tell us, Jean-Pierre: what did Monsieur Smith look like?"

Jean-Pierre thinks a moment. "He is a short man, and almost bald. His manner is a bit nervous. Surprisingly, despite the temperature, he chose to wear a wool suit. He also wears glasses—the ones that are circular in shape and tortoise shell in style."

At that moment, there is a knock on the door.

I open it. A bellhop hands me a suitcase. *"Pour Monsieur Craig. Compliments d'un vieil ami."*

"This was sent from an old friend?" I turn to Jack. "But no one knows we're here. Were you expecting anything?"

He shakes his head.

The bellhop shrugs and walks away, leaving me holding the bag.

And it's ticking.

What the…

Jack hears it too. He grabs it out of my hand and runs toward the door leading out onto the terrace.

Shocked, I watch as he slings the case with all his might toward the sea.

It drops into the water—

Just in the nick of time. Still, the explosion deafens us.

A tidal wave hits us. Jean-Pierre and I are thrown backward, like rag dolls.

My head slams into the wall. Before I pass out, the last thing I remember is Jack flying through the air toward me.

My angel.

2

Ghost Story

Everyone has at least one ghost story.

Perhaps yours includes a relative, not long deceased, who rose from the dead in order to give you some cryptic message that still stymies you to this day. (You can't wait to run into her again in the netherworld, if only to discover what the hell she was talking about.)

Or maybe you spent the night in some haunted hostelry, only to discover that your suite came equipped with a king bed, free HBO, a mini-bar, and its very own apparition!

Yada, yada, yada—we've heard it all before. If you really want to impress us, you're going to have to embellish your own tale from the crypt with some hair-raising anecdotes. Here's how.

First, come up with a bigger, badder spook. A run-in with Casper the Friendly Ghost is a snore.

Next, ratchet up the suspense. Set the mood and build to the actual sighting. In other words, do whatever it takes to get them to lean in, listen up, and freak out.

And finally, make it a happily ever after—for you, not the ghost.

~

"DONNA…DONNA, PLEASE, *WAKE UP*!" JACK'S ANXIOUS PLEAS rouse me from my black oblivion.

My eyelids flutter open to find his face hovering over mine. Concern for me is etched deeply in his brow.

There is a bruise on his forehead. When I touch it, he flinches.

I shake my head, angered that I've hurt him. Droplets fall onto my shoulders. I shiver at the memory of the wave that washed over me. Then I realize I'm shaking because I'm wet. Oh, my God—it wasn't a bad dream after all.

"When the wave hit me, I slammed into you," Jack explains. "We knocked heads."

"Ouch! I'm sorry, Jack." Instinctively, I reach up again, but I stop myself just in time. Jean-Pierre! Is he…"

"I am here, Madame." I turn to find Jean-Pierre sitting on a chair behind us. He holds a damp compress over his eye. "There is much damage to the room. All of your things are ruined."

I frown. "It's the least of my worries. Someone wanted to kill us. I'd like to find out why." I rummage through the ruins of our room for something to put on that isn't sopping wet. As luck would have it, a pair of my shorts are hanging off a torchiere lamp. I salvage that, along with one of Jack's button-down shirts hanging in the closet, and then snap my fingers at Jean-Pierre, indicating that he is to turn around while I dress.

He obliges with a blush.

Not Jack. He flops down on the bed, which was pushed by the wave against the back wall, and takes in the view—me, as opposed to the shoreline. "If we're going to catch Mr. Smith, first we have to know what he looks like. Jean-Pierre, what are the chances of us viewing archival footage from the hotel's security cameras?"

"I will take you there now. At least once a week I am asked to relieve the hotel's security guard; therefore, I'm allowed to access it."

The only shoes I can find are heels, so hey, they will have to do. But before I can bend down to strap my foot into it, Jack is kneeling at my side. Without a word, he takes it out of my hand. Gently, he places my foot into it.

When he feels the touch of my finger behind his ear, he looks up at me. There is no smile on his face, just adoration.

He is my Prince Charming.

More importantly, he is my life partner.

Yes, I trust him with my life.

My fairy tale spell is broken when Jean-Pierre beckons me from the door. "This way, Madame."

The honeymoon is officially over.

"It can't be him," Jack murmurs.

A chill goes up my spine. "Who is it?"

"Pinky Ring." Jack is so shocked that he lowers himself into a chair.

I've never seen him so awestruck. I touch his arm to

bring him back to the here and now. "I...I don't know who you mean."

"He's a former East German Stasi colonel who was recruited by the Quorum. I chased him down years ago, in London. When he came west, he hid under an alias. Acme never discovered what it was." Jack frowns. "I watched as he was hit by a bus and then again by a car. By the time I got to him, he was dead. I took his Quorum ring. It contained intel about the Los Angeles attack that put us together." He freezes the video frame before leaning in for a closer look. "Looks like he's gotten ahold of another ring." He points to the man's hand.

The ring is the twin of one I took off Salem: bling given to only the highest-ranking members of the Quorum. Unlike Salem, who wore it on his right ring finger, this man wears his on the smallest finger of his right hand.

Salem died, as did this man. So, how could it be that we're seeing them now?

The man is exactly as Jean-Pierre described him: short, fidgety, and immaculately, albeit inappropriately, dressed for Biarritz's sweltering climate.

On the other hand, the posh woman with him would turn heads in any part of the world. A white sundress drapes her tanned, slim body, which glides along on her four-inch heels as if floating on a cloud. Unfortunately for us, she wears large sunglasses and a hat that covers her hair, obscuring any obvious identifying features.

Still, there is something familiar about her.

After the couple is given their suite's security key by the desk clerk, they make their way onto the beach path that leads to the cabanas.

"I think I know her—but I can't put my finger on it," I point out to Jack. "How about you?"

"You're right. I wish we had a better shot of her. Jean-Pierre, can you move to a different security feed?"

With a click of a button, we watch as they reach the door to their cabana. As it turns out, it's just two away from ours.

Pinky Ring's hand alights on the woman's shoulder. She shrugs it off.

All this time the bellboy has been waiting patiently behind them, suitcases in tow. His mouth rises into a smirk.

Angered that the bellboy witnessed the rebuff, Pinky Ring waits until the bellman puts their bags into the room before tipping him at the door: a single Euro.

The bellman waits until the door closes, then proffers the greatest insult: hitting his bicep with a Spanish slap.

And yes, the valise that held the bomb was among Pinky Ring's things.

Case closed.

Jack shakes his head, still stunned. Finally, he turns to Jean-Pierre. "This is the footage where they arrive at the hotel, am I right?"

"*Oui,* Monsieur."

Jack taps Jean-Pierre on the shoulder. "Pull up the security camera at the time of their departure."

Jean-Pierre nods. It takes a few moments to find the approximate timestamp in the feed, but soon he has it up.

Pinky Ring has changed into a tuxedo. However, he is sunburned looking now, much like a lobster plucked from the sea. He trails his lady friend down the steps of the hotel, toward the curb.

Both he and his date wear Venetian facemasks. Her beige armless skintight sheath is sheer, but a spray of diamonds meanders over her breasts and down the center of the dress, front and back, providing some semblance of modesty. It also has a high slit on either side. Her head is wrapped in a matching turban, obscuring any idea of her hair color or its length.

There is certainly something familiar about her. I wish I could put my finger on it…

The bellman struggles with their bags. The one holding the bomb is not among them.

A limo pulls up. The driver jumps out in order to hold the door for the couple, then pops the trunk so that the bellman can stow their bags.

This time, the bellman gets nary a farthing for his efforts.

He lifts his right hand. Two of its fingers are raised into a backward V: the international symbol for "vuck off."

They drive off, but slow when they are level to the ruckus on the beach. Jean-Pierre frowns at the thought that he may have been set up.

The limo goes another half-mile before turning left onto a cross street. I tap the screen. "There! Why didn't they turn right, toward the airport?"

"Good point," Jack murmurs. "Jean-Pierre, where does the left side of the street take them?"

"To the beach pier."

Jack grimaces. "So that they can access a taxi yacht, to go to, say, the party on the *Divide and Conquer?*"

I smile. "I've always wanted to crash one of Biarritz's renowned society soirees."

"But not this one, Madame! The women who attend are strictly there for the pleasure of Monsieur al-Sadah and a select group of his friends, all of whom have '*la dependence amoureuse.*'"

"A love addiction?" Jack's mouth draws into a smirk.

I can't help but laugh out loud. "When it comes to al-Sadah, I know how to nip it in the bud." With, say, another bullet. This time, in the head. It may be messier, but there should be no doubting the result.

Jean-Pierre shakes his head. "I am putting it politely. Every guest brings a *putain*. She is expected to…er, 'perform,' either with the gentleman whom she accompanies, or another guest of his choosing."

"Orgies?" I try not to laugh. "How perfectly retro!" Well, if that's the case, my shorts and a T-shirt won't get me any further than the gangplank. "If we're going to crash Salem's party, all I need right now is a gown."

"You plan on attending?" The question comes at me from both Jack and Jean-Pierre.

"Nicolette was last seen heading for the *Divide and Conquer*. Her friends may still be there. And now Jack's pal, Pinky Ring, is on his way there too. When all roads lead to Rome, why not? I assume the hotel's couture salon is already closed?"

"Yes! I have a key, if you want to make a purchase." Jean-Pierre looks confused.

"Can you also get us into the hotel's pharmacy?" Jack asks.

Jean-Pierre nods.

"Good, because we'll need a few syringes, and some Rohypnol. If we're going to bring them to justice, we have to take them alive"—Jack grins—"but not necessarily conscious. When they wake up, we'll get our answers as to how they rose from the dead."

Jean-Pierre scowls. "If this man—Pinky Ring—is a friend of Monsieur al-Sadah, he will never be brought to justice! As you saw for yourself, the police here bow and scrape to billionaires."

Jack pats his arm. "Both men are international terrorists. Their crimes are numerous." Turning to me, Jack adds, "I'm calling Ryan to tell him that we'll be facing off with a couple of dangerous suspects. I'm sure his move will be to alert Interpol for back-up."

"If what Inspector Clouseau—I mean Duclos said is true, al-Sadah is shipping out in the morning; we've got to move fast, with or without back-up," I remind him.

"But, if one of those men killed Nicolette..." Jean-Pierre's eyes open wide. "Madame, you must not be left alone with either of them!"

"Don't worry, Jean-Pierre; Donna can more than take care of herself. And besides, I'll have her back." Jack puts his arm around me.

"So will I." Jean-Pierre's face hardens with resolve. He turns to me. "If it will help to find your *fantôme* and bring Monsieur Smith to justice for Nicolette's murder, I will make sure you get on that yacht."

He grabs the keys we need from the hotel manager's desk and we're off.

JACK DIALS RYAN'S PHONE NUMBER. GOODBYE TO ANY MORE mindless sun-filled days spent sipping great martinis while making slow, intoxicating love.

Do we really need to poke the hornet's nest of reality?

Too late. Ryan picks up with a click. "Why the call, when you've got another seventy-two hours of nuptial bliss coming to you?" His words are playful, but I detect a bit of wariness in his voice.

He knows us too well.

"We've stumbled into a situation here, boss," Jack replies.

Ryan sighs. "If I remember correctly, the last time you were in the south of France, the 'situation' involved three blondes, a chimpanzee, and a lobby boy from the Cannes de Croissette."

Well, this little never-before-divulged tidbit in Jack's past has certainly gotten my full attention.

Jack turns bright red. "Um…yeah, well, this is a bit more serious than that." I guess he realizes that if there was ever a time to change the topic it's now. "By coincidence, we've sighted a couple of apparitions."

Ryan is silent for too long. Finally: "We must have a bad connection. Could you repeat that?"

"Dead men walking—two, to be precise: Salem al-Sadah and Pinky Ring."

"What the…No way in hell! Jack, you were there at both exterminations, and Donna was there for one of them as well!" Even with an ocean and a continent separating us, I can easily envision Ryan's reaction to our unwelcome news: lumbering back and forth in front of his mirrored window walls while running his hand through the invisible hair on his long-bald head. "This isn't the Day of the Dead!"

"Ryan, trust me, if we hadn't seen this with our own eyes…" I hate that my voice trembles as I say this. "An Acme crew did Salem's wet work. I presume they confirmed the kill before fixing it to look like natural causes."

"Affirmative." Ryan still sounds shocked as he mulls over the possible repercussions to this predicament.

"At some point, Salem's body had to have been discovered by his bodyguards, am I right?" Jack asks.

Ryan thinks for a moment. "We broke the news to POTUS the very next day—your wedding day. Salem's family departed POTUS's West Coast compound immediately. But now that you mention it, I don't remember a formal announcement, either through diplomatic channels, or in the media." There is a rustling sound on Ryan's end as he covers the phone with his hand. It barely mutes his muffled yell: "Emma! Pull up everything you can on Salem al-Sadah since his untimely demise—and then get in here pronto. Bring Arnie with you!"

Emma Honeycutt Locklear handles our mission team's communications intelligence. Her husband, Arnie, heads up tech ops. As always, glad they have our backs.

It's time that someone shed more light on the man of the hour. "What about this Pinky Ring person's body?" I ask. "Do we know where it ended up?"

"A pauper's grave, somewhere outside of London, if I remember correctly," Ryan replies. "Your illustrious British team member, Dominic Fleming, is there now, to receive the Order of the Bath. I'll get him to verify the death and burial, and pull DNA samples that can be tested in Acme's lab."

"A knighthood? *That wanker*?" Jack is practically stuttering.

"He's got to have something on one of the Royals," I mutter, just loud enough for Jack to hear me. In any event, it's time to get this show on the road. "Ryan, the party on the *Divide and Conquer* is taking place now. With your blessing, we'll infiltrate Salem's shindig—and if necessary, we'll secure the suspects."

"Do it," Ryan commands. "But have your cellphones with you at all times. That way, Arnie can use your phones' GPS to track you. He can also hot mic them too, so we can listen in. If one of you gets in trouble, we'll relay intel to the other."

"If you can get ahold of a couple of mini Bluetooths, we'll be able to give you voice commands," Emma points out.

"Good thought," Jack replies.

"I've pulled up the *Divide and Conquer*'s deck plan," Arnie announces. "There are two diesel and two electric motors coupled with gas turbines. Its hull holds a Bentley Azure T and a Hummer, as well as a Hustler 41Razor speed-boat. Hey well, whattaya know? Salem's super yacht also has Green Star certification because its design gives it low power consumption and reduced emissions—"

Emma snorts at this. "One of the world's biggest arms dealers is into saving the planet? Horse hockey." She pauses then adds, "Hey, do you think you can get a computer close enough to the superyacht's WiFi? If so, we may be able to hack its security system in order to guide you through the ship, and to monitor Salem's guards."

"*Pardonez moi*, Mademoiselle Emma," Jean-Pierre chimes

in. "I bring my laptop with us on the hotel's yacht. You could guide me from there on how to do so."

"*Merci beaucoup*, Jean-Pierre," Emma purrs.

"Donna, since more than likely you'll be apprehending Salem, please remember: we can't get intel from a dead man," Ryan warns me.

In other words, bring the suspects in alive.

Like Pinky Ring's and his date's, the masks Jack and I choose hide only our eyes.

Mine is gold lamé, like the slip of a dress I now wear: sheer, tight, backless, with a front slit that leaves little to the imagination.

I've chosen a short platinum blond wig, the exact color and cut of Nicolette's gamine bob. My goal is to elicit a double-take or two—from her lover, and her killer.

Are they one and the same? I'm bound and determined to find out.

Has my most recent nemesis come back to life? It's yet another question I hope to have answered tonight.

I spot a gold lamé wristlet clutch that matches the dress. I slip three syringes filled with Rohypnol and my cellphone into it, nodding to Jean-Pierre to indicate that he should put it on our tab...

I guess I should look at the price tag—

Over a thousand dollars?

Yowza.

Solution...

Got it! I'll put it on my Acme expense report.

Granted, Ryan will go into cardiac arrest, but hey, the clutch matches the dress so it's a must-have, right?

Besides, if I bring Salem and Pinky Ring in alive, he'll be only too happy to let me keep it.

Considering that both targets have proven to be difficult to kill off in the first place, that shouldn't be so hard.

3

Body Parts

When you're dead, you may not care that biomedical companies wouldn't mind getting a piece of you: specifically, your skin and bones.

And because they offer around a thousand dollars for some of either, your family might be interested too. (A good reason to stipulate in your will that every inch of you is laid to rest before your estate is distributed to your greedy little beneficiaries.)

By the way, while you're alive, it is legal to sell off some of your body parts.

These figures are at the very top of the market, so if you're in need of a little cash, you may want to consider parting with some regenerative...er, parts, such as blood ($120), hair ($3,000), plasma ($4,800), sperm ($12,000), ovarian eggs ($24,000), and bone marrow ($18,000).

There is also a market for breast milk ($23,000) and (prepare to gag...or better yet, bag) feces ($13,000).

However, the big bucks go for certain organs that are illegal to *sell. Case in point: kidneys go for as much as $200,000 per on the black market in many countries, including the United States.*

Now, ask yourself, is the money truly worth it? I mean, God forbid, should the twin of the sold organ fail, where would that leave you?

The sad but true answer: resting in pieces.

JEAN-PIERRE DOCKS THE HOTEL'S FORTY-NINE-FOOT FERRETTI 480 alongside the *Divide and Conquer's* gangplank. With the party already underway, there is no line to speak of: just a couple of male guests, dressed in tuxedos, who are accompanied by breathtakingly gorgeous paid escorts.

"This is a lot bigger than the yacht POTUS wanted to sell to Salem," I mutter. I know this because I was on Salem's tour of the vessel while it was docked outside of President Lee Chiffray's bayside villa on Balboa Island, California.

Salem passed on the yacht. Instead, he propositioned me.

Jack claims that it was exactly what Lee wanted all along.

I beg to differ. In any event, it gave me an opportunity to abscond with Salem's ring—something worn by all leaders of the Quorum. Underneath its crest was intel on his plan to infiltrate the summit.

Jack bumps into one of the men who is much too busy frisking his date for any hidden treasure that might be stowed where the sun don't shine to notice my husband's sleight of hand inside Frisky's jacket pocket.

Jack's prize: the invitation that will get us beyond Salem's goon squad.

Jack proffers the invitation to one of the goombahs, who

checks it against the guest manifest before offering Jack a small clear packet of tiny beige pills. Jack takes it in stride, slipping it into the upper inside pocket of his tuxedo.

The dude also hands me a filled champagne flute. I smile slyly as I take it.

We saunter into the party while Frisky argues with one of the security detail over his right to join the rest of the Masters of the Universe on the Good Ship al-Sadah.

Jean-Pierre sails off, but not too far. He kills the engine and his lights while still close enough to grab the *Divide & Conquer's* WiFi signal. I've noticed that he's in a very dark mood. I think it's finally dawned on him that Nicolette is gone forever.

Nothing we can do will bring her back.

If only the same could have been said for Salem and this Pinky Ring guy.

FROM MY OWN INTIMATE KNOWLEDGE OF SALEM, THIS PARTY IS his best wet dream come true.

On the middle level in the yacht's three-story ballroom, a female deejay, nude except for a *Hello Kitty* mask and sky-high platform pumps, is gyrating to Beyoncé's *Formation*, as if it's the perfect national anthem for all the women onboard—

As if being at a john's beck and call is the epitome of female empowerment.

The yacht is filled with wall-to-wall bodies, most of which are in some form of slap-and-tickle clinch if not outright public fornication.

The women have made it easy for their dates, having shed their clothing along with their inhibitions. Only masks and heels remain.

Apparently, voyeurism is also a big a turn-on to this crowd. Those who don't partake in the amoral antics have no qualms in watching and gauging the joy, pain, and ecstasy of others.

I'm about to take a sip of champagne when Jack takes it out of my hand. "Something is off," he mutters. "Look at the women."

He's right. These ladies are much too placid. Some are so limp that they are barely standing up on their own. Their masks can't conceal the blank gazes in their eyes.

They have been drugged.

Jack slips the champagne flute onto the tray of waiter inching his way through the crowd.

Considering how many men are popping pills from their tiny swag packets, they must be drugged too—but whatever they've taken gives them the opposite effect. Granted, sexual desire is always a strong motivator. But these guys think nothing of grabbing, pinching, and rubbing any body part within reach.

When you have enough money to match your libido, partnerships are easily renegotiated. One woman is interchangeable with the next. We watch as one guy actually tosses in his Bulgari Magsonic Tourbillon to sweeten the deal.

"Gee, what a sport," Jack growls.

We may not be putting on a show, but we're being watched.

I look at the top deck to see that Salem al-Sadah's eyes roam the crowd below him.

Yes, I am positive it is he. I'd recognize that face anywhere: dark skin, the arched nose flanked on each side by high, sharp cheekbones. As tall as he is, his straight-backed stance gives him a regal air.

Evil should not be so handsome.

How is it that he is still alive?

He has an arm around two women with long auburn hair —twins, who are naked except for the strands of pearls around their necks. While the woman on his left fondles his nipple underneath his dress shirt, the one on the right kisses his neck.

The lascivious smile fades at the sight of me. His look is that of shock and anger. As his deep-set eyes drill into me, a shiver of dread runs up my spine.

He thinks I am she: Nicolette.

Obviously, he's not too happy that Pinky Ring failed to terminate her.

With an imperious wave of his hand, he signals me to come to him.

My response is a slight shake of my head as I whisper, "Come and get me."

He pops a pill, then makes his way down the grand stair-case, dragging the pouting girls with him.

Jack's poker face conceals the concern I hear in his voice: "I'll shadow. But Donna, be careful."

"You don't have to ask twice," I promise him.

Jack wraps a proprietary arm around my waist. Together, we wait for the inevitable: Salem's proposition.

~

"AH...I DON'T KNOW YOU AFTER ALL." SALEM'S PROCLAMATION does not ring of disappointment. "But perhaps I should." Taking my hand, he kisses it on the knuckles before turning it over. Salem's tongue rolls from my palm and up my wrist. When he turns his head to watch my reaction, he asks, "Would you like me to do more of that?"

What I remember about Salem is that he likes a conquest. "Thank you, but I have a date for the evening." I wipe Salem's spittle on my palm onto the back of one of the twins.

Salem laughs heartily at this. However, his acknowledgement to Jack is no more than a cursory bow as he growls, "We've never met."

Jack smiles at Salem, but he knows better than to hold out his hand. "Allan Woodcourt."

So, Frisky's real name, on the invitation Jack swiped, is the same as a character in *Bleak House.* Go figure.

"Ah, yes, of Brandon and Lyle! Your investment firm is interested in financing Graffias Industries' latest product, is it not, Mr. Woodcourt?" Salem's eyes stay on me, even as he addresses Jack. "And yet, Mr. Brandon could not be here for our private launch party? This disappoints me greatly."

Jack takes this and runs with it. "It could not be avoided, Mr. al-Sadah. He sends his regrets, and me in his stead."

"As well as this lovely lady to accompany you." Salem's finger traces the curve of my jaw. "Mr. Brandon is quite thoughtful indeed."

Although Jack's eyes harden, his smile doesn't waver. "This is my associate, Honoria Dedlock."

You've got to love a man who knows his Dickens.

Despite Salem's frosty demeanor, the Doublemint Twins' reactions to Jack are much friendlier. One licks her lips at him, as if he's dessert. The other drapes herself over one of his shoulders. Her fingers are undoing his tie.

Jack ignores her. His eyes never once leave Salem, as if daring him to stare back.

"While I take your, er, 'associate' on a tour of my yacht, Sophie and Isabelle are sure to provide you with an interesting diversion."

"Thanks, but I'd like to take that tour too." Jack's steely tone implies he won't take no for an answer. "What's the old saying? Oh yeah: 'when it comes to yachts, it's not just the size that matters.' I'll bet this ocean-going beauty is tricked out with some interesting gear."

Salem is not used to being dismissed—and in front of women, no less. Rage darkens his face. He takes a step forward—

And so do I. My move puts me between Jack and Salem. I slide close enough to Salem to imitate the move I saw one of the twins make earlier, that is, to tweak his nipple under his tuxedo jacket. "Allan, I don't mind. I'm sure you won't mind a little change of pace, too." I lean over and give Jack a long, lingering kiss.

When I pull back, I'm smiling. I can't afford to let the worry in Jack's face be reflected in mine—not if we're to complete our mission and bring Salem to justice.

Besides, I've got Acme backing me up. And the first chance I get, Salem gets pricked with the Roofie-filled syringe.

Jack knows this. It's why he doesn't punch Salem in the gut when our host steers me toward the grand staircase.

Isabelle and Sophie set upon Jack like wolves on a sacrificial lamb. He does his best to keep his eyes on me, but can't for more than a few quick moments as the crowd envelops us.

I DON'T THINK JACK SEES IT WHEN SALEM DETOURS US TO THE right of the staircase, into an alcove. It holds an elevator. He pulls a tiny brass key from his tuxedo pocket and turns it in the lock beside the elevator. It opens silently.

Before I know it, he shoves me inside, and against the back wall.

His mouth grinds into mine. I try to push him off, but he slaps me across the face so hard that my head ricochets off the wall, knocking the tiny Bluetooth out of my ear.

It pings as it hits the floor, but he's too busy fondling me to hear it.

Sadly, I'm too far away to grab it. Still, I struggle as hard as I can to free myself, but Salem seems to have the strength of three men. With one broad forearm, he pins my arms above my head, ripping the chain strap of my clutch off my wrist, and tossing it onto the floor.

His other hand yanks my hair—

And my wig comes off in his palm.

He stares down at it, then back at me.

"Why…you're…" He laughs uproariously.

Oh, hell. He recognizes me.

He must also remember what I did to him the last time we saw each other.

Well, I remember what he did to me too.

I remember his rough touch. His promise of pain. And his total disregard for life.

That last nasty little trait cost him his own–or so I thought.

When he moves in to smother my mouth with his, I hear everything in my clutch purse crunch beneath his foot: the syringes, not to mention my cellphone.

Damn it! How will Jack be able to find me? I'm now naked, figuratively. (But, I dread, soon literally.)

It's up to me to save myself.

MY GUESS IS THAT WE'RE NOT GOING UP TOWARD THE PRIVATE cabins, but down into the hull of the ship. Quite frankly, it's a wonder I feel any gravitational pull on my body at all, what with all the poking, prodding, and grabbing Salem is doing, all the while crooning sadistic taunts as to what he'll do with me when we get to (as he so lovingly puts it) "one of my many torture chambers."

Finally, the elevator door opens into a wide hallway. Salem's elbow goes around my neck, making it easier to drag me along.

Like the main ballroom, strobe lights plunge the hall into a freeze-frame chiaroscuro of darkness and light. When my eyes finally adjust, I realize that each room we pass is some sort of torture chamber. Every now and again, Salem will stop in a doorway in order to admire the sex play of his guests.

One of the rooms seems to run on forever, both in its length and depth. Inside, it looks like a free-for-all of sex and pain. The walls are lined with shackled captors, both male and female. Their varied stages of undress are the result of the whip slashes on their blood-striped backs.

Not all of their shouts are muzzled by the various accoutrements placed between their lips. The ones who can scream have gags made of metal fingers or plastic rings that leave their mouths open for anything their torturers want to shove into them. If their torturers' engorged cocks are any indication, they'll soon be silenced too.

Some of the onlookers are too engrossed in their own sexual machinations to watch the flogging action. They're stacked three or four deep on the floor. If so many of them weren't thrusting, wriggling, and moaning, their orgy could be mistaken for a mass grave.

In another room, a naked woman is bent, spread-eagled, over a vinyl barrel horse. Her wrists and ankles are chained to the hardwood floor. Her torturer—a man thick in the neck, broad in the shoulder, and taut in the abs—wears only leather chaps and an executioner's mask. Her head jerks back each time he strikes her back with a cat-o-nine-tails. Her screams pierce the air.

The guests watch from the couches scattered throughout the room. For the most part, the female observers flinch with each squeal from the bound woman. Their eyelids are raised only to half-mast. Whether this indicates a clouded stupor, abject fear, or numbed resignation, I can't say.

On the other hand, the men—many who have already shed their tuxedos—cheer him on. Some are so riled up that they emulate his moves, smacking the women at their sides and in their laps with their hands or some of the torture toys scattered around the room.

Every now and then, one of the men will gobble yet another pill. If his submissive struggles to get away, he'll force her mouth open in order to pour the dregs of the closest champagne flute into it.

So much is poured into one of the women that she convulses. Her captor's attempt to revive her is to pump her chest, but touching her breasts brings him to climax as she takes a last sad gasp.

She is Nicolette's friend, Suzette.

This is not how I want to die.

Suzette's rapist doesn't notice, and likely doesn't care, that she isn't breathing.

Salem does, and he isn't happy about it. He punches a wall intercom with his fist.

It squawks, "Yes, honorable patron?"

"Chamber Eight. A guest is no longer with us. Remove her playmate as well."

A mere moment later, two of Salem's security guards have entered the room. One swings the dead girl over his shoulder while the other tries to nudge the man toward the door.

Seeing Salem standing in the threshold, the man angrily heads our way.

I suddenly realize that the man is Pinky Ring.

"How dare you, Salem!" he screams. The words are English, but his accent is German. "I won't have it—not after what I did for you tonight—"

Salem lets go of me in order to grab Pinky Ring by his throat and slam him against the wall. "Shut up, you little fool! Not in front of *her*."

Pinky Ring's eyes slide in my direction. Although

gagging, he must like what he sees because his pout turns into a clown's grin. "Please don't remove me from all the fun and games. I'll…I'll behave, I promise! And I'll give you my vote against…against The Other."

His declaration intrigues Salem enough that he releases the choke hold on Pinky Ring. Still, to play coy, he shrugs. "You mean to tell me that I didn't already have it?"

"The Other can be quite persuasive too, as you know all too well." Pinky Ring straightens his bowtie, but his eyes shift to me. "Yes, you'll have my vote—if you throw this one in as part of the deal."

"You little imbecile!" Salem chuckles raucously. "Perhaps, when I'm done with her. So then, do I have your vote?"

Pinky Ring's beady little eyes slide my way. He moves in for a closer look—too close in fact.

He cups my breast, as if that might jog his memory.

It won't since we've never met. As a way of reminding him of this, I slap his face.

He yelps in pain. He draws back his hand to retaliate, but Salem grabs it before it makes contact. "Forget it. She's mine to punish. Go pull another woman from the pens."

As he crushes Pinky Ring's hand in his fist, the smaller man whimpers, "They've been passed around too much! And they certainly don't have her desire to live."

"We have a few new ones in there. Whomever you choose, you'll be her first." Salem's arm goes around my waist in order to jerk me along to another door further down the hall. It is closed.

Out of the corner of my eye, I watch as he taps in the necessary code on its numbered lock:

19*29#

It slides open to reveal a room holding wall-to-wall cages. They are so small that the captives—both men and women—are on their hands and knees. Their mouths are gagged, and most are naked.

Water bottles are strapped to the rail of each cage, as if these people are lab rats. I imagine the liquid is drugged, which is why they are so docile.

The women who are still dressed whimper the most. When one of them realizes the door has opened, she bangs on her cage with her bound wrists.

Salem goose-steps me to the wall. There, he reaches up with his free hand in order to pull down a short metal rod: it's a cattle prod.

He takes it over to the woman's cage and smacks her hard across the shoulder. She shudders from the jolt of electricity that runs through her body. Her eyes roll up into her head before she passes out.

The others cower in the farthest corners of their pens.

"Too bad. She was the prettiest," Pinky Ring murmurs.

I recognize her. She is Jean-Pierre's friend, Gigi.

"The auction starts at midnight. I anticipate she'll go for ten million Euros." Salem cocks his head as he scrutinizes her. "Then again, I may keep her"—his gaze shifts my way —"if this one doesn't last the night." He jerks me close enough that his whisper is hot on my neck. "What do you think, my pretty? Are you up for some fun and games?"

He wants me to be frightened of ending up like Gigi. He wants me to barter for my life; to beg him to let me go.

I want to make him pay for all the suffering he causes.

I want to kill this son of a bitch.

I summon a smile. With a throaty laugh, I murmur, "Lead the way."

His grin grows into a leer. "After the head games you've played on me, naughty one, I'd say be careful what you wish for."

His arm goes around my waist again. He's strong enough to lift me off my feet as he strides purposefully out the door, to another at the end of the hall.

I carefully watch as he opens the door with the same six digit code as the one he used to access the slave pens:

19*29#

As Salem shoves me inside, the door slams loudly, echoing through his private torture chamber.

LIKE THE OTHER ROOMS ON THIS LEVEL OF THE SHIP, THERE ARE no portholes, and its walls are padded—to muffle any screams, I imagine. Only in here, the walls of the room come to a V at one side. From that I deduce that we are at the bow of the ship.

The fluorescent lights from overhead cast deep ugly shadows of the only things in the room: the two chains that hang from the center of the ceiling, and above a stainless steel table to one side are several items: a cattle prod, a Taser, pliers, and a cleaver—undoubtedly there to torture this twisted bastard's unfortunate guests.

With more than a little luck, one of his torture tools may save me.

More goodies hang on a wall: whips of various shapes and sizes, spreader bars, more chains, choke and jolt collars, straightjackets, paddles, butt plugs, and dildos. On another wall, floor-to-ceiling shelves hold every high heel imaginable.

"I see you've taken great care to indulge your foot fetish," I declare.

He walks over to the shelves. From one on high, he pulls a pair of red four-inch sandals, from Yves St. Laurent.

Yes, I remember those shoes: When Salem and I last met, he'd chosen a similar pair for me. I was still wearing them when I stepped over his corpse. I hope tonight I will experience a déjà vu moment.

He holds them out to me. "These suit you. Put on the right one, then the left."

"Don't you want to do the honors?" My God, he made such a big deal about it last time: getting down on one knee, lifting my foot to it, unstrapping the shoe I wore. Ah, good times.

He frowns. "No. I remember…something…but it did not go well."

No gentle reminders from me. Far be it from me to get on his bad side now.

I take the shoes from him. He watches me as I step into them. When I bend to adjust the strap of one, his hand slides over my backside. He pauses to see what I do.

Nothing.

He slaps it so hard that I lose my balance.

At that, he laughs.

Thank goodness the other shoe's strap doesn't need adjusting. I hold my hands behind my back, faking the fact that I'm duly chastened.

He walks over to the wall holding the sex toys and chooses a three-pronged whip.

He doesn't see me pick up the Taser gun. My hands are behind me again before he has a chance to turn around.

As he faces me, I say in my best little girl voice: "Are you going to let me choose my poison?"

"Why don't we take turns, my dear?" He snaps the whip in the direction of the wall. "What is your name, anyway? Not that it matters. When I'm through with you, your name will be a distant memory to you—"

He doesn't remember me.

But…how can that be?

"—by the time you join the other women chosen for our new little enterprise."

"By that, do you mean the slave auction that you've got going on here?"

He chuckles. "No, no! The auction is *petit amusement*, not the business of the day, by any means! You came here because you don't mind a little roleplaying. Our organization is giving you the ultimate opportunity to do just that—"

Suddenly, the ship rocks violently.

The lights go dark.

I crouch low. The great news: He can't see me.

The bad news: I can't see him either.

In the meantime, a dull and steady alarm moans through the hull's intercom system. Whatever happened must be serious enough to abandon ship.

Salem makes the first move, swinging the whip.

It catches my arm. When I grunt from the pain, he snickers. Hearing another whoosh, I duck in time to miss his next strike.

My retaliation comes with a jolt from the Taser.

I realize I've struck gold—or something more precious to him—when it lights up the room for a moment, showing me where he now has a terrible owie: On his chest.

The shock throws him backward, into the steel table. As it rolls away, the items that were arrayed upon it clatter to the floor.

No doubt he's down for the count—

Which means I should get the hell out—*now.*

I head for the door, when suddenly the yacht rears up on one side and tosses me in another direction. Shit, whatever hit it must have made some big gash in its hull. We must be taking on water.

Suddenly, Salem grabs ahold of my ankle. He jerks me onto my knees and is pulling me toward him.

What the hell? He should be out cold, considering that the Taser has enough power to immobilize a raging bull! What are those pills he's popping?

The thought hits me too late that he may have a few more weapons at his disposal. I reach down and zap him again with the Taser, then I scramble away.

He howls a string of curses in something other than English: another advantage to being multi-lingual.

It's so dark that I've lost my bearings. Still I rise to my feet in order to inch my way in what I hope is the opposite direction—

Only to be burned on my calf by a jolt of electricity from the cattle prod. Now it's my turn to cuss up a storm.

The yacht gives yet one more lurch as it heaves to one side, and sends us rolling. In the dark I can't tell which way is up—

Until my back hits the door handle. Fucking *ouch!*

I hear the sound of something slicing the air. It pierces the wall to the right above my head. Very carefully I reach for it—

And cut my finger on the blade of the cleaver.

I can't stifle a yelp. Damn it, I've given myself away because I hear him scrambling toward me.

Although in pain, I wrench the cleaver from the wall, swinging it as hard as I can in Salem's direction.

I hit something because he roars, "My fingers! ...Why you...you *cunt!*"

With whatever fingers he has left, he pulls me toward him. Now they are around my throat. I claw at his wrists as he chokes me, but I can't make him stop. Soon my mind wanders to all the things that I should be doing:

Lying in the sun. Listening to the waves lap at the shore.

Laughing with my children.

Making love to my husband.

Instead, I let my hands drop to my side. At the same time, my hand falls onto the pointed pliers.

I scoop them up—

And stab him in the neck.

I must have hit his jugular vein because my arm is sprayed with his blood.

I feel his hands falling away from me. He gasps, but he cannot speak.

He blacks out.

The yacht convulses again—even harder this time. Once again, I'm slammed against the door.

Frantically, I tap in the security pad with the code Salem used to open it, and turn the handle swiftly.

Thank God it opens. For a second time, I'm spared death beside a man I've now killed twice.

The hallway's emergency lights are dim, but working. The *Divide and Conquer* is at such a precarious angle that I tumble into the hallway, along with some of Salem's deadly toys.

A finger rolls past me. It wears the ring with the Quorum crest.

I pick it up and run with it. Mission accomplished —sort of.

I OPEN EVERY DOOR THAT IS UNLOCKED, HOPING TO FIND JACK. Most of the rooms are empty, so at least some of the women were aware enough to make their way to a higher bridge, even in their drugged states of consciousness. I wonder how many were helped by their rapists. My guess is very few.

By now, several feet of water fill the hallway, as we tilt to the left—the port side of the yacht.

I come across a door that is locked. I recognize it as the one holding all the captives in cages.

I try Salem's code and it opens.

I sidestep the cages as they tumble forward. The prisoners can't reach the latches that open their cage doors, but I can, and I do. Some of the women have already disconnected the IVs that have been drugging them, and are ready to run or swim for safety. Many assist those who are still too dazed to help themselves.

As I watch the last woman stumble out the door, I realize that Gigi isn't among them. Did Pinky Ring get his way with her after all?

Hopefully, Jack accomplished his goal of stopping that cruel little toad.

The water is now waist high. I'm about to join them in swimming to safety when I notice another closed room behind a set of double doors. At this point, the hallway is tilted so precariously that the doors are now above my head. To reach the lock pad, I have to jump up and grab the handle.

As I hang onto it with one hand, I once again punch the code on the lock pad with the other.

When the doors slide open, I am smacked down into the water by hundreds of foot-long by foot-wide clear plastic packets filled with the tiny beige pills.

The packets may float, but I don't. I pop up for air, pushing the packets out of the way, but there are so many of them and there is only four feet of air in the hall. Soon, I'm completely submerged again.

I'm drowning.

No. I won't die this way.

A glimpse of hope is the metal railing along the wall that now serves as the roof above me. If I reach it, I can follow it up the stairs.

With all my might, I push down until I hit the wall that now serves as the floor, only to kick myself to the top. I extend my hands over my head in order to grasp for the railing—

I miss.

I gasp for air again. Considering that the hall now has only six inches of air to spare, there won't be a next time.

Before my hand disappears underwater, I feel something grabbing it—

Another hand.

A second later, an arm goes around my waist.

I turn my head to I see my savior: Jack.

My angel.

We suddenly sail through the water toward the steps. We're moving at lightning speed.

I look down to see that Jack has a nylon rope around his waist.

Jean-Pierre is pulling us toward the steps. I knew those broad shoulders were more than just man candy.

Jean-Pierre's brow, furled in fear, relaxes when he sees me with Jack. His arms work even more furiously to pull us all the way up the stairs to the next deck.

By the time we reach him, I'm choking on all the salt water I've swallowed. Still, it doesn't stop me from slobbering them both with kisses.

"Run now, kiss later," Jack commands me. "Let me give you a hand."

Instead, I hand him a finger—Salem's.

When he realizes what he's holding, he laughs. "I think Ryan was expecting a full extraction."

"My bad. This will have to do."

He knows better than to argue. Holding my hand, he leads the way.

MOST OF THE SECOND DECK IS STILL ABOVE THE WATER LINE. "The hotel's tender is starboard," Jean-Pierre explains. "Unfortunately, Madame, you'll have to jump back into the water and swim to it."

"And the sooner the better," Jack warns. "The way this luxury coffin is taking on water, it's going to capsize in no time—if it doesn't blow first."

I nod. "Lead the way."

Jean-Pierre jumps first. He treads water while Jack and I follow suit.

Our boat is a good twenty yards away, but I swim it joyfully, knowing full well the disaster we just escaped.

After we clamber onboard, Jean-Pierre takes the wheel while Jack wraps me in one of the hotel's robes.

I kiss his cheek. "Thank goodness you found me when you did."

"Frankly, you should thank Jean-Pierre and Emma for that. With Emma's instructions, Jean-Pierre was able to hack the ship's security cameras. Even after Acme lost audio on you—and you with them—Emma could track you from the elevator to Salem's torture chamber. Emma turned off the lights in the hope that you could dodge Salem long enough that I'd have time to get there." He moves a damp tendril of my hair behind my ear. "As always, you were able to take care of yourself."

"That may be the case, but I hope you never stop trying. Next time, I may not be so lucky."

"Until I take my dying breath." Jack's voice cracks as he makes this vow.

"Why did the yacht take on water?"

"When Arnie hacked the yacht's navigational system

software, he thought he'd make it easier for Interpol to board it by bringing it to shore. Unfortunately, he's not that great a SIM pilot—especially when he's input a speed that is twice as fast as it should be in a crowded bay. He turned to avoid sideswiping another super yacht and instead got rammed head-on by a joyriding speedboat."

"I presume that you couldn't find Pinky Ring in the melee."

Jack scowls. "Sadly, no. The evacuation was a madhouse. The other yachts were gracious in making room for Salem's waterlogged guests. I didn't see which one of the rescue boats took him."

"Well, I had a run-in with him." I shudder at the memory. "He wanted me for a little fun and games of his own, but Salem insisted he take Gigi instead."

"So, she's alive!"

"Yes—but barely. Jack, the hull also held a room full of captives—both women and men—in cages."

"Sex slaves?"

"Yes, some of them were going to be sold to the highest bidders tonight. But Salem indicated that some were facing a worse fate—some sort of experiment on a very large scale. The Quorum is seeking financial partners for it." I shake my head in wonder. "And another thing: he didn't recognize me! Even without the mask and the wig, he didn't realize who I was."

"Keep in mind: his last run-in with you almost killed him. Maybe it was traumatic enough to give him amnesia." He smiles. "I have the opposite experience. When I'm with you, I forget that other women exist."

His sweet lie earns him a kiss.

We linger together blissfully lip-locked until Jean-Pierre shouts, "Madame! Monsieur! Pinky Ring—he is standing on the dock!"

The little cretin is not alone. The mystery woman is hustling Gigi into a waiting limousine.

When Jean-Pierre sees Gigi, he puts the boat in top gear.

Instinctively, Pinky Ring looks up. He frowns when he sees Jack. Does he recognize him? Suddenly he draws a gun and fires—

Jack and I duck.

The bullet hits Jean-Pierre.

Our boat shoots beyond the dock.

I crouch down beside Jean-Pierre. The wound is on his shoulder. Quickly, I grab a towel to staunch the blood streaming from it.

In the meantime, Jack grabs the wheel and flips us back on course.

By the time we reach the dock, the limo is gone. Jack and I carry Jean-Pierre's unconscious body onto the dock.

Duclos and his partner are the first officers to answer our emergency call. Recognizing Jean-Pierre, Duclos exclaims, "Ah! You see? As I said, he killed the girl. But because he cannot live with his guilt, he shoots himself too."

I slap his face before Jack can stop me.

The only thing that keeps me from jail is the arrival of Interpol on Salem's helicopter pad.

We insist that the pilot first take Jean-Pierre to the nearest emergency hospital.

As we fly off, I look down at the *Divide and Conquer*. The bow is now the only thing above the water line.

It is a fitting crypt for Salem.

4

Family Plot

The family that plays together stays together.

But they shouldn't die together. Someone should be left to bury the bodies, right?

Yet another reason to have secured a family plot before any unfortunate moments arise. When doing so, here's what to look for:

First, remember: those who die first get the choicest plot in the family lot. But there are times when it doesn't pay to be first. (Yes, this is one of them.)

Next, make sure it's on high ground. Why? Simple! You don't want a heavy rainstorm to send your dearly departed loved ones floating downstream—unless you're worried that a court order to exhume one of their bodies will provide evidence needed to put you away for life.

Also, no matter how rotten one or more of your relatives had been in life, it's very poor form to request that they be placed in one mass grave.

And, finally, don't be stingy about the casket. Remember: the stronger it is, the less likely it'll leak any unwelcome secrets.

~

CHERRY PIE IS A NORMAL TREAT FOR THE TYPICAL AMERICAN family. Ergo, I, the mother of the Craig family, am making a cherry pie.

It doesn't matter that it is three in the morning, or that the rest of the household is sound asleep.

In fact, I prefer it. This way, I can focus with precision on the task at hand instead of the countless other events that vie for a mother's attention, often beckoning her to acknowledge, reward, and reciprocate as her pie goes up in flames.

This early in the morning, I won't be tempted to stop rolling out pie dough in order to match Trisha's constant petting with a flurry of kisses.

In the still of the night, I won't be so fascinated by Jeff's nonstop verbal replay of his latest baseball pitching victory that I forget to add almond extract to the mixture of sweet and sour pitted cherries already tossed with sugar, vanilla, lemon juice, and a little cornstarch.

At the break of dawn, I'll find it easier to crisscross strips of dough over my pie's filling if I don't have to resist the urge to laugh at Mary and Evan's flirtatious banter.

And I'd certainly miss the oven timer if I let Jack have his way with me in bed—

Admittedly, it's not easy choosing between great sex and great pie.

This time, the latter comes first. The former is my just desserts.

AS IT TURNS OUT, I'VE MISSED THE FORMER ANYWAY, HAVING fallen dead asleep just after putting the pie in the oven.

Sunlight streaming through the kitchen window wakes me up. Or is it the sound of Jeff's voice as he explains his new fastball technique to Evan?

Maybe it's because Trisha is gently stroking my cheek and whispering in my ear: "Dad says it's okay for us to have pie for breakfast, but only if you say so too. Can we, please? Pretty please?"

I nod, but then immediately wince to find Aunt Phyllis brewing—make that burning—the coffee, while Mary cuts the pie into generous wedges.

Oh, my goodness! I guess I burned it—

No, it's a perfect golden brown.

But, where is Jack?

Before I can turn around to find him, I feel his arm around my shoulder, and then his lips on my cheek.

Instinctively, my mouth turns to his. Our kiss is gentle but lingering. When we draw away, we find our children scrutinizing us. There are shy smiles on their faces and joy in their eyes.

My hand beckons them to us for a group hug.

In no time, I am enveloped in their loving arms.

They've missed me—and not just because of my pie. But my having baked one makes this homecoming so much sweeter.

"MOMMY, WHILE YOU WERE GONE I HAD A VERY BAD DREAM," Trisha's dire declaration is mumbled through a mouthful of pie.

"Do you want to tell me about it?" I ask, as I try not to gag while gulping down the last of Phyllis's bitter brew. Instead, I lean into my aunt, who sits beside me—my way of reassuring her that I appreciate all she does for Jack and me while we're away.

Phyllis pats my arm appreciatively. "Our baby screamed the last three nights in a row! I offered to climb into bed with her, but she wanted to be a big girl and tough it out."

Trisha nods, but when Aunt Phyllis gets up and goes to the counter for yet another cup of coffee, she cups her hand to my ear and whispers, "Really, it's because Aunt Phyllis snores. Mommy, can you come sleep with me instead?"

"If you want, yes, of course," I promise. "Honey, would you like to talk about it?"

"I asked her that too, but Trisha wanted to wait until you came home," Mary squeezes her little sister's hand.

"Well, your dad and I are here now," I say, hoping my smile encourages her.

Trisha blushes. "Daddy may be mad when he hears about it."

Jack shakes his head. "I could never be mad at you, sweet pea. *Ever*." He crosses his heart to make his point.

Trisha nods slowly, but her lip quivers. "Okay..." She sighs. "It's the same dream all the time, only it doesn't seem like a dream because it's *so real*! In it, my other daddy—the bad one—is in the room with me."

Everyone's fork freezes in mid-air.

Mary frowns. As the oldest of my children, her memories

of her biological father took longer to fade during his five-year absence from their young lives. When Carl resurfaced, she had the hardest time reconciling his desertion with her adoration of Jack. Carl's terrorist acts may have given her yet another excuse to hate him, but he was still her father.

Trisha's nightmares are yet one more reminder of how Carl tore our family apart.

On the other hand, Jeff leans in, fascinated. His way of dealing with his own close call with terrorism is to approach it dispassionately, and to research it methodically.

Would it be better if his sisters took the same approach? It's hard to say. Each of us has processed the same trauma in our own way.

My solution was to become an assassin. Literally, I killed the cause of our distress. But I would not want my children to have taken that path.

Apparently, Trisha's is to dream about the father she never knew. Will talking about it make what few memories she has about him fade? Perhaps, which is why I ask: "What happens in your dream?"

"He stands at the foot of my bed, and tells me how much he loves us all and misses us, and how he wishes he'd never left us, especially since he missed me being born." She wipes away a tear. "The first night he came, I told him that we aren't mad at him anymore, now that he's gone. But then, last night he told me that if we wanted him to, he'd come back. All we have to do is say so." Tears glaze her eyes. "Mommy, I don't want him here, but I don't want to tell him that because it might hurt his feelings." She pauses. Out of the corner of her eye, she looks at Jack. "Besides, we already have a daddy, and we love him very much."

Jack pulls her close for a hug. "He isn't coming back, Trisha. And your mother and I will always be here to love and protect you."

She nods emphatically. "I know. I just don't want to hurt his feelings."

"You can't because he's not real," Jeff assures her.

"But...I saw him!" Trisha insists. "I swear!"

Jeff shakes his head. "No, you didn't. He's...what do you call it? Oh yeah, a figment of your imagination."

"Sometimes our subconscious—that is, a part of our minds—brings up sad thoughts when we sleep," I explain. "It's one way to deal with unhappiness."

Trisha furrows her brow at this new information. "He won't come back then, ever?"

"Never." Jack's declaration isn't angry, but matter-of-fact.

"Never," Mary agrees. She places one hand over her sister's, and another over Jack's.

Her actions confirm what I'd hoped: her own issues regarding her father are laid to rest, once and for all.

Carl rests in peace now. How long must we deal with the damage he left behind?

Trisha's relief comes with a smile. She holds up her milk glass. "I'll drink to that."

Me too. Later tonight. With something stronger than milk. And much less bitter than Aunt Phyllis's coffee.

Jeff turns to Jack. "Dad, can you come to my game this afternoon?"

Jack tousles our son's hair. "Wouldn't miss it for the world."

Jeff nods toward Evan. "Evan's been assisting Coach Haskell."

I turn to Evan. "That's sweet of you."

"Mr. Haskell also coaches my lacrosse team at Hilldale High, remember? He's been a great influence on my goal keeping technique. When he asked me, of course I said yes. Besides, I figure it'll look good on my college applications." Evan shrugs. "Speaking of which, I've earmarked a few colleges that I'd like to apply to—that is, if they can take me on either a lacrosse or an academic scholarship."

"Do you mean to tell me that the executor of your mother and father's estate still won't let you access your trust?" I ask angrily.

"The trust is tied to the income created by my father's tech conglomerate. The executor, Mr. Asquith, claims that it's taken on heavy losses since Dad's death, and that the board of directors insists it be sold. But so far, there have been no takers."

"I find that hard to believe," Jack murmurs.

"Me too," Evan assures us, "I questioned him about potential acquisition partners. I even did some of my own research about it, but he pretty much told me to mind my own business."

"The sale of your family's company *is* your business."

"My words exactly. But he laughed it off, claiming it's a down market for tech"—he rolls his eyes at that obvious fallacy—"and that I should focus on my grades instead, if I want to get in to any college at this point." To avoid looking us in the eye, Evan looks down at his hands. "Even my parents' alma mater, Adams Morgan University, has cooled off on the idea of my admission after Mother was convicted of plotting Father's death."

"That's crazy!" Mary declares emphatically. "And if they

are so stupid to deny a legacy with your grade point average, other colleges will be fighting to have you."

He shakes his head. "It's not that easy. Even with great grades, if I can't get a scholarship, my need for financial assistance may knock me out of the box. But I'll certainly try my darnedest. And with that in mind"—he looks at Jack—"I hope either you or Donna would do me the honor of accompanying me on some of my visits to a few of the colleges on my hit list. I know you've got a full house here, but I figure if I tour the campuses before my senior year at Hilldale is underway, it'll be easier on everyone, schedule-wise. From what my counselor tells me, going to the schools—and even better, showing demonstrated interest in them—is an important determinant as to whether or not you'll be accepted."

"'Demonstrated interest?'" Jeff snorts through a mouthful of pie. "What the heck is that?"

I frown my warning for him to butt out, but I've got to admit I'm wondering the same thing.

"It means going full-court press to show your interest in the school: ask intelligent and specific questions, demonstrate and take on a couple more written essays that show your knowledge of the school, your chosen profession—in my case, biotechnology—and how you as a student will add value to that field of study." Evan rubs his forehead at the thought of all the work that is in front of him.

Jack nods slowly. I know what he's thinking: besides the usual struggle to keep the Craig household as normal as possible, the mystery of Salem and Pinky Ring's resurrections have thrown our lives off kilter.

I squeeze Evan's hand. "We can certainly go along to any

of the local schools on your list. It's just a few hours out of our day."

He smiles back at me. "That would be UCLA and USC. Both offer biotech degrees. I'm also applying to Berkeley and Stanford for the same reasons."

"Exemplary schools, and quick over-nighters, if Aunt Phyllis doesn't mind holding court here."

Aunt Phyllis hugs Evan's neck. "Not if it gets this one out of my hair—except for holidays—and summer break, of course. Hey, we can hang together during spring break, too! Par-*tay!*"

It's my turn to roll my eyes. "What Aunt Phyllis is trying to say, Evan, is that we'll always be your home away from school. What East Coast schools do you have on your list?"

"Other than Adams Morgan, you mean?" He shrugs. "Considering my current financial situation, I've kept a very short list. As much as I'd like to apply to Harvard, Northeastern, and MIT, I think they'll be long shots."

"You should still do so. It's times up to bat," Mary insists. "The counselors say to go for at least ten schools."

"I'll add a couple of community colleges to the list." There is no sarcasm in Evan's tone.

I shake my head. "You'll do nothing of the sort. Harvard, Northeastern, and MIT are all in Boston. That's a quick train ride from DC. We may have a reason to be in Washington anyway. If so, you can come along."

"Me too? ...I mean...that I'll need to tour colleges the following year, anyway..." By the way Mary looks at me with puppy-dog eyes, I can easily guess the real reason she wants to tag along.

Jack covers his smirk by raising his coffee mug to his mouth—

But then he winces at its bitter taste.

That's what he gets for leaving the ball in my court. "Dad and I will give it serious consideration. We'll discuss it again when we get back from the office."

Mary smiles sweetly at Jack. A good politician knows that it's never too early to start campaigning.

This time, when Jack chokes up, it has nothing to do with the acidity of Aunt Phyllis's brew.

5

Grave Digging

Grave-digging is an honorable profession.

I mean, come on: it has to be, otherwise the streets would be strewn with the putrid scented, puss-filled and maggot-engorged unsightly corpses. (Hopefully, gentle reader, you didn't find that description too off-putting. If so, consider the source...)

Should the vocation interest you, here are a few cautionary considerations:

First, you've got to be able to count: at least to four (feet wide) by ten (feet long) by six (feet under. In some states, graves with as little as a four-foot depth will do).

Next, you can't be afraid to sling a shovel or a pick ax. Consider the upside: you'll build up a fine set of biceps and abs for when bathing suit season arrives!

Also, it's important that you wear the right attire: old jeans and T-shirts or sweats, with a good pair of sturdy work boots. In other words, time to put away your haute couture! (Besides, if you see a ghost, the last thing you need is to wet yourself in a new pair of Valentino silk flair-legged high-waisted cady trousers.)

And, finally, you can't be afraid to work in a cemetery at any time, day or night. However, if toiling away in a small town of dead folk gives you the heebie-jeebies, there are many uses for your shovel and pick axe among the living, albeit most assassins don't make a shovel their weapon of choice. But, hey, feel free to start a trend.

"PINKY RING'S CASKET IS AS EMPTY AS KHASEKHEMWY'S TOMB," Dominic Fleming's stentorian proclamation rings throughout Acme's conference room. "Shall we presume that he has risen, like Banquo's ghost?"

I, and the others in the room, do our best to keep from bursting out with laughter. It's hard to take Dominic seriously while he still wears the flowing crimson satin mantle in which he was knighted, along with the sash, and the humongous bling known as the Knight Grand Cross.

Arnie can't help but snicker, setting off an avalanche of chuckles (Jack), guffaws (Abu), and outright giggles (Emma and me).

"Enough, people!" Ryan roars. "This is not a laughing matter."

He refuses to speak again until all sound is stifled. We've just calmed down when Jack notices that one of the satin mantle's tassels is caught under Abu's chair.

When it rips, Jack lets loose with a wicked snort.

The room explodes once more with laughter.

Incensed, Dominic sputters epithets that make no sense

at all to an American ear—something about "Sweet Fanny Adams" (whoever she is) and how naffed we are (yep, sounds dirty to me too) and that we can all "get on your bikes" (*totally* lost in translation). Dominic saves the worst of these little gems for Jack, whom he calls a "gormless duffer" who'd better "put a sock in it" (okay, I get that one) or he'll give Jack a "knuckle sandwich" (frankly, I think our British cousins stole that one from us).

Jack must be fluent in Brit-eese because, suddenly, he's nose to nose with Dominic. "I'm game, you bloody little tosser—"

"Enough already!" Ryan roars before knuckle sandwiches are exchanged.

He can be *such* a Buzz Kill Betty.

Still, we are duly chastened. I prove this by raising my hand.

Ryan's eyes narrow. "This better be pertinent."

"It is," I insist meekly. "I want to know if the lab has gotten back to us with a DNA analysis from Salem's finger."

"Yes." Ryan's scowl deepens. "The sample is verified as belonging to him."

Jack slams his fist on the conference room table. "It just doesn't make sense! He was stone cold dead when we left his suite in the Beverly Wilshire. And the cleaners' report verifies the extermination!"

Ryan throws up his hands. "I can't explain it either, but the scientific verification is all there. The fact that Pinky Ring's grave is empty puts any assumption that he was exterminated to rest." He winces. "Pardon my pun."

"So, both Pinky Ring and Salem were never exterminated?" I shake my head in awe. "It's crazy! It's…" I take a deep breath to calm myself down. "Okay, let's just say these two guys somehow walked away with a new lease on life. How does it explain that *Salem did not recognize me*?" I let that sink in. When no one speaks, I add, "Remember, I was the person who shot him—*in the chest—and left* him for dead just a few weeks prior!"

"Maybe with the blunt force trauma, he suffered from some sort of amnesia?" Emma asks.

I shrug. "Okay, maybe. But come on—wouldn't his hearing my voice, or my being in his presence, jog some memory of the incident?"

"From what we heard when you were still mic'ed, he admitted that he thought you looked familiar," Arnie points out.

I shake my head. "That was when I was wearing the platinum blonde wig that was cut similarly to Nicolette's."

"You say he chose the exact same pair of shoes for you as last time? My guess is that he was playing a head game with you," Dominic reasons. "Or, maybe it was purely coincidence. To be honest, dearie, you're not really all that memorable."

I clench my fist under his nose as a reminder that I too can throw a few knuckle sandwiches.

He raises a hand in order to cover his glorious cheekbones. "Truly, old girl, I meant it as a compliment! Your lack of any exquisite features allows you to be nonexistent. You are as anonymous as a charwoman in the East End. As invisible as a wallflower at a cotillion—"

I'll admit it: I don't take compliments well. This time when I raise my fist, Jack grabs my wrist so that I may work on this tiny fault somewhere other than a federal prison.

As an insight hits him, Abu snaps his fingers. "Or, maybe Salem did it because, slowly and surely, the memory of you was coming back to him."

"I…I don't know." I shrug helplessly. "Maybe. I mean—well, he did say something intriguing at the very moment I put the high heels on my feet. How did he put it? Oh, yes! He said it reminded him of something, but that it didn't go well."

"Maybe he was having a déjà vu moment," Abu replies.

"Now that he's really dead, we'll never know what he meant by it." Ryan's clipped tone indicates his disappointment that Salem isn't here with us right now, under interrogation.

"What about the pills we brought back with us? Why did Salem have so many in the hull of the ship?" Jack's question gets me off the hook—for now, anyway.

"Pills—and all those sex slaves!" Emma shivers. "They would have drowned if Donna hadn't released them."

"Salem was using both as bartering chips with some of the other power players, some of whom were on the yacht with us last night," I declare. "Like Salem and the rest of the men, Pinky Ring was hopped up on the stuff. It's why he killed Suzette. Salem was going to throw him off the yacht until Pinky Ring promised to vote with him on some issue, against someone they called 'the Other.'"

"We downloaded the security footage from the ship's computer," Ryan replies. "Emma and Arnie's teams will run facial recognition on everyone at the party. We'll use it to ID the men who may be Quorum clients. As for the women, many may show up on Interpol's missing persons database."

He tosses a packet of pills at each of us. "And by the way, turns out that it's Captagon."

"What exactly does it do?" Emma asks.

"It's composed of two drugs: amphetamine and theophylline," Abu explains. "An American pharmaceutical firm produced it up until the nineteen-eighties, as a legal controlled substance for attention deficit disorders. For over a decade now, the Lebanese have captured the Captagon black market. Unfortunately, ISIS has taken over the production of it. Since the conflict in Syria, Captagon production has skyrocketed. ISIS keeps their young recruits hopped up on it. The jihadists are like zombies. They don't feel the need for sleep, and they'll fight on for days at a time." He shrugs. "They also consider it an aphrodisiac. So not only are they numbed to all the carnage, they rape with abandon. To keep their zombie fighters happy, ISIS has farms of women who are used as sex slaves. Sex is a great recruitment tool."

"Perhaps Salem was bringing more of it into Saudi Arabia so that it could be distributed into the Middle Eastern war zones," I reason.

Abu shakes his head. "More than likely he's exporting it *out* of the Middle East. Similarly sized shipments have been discovered on other private yachts and jets of wealthy Arab businessmen who are known to straddle both sides of the political discourse."

Ryan frowns. "Believe it or not, you stumbled upon our most recent assignment."

Jack and I stare at each other before turning to face him. "How so?" Jack asks.

"When Arnie hacked into the *Divide & Conquer's* computer system, he pulled up something even more important than the yacht's security codes and schematic. Arnie, why don't you fill them in on it?"

Preening under Ryan's rare praise, Arnie says, "On a whim, I decided to snoop around Salem's personal computer. He'd received an encrypted file within a very recent email. I guess he hadn't had time to upload it into his secure cloud because his hot and heavy party—or should I say orgy—was underway."

"What's in the file?" I ask.

Arnie nods toward Ryan.

"I've been waiting for you and Jack before briefing the rest of your mission team. The file contained white papers from a top-secret project run by the Defense Advanced Research Projects Agency," Ryan replies. He pauses, then adds, "DARPA is creating a prototype for a 'super soldier.' It's called 'Operation Hercules.'" His pause comes with a frown. "The Quorum somehow got wind of it, then breached the program's security measures. I made POTUS aware of this. In turn, he's given Acme the mission of discovering how the breach was committed, and how much of the program has been compromised."

"Wait...'super soldiers?' You mean, like, cyborgs?" Arnie asks. "Awesome!"

Ryan frowns. "No, of course not. We're talking about human assets who will undergo some physical and mental enhancements so that they'd be larger, stronger, and smarter before going out into the battlefield."

I shiver as the memory of the new and improved Salem comes to mind. "Is Captagon part of the program? Is that why the yacht's hull was filled with it?"

"The white papers don't mention Captagon. Unlike the

Quorum using drugs for a false, addictive high, DARPA's goal is more holistic—that is to say, body, mind, and soul," Ryan counters.

"That sounds so airy-fairy," Jack mutters.

"In fact, it's pure science, not science-fiction," Ryan insists.

Jack's eyes narrow. "In what way?"

"Three teams of scientists are working on different portions of the project. Up until the presentation to the NSC oversight committee, they worked around the clock, independently—in fact, in different secure locations—and completely unaware of each other." Ryan hits a key on his computer that brings up our mission's case file notes on one of the conference wall's video screens.

The first page shows a man in his mid-thirties. He wears the Valley's ubiquitous uniform of a man of his stature—that is to say, black long-sleeve T-shirt, worn over jeans and sockless loafers—and sports tortoise-shell glasses, a pony tail, and just enough boho scruff on his lantern jaw to pass as a hipster.

He stands beside a man with one arm that is of normal size, and another that looks doll-like. "An important component of the project is stem cell research, especially as it pertains to DNA editing," Ryan explains. "One team is conducting research on regenerative bioengineering. It's headed up by Doctor Rudy Brooks, who works at DNA 10Squared, a biotechnology firm and DARPA contractor on several projects. The company is located in Palo Alto."

"How will it be used?" Emma asks.

"Great question. Imagine if a soldier who lost a leg because he happened to step on an IED could grow a new one within a few days," Ryan explains. "It's worked success-fully in lab rats. This veteran—who, as you see is an amputee—volunteered to be a human test subject. His new arm is already growing."

"What you are talking about, old man, are biolimbs," Dominic pipes in. "My God! Imagine its use in the private sector!"

Ryan nods. "Like most of our military's innovations, it will eventually impact civilian lives in a significant way. There are over two million amputees today in this country. Close to one hundred and fifty amputations happen every year. Think of how their lives will be affected." He shakes his head at the wonder of it all. "Another application for his research is genome-editing technology."

"What is that, exactly?" Abu asks.

"A lab tool called a CRISPR allows scientists to manipu-late DNA in the nucleus," Ryan continues. "Imagine tiny 'molecular scissors' guided by satellite navigation that have the ability to reach within any cell—be it sperm, a one-celled embryo, or an egg—and either insert good DNA, or snip out the bad stuff prior to replication of DNA in the next generation."

I shake my head. "It sounds as if we're now playing God."

"Humans weren't supposed to fly either," Ryan argues. "Today, going to the moon is an afterthought. Imagine if you were able to snip the BRCA1 breast cancer out of your DNA, and in doing so, eradicate it in your descendants. Would you do so?"

The vision of my mother's final days on earth come to mind. "Without hesitation," I murmur.

"For DARPA, this generation of super soldiers will be surgically enhanced. But the next generation will be created at inception," Ryan points out.

"Gee, whatever happened to free will?" Emma mutters. "I mean, what if the dude wants to dance ballet instead?"

"Trust me; he'll get offers from every dance company in the world," Dominic declares.

"He's right," Ryan adds. "And diseases such as cystic fibrosis, hemophilia, muscular dystrophy, and sickle cell will be things of the past."

I shrug. "The commercial application will be a stockholder's wet dream, not to mention parents who want a designer baby."

"Do the agency's experiments include DNA editing with other species?" Emma asks warily.

"By that, do you mean is it creating chimeras?" I wonder out loud.

"Half man and half beast? That's pretty scary!" Abu shakes his head at the thought.

"Let's not get ahead of ourselves, people. DARPA doesn't want mutants. The ethics issue alone would kill the program," Ryan warns. "It'll look more like this." He hits the computer key again.

A different picture appears. An older gentleman—portly, with a goatee—is working with a man wearing a prosthetic arm. The man's head is taped with electrodes. He appears to be lifting a heavy weight. "This is Dr. Norbert Welles, who heads up the second group of researchers who is working on neural implants that can control robotic prosthetics. He's the founder of MesmerMind, a start-up based in San Francisco."

"A reboot of the Bionic Man?" Arnie's fist pumps the air. "Awesome!"

"This isn't one of your comic book fantasies, Arnie," Ryan growls. "This is real life."

"What does the third team's research entail?" Jack asks.

"Memory modification," Ryan answers. "Operation Hercules is providing the most comprehensive research that has ever been conducted in the physiology of memory. Dr. Shelley Wollstonecraft leads this team. She works at UC Berkeley's BioEngineering Department."

He taps the key once more. This time, a woman appears on the screen. She is in her mid-thirties, and stunningly beautiful. Her long dark hair curls to her shoulders. Dr. Wollstonecraft stands beside a CT scan of a green-hued brain. While in mid-conversation with someone not in the photo, she points to an area of the cerebral cortex that is highlighted in a vibrant red color.

"What exactly is memory modification?" Dominic asks.

I presume it's what every woman who has had the misfortune of being sweet-talked into having sex with Dominic must do in order regain her self respect. Still, I wait for Ryan's answer.

"Consider the changes that would occur in our lives if there were a way in which we could effectively block bad memories," Ryan explains. "Like those which cause veterans Post Traumatic Stress Disorder."

"Cool! Sort of like the movie, *Eternal Sunshine of the Spotless Mind*!" Arnie proclaims.

"Yes…I mean *no*!" Ryan rubs his eyes as if doing so might make his annoyance with Arnie somehow disappear. "Again, this is real life. If the research holds, Operation

Hercules' assets will be emotionally unified in their mission. And, once again, their success means civilians soon reap the benefits of the research as well. Be they combat vets or everyday citizens who have found themselves in trying circumstances, over five percent of our country's citizens have experienced some form of Post-Traumatic Stress Disorder. It will also help the millions of others who've suffered some crippling phobia, or a debilitating anxiety—not to mention those with addictions."

Still in doubt, Emma shakes her head. "Come on, Ryan! What we're talking about here is mind control!"

"What's wrong with the good old-fashioned way of dealing with mental health issues—you know, like talk therapy, or a correctly prescribed program of drug therapy?" Dominic asks.

"Again, it's memory modification, Emma. And, to answer your question, Dominic: pyscho-phramaceuticals and behavioral therapies don't do as good of a job. All pharmaceuticals have some form of side effect. And, unfortunately, behavioral therapy often lapses over time."

"With advances in medical technologies, both drug and behavioral therapies can, and will, be tweaked with the patient in mind," I counter.

"That may be the case, but no time soon—unless we're able to crack the last frontier: the human brain, which is exactly what Dr. Wollstonecraft is doing," Ryan replies. "PET and MRI scans allow neuroscientists to monitor the brain's metabolic changes and blood flow, but this technology can't measure neuron activity." He sighs. "That's where Dr. Wollstonecraft's project comes in. She and her team have already identified and mapped pathways where the brain creates, archives, and recalls memories. By the end of the month, their research will be validated by human test subjects."

"Since we police the world—for peanuts to our allies, and at the expense of a living wage to our military personnel —I guess super-sizing our soldiers is one way to throw them a bone," Emma mutters. "But how will these so-called modifications affect them after their tours of duty?"

"Great question," I murmur.

Obviously, Ryan doesn't share my opinion, because he ignores it. Instead, his eyes shift from one of us to the other. "Ladies and gentleman, our world is swiftly moving beyond conventional warfare. If we are going to fight fanatical terrorism without the collateral damage of innocent victims, we need to be smarter, stronger, and more select in tracking down our enemies: on a case-by-case basis. Operation Hercules is the answer. And DARPA—not to mention POTUS—has put the program's security in our hands."

Our mission team can succinctly read in Ryan's tone: *Get onboard, or get out.*

After what Jack and I have seen these past forty-eight hours, we really don't have a choice.

Jack shrugs his acceptance of the inevitable. "Okay, we're in. Tell us about the security breach."

"It was old school: there was no technological hacking because all three teams kept their notes on paper, and under lock and key. To assure this, anyone working on the project was kept under twenty-four-hour surveillance from day one."

"Who had access to the papers?" I ask.

"The project's three lead scientists presented white papers on their projects on Thursday."

"That would have been the day before Salem hit Biarritz," I reason. "Who is on this committee, and where did it meet?" I ask.

"The scientists presented their findings to POTUS, Director of Intelligence Marcus Branham, and the director of DARPA. The meeting was too large to hold in the Oval Office. My guess is that it took place in the West Wing's Roosevelt Room," Ryan reasons.

"Don't leave us in suspense," I chide Ryan. "Who are our prime suspects? Make my day and tell us it's Todd and Blake."

"No, sorry. It's Dr. Brooks, for one," Ryan says. "And Dr. Wollstonecraft." He takes a deep breath. "And, er, President Chiffray."

"Lee? Why am I not surprised?" Jack mutters.

He doesn't need a reason to be at odds with Lee. He's already got one:

Me.

"In his defense, Jack, only POTUS and his new Director of Intelligence, Marcus Branham, knew that each of the officially released copies has a light-sensitive halo that is invisible to the naked eye. Scanning, photographing, or photocopying will set off a silent digital alarm that allows the compromised copy to be identified with the time and date of the breach. And, by the way, it was POTUS who insisted that Acme be hired to investigate the leak, since we were the ones who exposed it."

Jack shrugs. What can he say? In this matter, Lee's actions speak volumes: he is not looking for a cover-up.

"I presume you haven't divulged to POTUS his role in the breach," Jack counters.

"You presume correctly. He only knows that a breach occurred, but not how and when. Frankly, I'd like to keep it that way. It assures his hands are clean during our investigation," Ryan points out.

"What are the time stamps on the breaches?" Dominic asks.

"The meeting lasted all day," Arnie replies. "All of the papers that were compromised happened sometime during the meeting, within hours of each other."

"Other than POTUS and Director Branham, are any of the other participants aware that breaches were detected?" I ask.

"No. And, for now, POTUS and I agree we should keep it that way to see if other theft attempts are made," Ryan assures us. "Interestingly enough, neither of the scientists' compromised copies was the one regarding their own research. Dr. Wollstonecraft's was of Dr. Welles's neural implant research, and Dr. Welles's was about the regenerative bioengineering research conducted by Dr. Brooks. POTUS's compromised copy dealt with Wollstonecraft's memory modification research."

"What are our marching orders?" Jack asks.

Ryan points to Dominic. "I need you to fly immediately to Biarritz to confiscate Salem's remains for analysis. I also want you to pick up Pinky Ring's trail from when he shot Jean-Pierre." He then turns to me. "Donna will go undercover within DARPA, as the public information officer assigned to the project. In that capacity, you'll have access to the scientists. Emma, Arnie as always, you're on ComInt and tech, respectively."

The Locklears nod.

"What about POTUS?" Jack asks.

"He's all yours," Ryan replies.

Jack smiles at the thought.

"Wait…on second thought, let's, er, leave him in Donna's capable hands. Jack, you'll provide backup on all three ops."

Despite Jack's scowl, Ryan dismisses us with a nod. "Remember, time is of the essence."

"I GUESS THE UPSIDE OF A TRIP TO DC IS THAT WE CAN TOUR Morgan Adams University with Evan." I say this in order to break Jack's silence on the car trip home.

"Yeah, wow, great idea. Having Evan along will give me something to do while you're entertaining Lee."

I stifle the urge to flinch at Jack's sarcasm. Instead, I shake my head. "What do you mean? Of course, you're going with me to see Lee."

"Ryan made it clear that he thinks you're perfectly capable of finding out what we need without any help from me."

"If that's the case, since I'm in charge of how I work the operation, I insist that you be there too."

He glances over at me. "Don't throw me a bone, Donna."

"Quit sulking. It's a turn-off."

The next thing I know, he's pulled over to the side of the road.

We are on the 405, arguably the least romantic road in all of California—

Unless the man you love puts his hand on your thigh—

And melts your heart with his searing gaze—

Before locking your lips in a heart pounding kiss.

Perfect. I have him right where I want him: in my arms.

He waits until we resume oxygen intake, then mutters, "Who did you say is sulking?"

"Certainly not you," I purr. "Good then, it's settled."

He laughs. "Oh, yeah? What's settled?"

"Your role in the investigation I'll be heading up: that of the compromised DARPA white paper that was in POTUS's possession."

Damn it, his frown is back. "And what, exactly, is my role again?"

"Hopefully, you'll be losing at golf to Lee on the Blue Course of the Congressional Country Club while I trace the route the white paper took in getting into—and for that matter, out of—the Oval Office."

"In other words, I'm the decoy—not you?"

I nod. "Yes—but only because your golf handicap is much better than mine."

"The last thing Lee wants to do is spend four hours on a golf course with me."

"You're wrong about that. Lee would agree to a foursome with Francisco Franco, Attila the Hun, and Joseph Mengele if it got him out of the White House on a beautiful Sunday afternoon."

Jack starts the car up again. As he pulls into the slow lane, he murmurs, "Nice to know you think so highly of me."

"I also think highly of Evan. And guess what? He'll be part of your golf foursome, along with Connelly McIver, the dean of Morgan Adams University—that is, after he and Evan have their photo op with the president in the Oval

Office. If the game these colleges play is 'who do you know,' Evan's connection to POTUS should go a long way to erasing his mother's misdeeds."

"Do you really think Lee will agree to this?"

"I'd say he owes the kid that much, and more. The only reason he now lives in the White House is because Catherine Martin took Carl's advice to make Lee her vice president. At the same time, it made Evan an orphan."

"Do you think Lee is just going to let you hang in his private office, twiddling your thumbs?"

"Oh, he'll soon realize that I'll be doing much more than that—say, clearing his name—and Babette's too, if he's lucky."

The latter would be wishful thinking on Lee's part. The First Lady of the United States is always high on my list of suspects. Not only does she have unlimited access to the Oval Office, her path to power crisscrosses the rise of the Quorum much too often to be coincidental.

Lee realizes this too. Still, he's bound and determined to protect her. Not just because of her connections with known terrorists—my first husband, Carl; her first husband, Jonah Breck; and Salem al-Sadah—would lead to the biggest scandal ever to rock the U.S. Presidency, but because she's pregnant.

He knows it's not his child.

Lee is living proof that love truly is blind.

"So you're going against Ryan's mandate and breaking the news to Lee that his compromised copy makes him a key suspect?"

"Frankly, it's the only way to clear the First Couple of any wrongdoing. The fact that he doesn't yet know it gives me an advantage. If he says no to my request to full access to everything and everyone who can shed light on what happened in the hours leading up to, and during, the Operation Hercules briefing, he'll look that much more guilty." I shrug. "For that matter, I'll need access to Babette too. So enjoy your golf game while I dig through this mess. If I'm lucky, I'll have what I need before Monday, so that I can join you and Evan when he's scheduled to tour the Adams Morgan campus."

"Not to bring up a sore subject, but as you know, Mary is dying to go along with us on these college tours," Jack reminds me.

I frown. "I know, but not this one to DC and Boston. There's too much at stake with this mission. We'll take her along to Stanford and Berkeley."

"That may not appease her," he warns.

"It'll have to do. Frankly, separating those two for a couple of days will do them both some good. Sharing their grief from traumatic events isn't the best reason to start—or for that matter, stay in a relationship."

"Oh, no?" Jack eyes me with disbelief. "What, are you crazy? It worked for us."

"Really? Is that what you think—that we were drawn together in a quest to make right the atrocities Carl committed in the name of the Quorum?" I open my eyes wide in mock disbelief. "Gee, I guess it's time to put that assumption to bed once and for all." I crook my finger, beckoning him forward. When his ear is close enough, I whisper, "It's the *cuddling*."

Jack thinks for a moment, then muses, "Maybe Mary feels the same way about Evan."

His smart-ass remark earns him a hard punch in the arm.

Jack is laughing so hard that he almost swerves into a big rig.

As the truck's driver lays on his horn, Jack hits the accelerator. In less time than it takes to say "cuddle" Jack's BMW i8 has us forty feet beyond that rig.

Note to self: put a security camera in the playhouse.

6

Paranormal Activity

Serious ghost hunters have specific tools to determine if paranormal activity is in the area. Should you suspect a ghost lives with you, a ghost hunter will show up with:

1. *Audio equipment with microphones that are sensitive enough to pick up ectoplasm readings. Why? Because ghosts' comments—known in this business as "electronic voice phenomena," or EVP—often cannot be picked up by the human ear.*
2. *Electromagnetic Frequency readers, because you cannot see EMFs with the naked eye. Popular devices include the KII meter, and the Ovilus X. (Which begs the question: were there previous versions of the labeled Ovilus I, II, III, IV, V, VI, VII, VIII and IX? If so, how accurate were they?).*
3. *The hunters will also bring ion detectors, infrared cameras, and Geiger counters.*

Ironically, despite the pings, tings, and whirrs made by all these gadgets, none have yet provided empirical evidence that our dearly departed are still here among us in some alternate dimension.

In other words, there is no real way to know if the ghost hunter you've contacted is legitimate, or if he's pulling your very real leg.

And still, we want to believe. Go figure.

THE HALL OUTSIDE THE OVAL OFFICE'S RECEPTION AREA swarms with busy people doing important things that will result in historic consequence.

When Jack and I enter with Evan, Dean Connelly McIver is already there.

The men are dressed in khakis and golf shirts under blazers. Their golf gear and shoes were already taken off their hands by the president's Secret Service detail. Besides being put through a security scanner, it will be stowed in the caravan that will take POTUS and his guests to the Congressional Country Club.

I'm dressed a bit more formally. Jack and I have to break the news to Lee about the sources of the compromised DARPA white papers, and to ask his permission to review the security video footage of those who were in the Project Hercules meeting.

Dean McIver doesn't rise from the oval-backed chair, but stays seated until Lee's new secretary, a sweet looking woman in her twenties, comes over and introduces herself as Eve Pettival. "The president looks forward to getting out on the links, but first things first—the photo shoot." Her arm goes out toward McIver. "Please, let me introduce you."

It's the first time Jack and I are meeting McIver, but I guess it's more accurate to say that Evan and he are to be *reintroduced*, since both of Evan's parents, Catherine and Robert, took Evan to every alumni event they attended at the university. This includes the one announcing the biotechnology scholarships funded by Robert, not to mention the well-publicized naming ceremony for the Robert Martin technology lab, built on Morgan Adams's campus with Robert's money.

After a tepid shake of our hands, McIver turns to Evan. Despite a heartier handshake accompanied with the robust declaration, "Ah, there's our boy!" there is a chill in the dean's voice.

Thank goodness Lee's welcome is much warmer to the poor kid.

Strolling purposefully out of his office, Lee reaches to shake Jack's hand, and then pecks me on the cheek. Evan, though, gets a warm hug. "Hey, Evan, long time no see," the president murmurs.

"You should make it out to California more often, Mr. President," Evan ribs him.

A smile lights up Lee's face. "Speaking of which, we'll be home later this week for a few days. Janie will be going through orientation at her prep school. I look forward to having you over to Lion's Lair for a round of golf there as well."

At this point, Eve introduces Lee to Dean McIver, who has been watching the exchange agog. Odd, since a man in his position at a major private university knows all too well that politics makes for strange bedfellows.

Then again, putting the name of the benefactor who just gave you yet another one-hundred-million-dollar gift for a previously named building obviously took some rolling around in the sheets too. Just this morning, Adams Morgan University announced that its new technology building will herein be called "the Lionel Broderick Technology Lab," effectively erasing any and all evidence of the Martin family's gift.

I haven't yet broken that news to Evan.

I may break McIver's arm instead.

"TURN A LITTLE TO THE LEFT, MR. PRESIDENT," GORDON Soames, the diminutive photographer who has been a White House staple through the last four administrations, cajoles his boss. "Ah, good! And you, sir"—he points to Dean McIver—"just a little to the right…perfect!" He takes a quick succession of shots. "Now, how about some smiles, gentlemen?"

When Lee smiles, his eyes shift toward me.

Grateful for this effort on Evan's behalf, I smile back.

None of this is lost on Jack.

I squeeze Jack's hand. He kisses the back of mine.

None of this is lost on Lee.

For a nanosecond, his smile wavers. Did the camera that is snapping away furiously catch it?

A moment later, Gordon motions for Evan to join them.

The boy hesitates before making the few tentative steps that put him at Lee's side.

Lee shifts in order to put Evan between he and McIver.

A frown of disappointment flashes on McIver's face, but only for a moment. Having to smile pretty for the camera with Evan at his side seems to have put him in an awkward situation.

Well, too bad. If he's going to let Evan down, it's much better that the boy discovers this early in the college admissions process.

As Gordon packs up his camera gear, Lee nods to his secretary. "We're off, Eve."

That's her cue to call the Secret Service with the message to ready POTUS's cavalcade.

Lee shakes McIver's hand again before giving Evan's shoulder a good squeeze. "If you and Dean McIver don't mind following Eve out, Jack and I will join you shortly. I'm sure you two have much to talk about."

Evan looks hopeful, whereas McIver practically blanches at the thought of being alone with the young man.

Eve nudges them out, closing the door behind them.

By the time Lee has turned around to face us, his smile has faded. In its place is a pained grimace. "I understand that you killed Salem—*yet a second time*. Want to debrief me on how something like this happens, Mr. and Mrs. Craig?"

EGAD.

Okay, so, how do you tell a guy that you somehow

missed a point-blank kill shot to the baby daddy whose death his wife still mourns?

In all honesty, I've got no idea—but here goes. "Yeah, well, about that…" I roll my eyes as I sigh. "We're, like, on this beach in the south of France when lo and behold a mega-yacht rolls up with the very last person on Earth you'd expect to be on it. Well, of course, we're curious, since one of us—*moi*— actually pulled the trigger on the guy, and the other"—I wave in Jack's direction—"came in a few seconds later and can verify the kill. Hours later, a dead girl turns up on the beach, and since rumor has it that Supposed-to-Be-Dead-Dude is throwing some big shindig on his tugboat, we think to ourselves, 'Selves, what say we crash it to see what's up?' So we do, and yada yada yada, he tries to rape me, yada yada yada, and so I—"

"Cut to the chase, Donna." Lee crosses his arms on his chest.

"With all due respect, Mr. President, you know as much about it as us," Jack growls. "But considering that Salem's personal email contained classified intel regarding Operation Hercules, there may be a connection between it and his Second Coming."

Lee's face turns white beneath his golfer's tan. "But how?…who…"

"Ryan told you what we know," I reply. "Or, knew at the time. In the meantime, some new clues have come to light—including the source of the leak regarding Operation Hercules. Really, there were three of them."

"You mean to tell me the Quorum has three cells planted within DARPA?"

"There were three compromised files." I pause and take a deep breath. "Including one that was in your possession."

Slowly, Lee sinks onto one of his office's divans. "There's no way it could have happened! The research has no digital trail. And the white papers came by military courier in a triple-sealed envelope. They never left the Oval Office, or the adjoining conference room. If they weren't in my hands— and mine alone—they were in my office safe."

"All the more reason Donna and I will conduct a step-by-step investigation, including interrogations with anyone who may have been alone in your office since the papers arrived."

"Of course, you've got my permission to do so." Lee shrugs. "A heads up: I haven't yet mentioned it to Vice President Drucker, for obvious reasons."

The biggest reason being that he doesn't feel the vice president has his back.

I've never met Vice President Thomas Drucker. As Catherine Martin's vice president-elect, Lee succeeded even before she took office. His party, the Democrats, strong-armed Lee to accept Drucker, the party's congressional whip. He is already a well-trained lapdog of the party's money-men, whereas someone with Lee's largesse in office means he can't be bought off the old-fashioned way: one donation at a time.

The trade-off was that Catherine would get a presidential pardon when Lee left office. With her death, he won't have to give it to her now, but he's still saddled with Drucker anyway.

I smile to reassure him. "I'll start immediately. If Vice

President Drucker wasn't in the meeting, I don't see the need to interview him." It's my way of saying he can count on me.

"He wasn't. In fact, there is no way he could have known about it."

"Good," I reply. "Hopefully some clue will reveal itself within the security camera footage that is available. I know the Secret Service sweeps the West Wing from top to bottom. Still, with your permission, I'd also like to inspect both the Oval Office and the Roosevelt Room."

Lee nods as he rises. "I'll ask Eve to pull the visitor manifest since last Thursday, which is when the meeting took place."

"Is there also some sort of video recording of the meeting?" I ask.

He shakes his head. "During this presidency, the walls don't have ears."

Understandable, but it sure as hell would make our jobs easier. Now is not the time to point that out, so instead I walk over to shake his hand. "Thank you, Mr. President. I know this must be a terrible blow to you."

Lee looks down at my hand, but doesn't shake it. Instead, he holds tight to it.

As if I'm his lifeline.

He gives me too much credit. At this point, I'm just trying to keep more corpses from popping up alive.

Lee finally lets go and walks out the door. As he tells Eve I'm to have access to both the Oval office and the adjoining private office until he gets back, and to round up whomever I need for questioning, Jack gives me a hug and a kiss on the forehead, for good luck.

Heaven knows I'll need it.

I watch from the doorway as Evan and the men move down the hall with Lee's Secret Service detail on their heels. Eve looks up and smiles at me. "The president has put me at your disposal. In fact, as we speak I'm running off the visitor manifest for the days in question. How else may I help?"

"Tell me the protocol for those who come into the Oval Office, and for that matter, the Roosevelt Room."

"As they enter, guests are asked to leave their cell phones in this basket"—Eve points to the one on the credenza beside her desk—"which they slip into a plastic bag, along with a Post-It bearing their names."

I nod. "Got it."

"When the president buzzes my intercom to allow them into the Oval Office, I'll open the door for them."

"Is the same system used for meetings in the Roosevelt Room?"

"Yes, for the most part."

"Eve, were there any security videos in action on the day in question?"

She thinks for a moment. "In the hallways, and in here"—she motions through the reception area—"yes, of course. But as far as I know, there aren't any security cameras in either the Oval office, or the Roosevelt Room."

What a shame.

"As soon as possible, I'd like to review the hall and reception footage, starting within twenty-four hours prior to the meeting, then twenty-four hours after. I'm sure it will take a couple of hours."

"I'll pull it up for you now." she assures me. "You can

watch it on the computer monitor in the president's private study." She points toward the door leading to a small room between the Oval Office and the West Wing dining room.

"Thank you. Please call me when it's been set up."

She nods and heads for her desk to make the necessary calls.

Ten minutes later, she invites me into Lee's study. She leads me to a laptop computer, and punches in a code, giving me the access I need.

"Thank you for that, Eve. I don't need anything else for now. However, should you run across anything that strikes you as odd taking place anywhere in the West Wing or the administrative offices, please pass forward your suspicions to me—and me alone. It is the only way to assure that the president has clean hands during our investigation. Do you understand?"

"Yes, of course." Her firm nod reflects her resolve to live up to this unusual request.

I wait until the door closes behind her before touching the computer.

The hunt begins for a terrorist in the White House.

THERE IS A DIGITAL FOLDER ON THE LAPTOP COMPUTER'S SCREEN. Inside of it are four video files: one that records the Oval Office reception area itself; one of the hallway between the Oval Office reception area and the Roosevelt Room; another of the anteroom between the West Wing's lobby and the press secretary's office that leads to the Roosevelt Room. The final one recorded the hallway leading from the chief of staff's office to the Oval Office, which has a door leading in to the Roosevelt Room.

A subtle choreography unfolds between the various security feeds: between the frantically paced comings and goings of the West Wing's metaphorical *corps de ballet*—administrative staffers whose steps are quickened with the urgency of the nation's business. But my eyes seek out the principal dancers—that is to say our persons-of-interest. I'm eager to see who they will be.

Even if they take their solos offstage, the time stamps on the breaches should give me clues as to who performed an espionage arabesque.

The set-up of the room commenced ninety minutes before the meeting. A young pretty assistant walked through the West Wing lobby and the Roosevelt Room anteroom, her arms laden with folders labeled with each of the attendees' names, and lined pads and pens bearing the White House logo. One of each was placed in front of an attendee's already reserved seat. When she left the room, she closed the door behind her.

About half an hour before the meeting started, she returned in order to escort two of the West Wing white-coated kitchen staff members through the door, along with a long cart with coffee, tea, fresh fruit, and pastries.

The Operation Hercules meeting started promptly at nine on Thursday morning. The project's lead scientists came early and filed in through the lobby anteroom.

I look closely at the two under suspicion: Rudy Brooks and Shelley Wollstonecraft. As they introduced themselves, their faces reflected recognition, as well as their surprise at seeing each other.

What I see next makes me shudder. Department of Justice Assistant Attorney Blake Reynolds, and Lee's National Security Council liaison, Todd Courtland, came out of Vice President Drucker's office just when the other two attendees—the director of intelligence, and the director of DARPA—walked toward the Oval Office with Lee.

Blake tried to indict me for treason along with Carl, because he refused to believe Carl doped me up in order to use me as a human shield during his escape from Gitmo. Todd is a conniving political animal, but I've yet to catch him doing something underhanded.

There's a first time for everything.

In the video, Blake and Todd exchanged knowing glances, but then went their separate ways: Todd, to his own office in the West Wing; and Blake, out the reception area of the West Wing, presumably back to the Department of Justice.

Within ten minutes, the security directors entered the Roosevelt Room. The West Wing aide escorted the scientists in from the anteroom.

I fast-forward to the next time the doors open: about twelve-fifteen, when the group breaks for lunch.

Before joining the others in the dining room, the scientists were shuffled into the Oval Office for their official photos with the president. Lee carried a folder with him.

The DOI and DARPA directors grabbed their phones to check messages as they moved toward the West Wing dining room.

I check the time stamps on the breaches. Apparently, they took place within the lunch hour.

During that time period, Lee and the two male doctors—

Rudy Brooks and Norbert Welles—moved from the Oval Office down the hall to the West Wing dining room. I notice Lee doesn't have his folder with him, so he did indeed leave it in his office. Had he put it in the safe, like he insists?

The third scientist, Shelley Wollstonecraft, walked back into the Roosevelt Room. When she left, she had her purse with her. With it in hand, she headed to the women's lavatory, near the West Wing lobby. Within five minutes, she'd rejoined all the men, who were already seated in the dining room.

Whereas there was hustle and bustle in the hallways, the meeting's attendees stayed put in the dining room.

The waiters roamed in and out of the room with various serving dishes and pitchers. When dessert was finally proffered, Rudy headed out into the hallway that goes from the dining room to the closest men's lavatory.

When he came out, instead of going back to the dining room, he made his way to the Roosevelt Room. He was there for only a few moments, but it was certainly enough time to take pictures with his cell phone.

Just as Rudy made his way out the door, the two members of the West Wing's kitchen staff were entering with fresh hot drink urns in their hands. They seemed startled to see him. To put them at ease, he laughed, and was kind enough to hold the door open for them. This time it was left open. A Secret Service agent stood at the threshold and watched them, so they are cleared from off my suspect list.

When they left through the lobby anteroom, the Secret Service agent was still standing by the door as Eve entered from the hall leading from the Oval Office. She placed Lee's personal mug in front of his seat, then said something to the Secret Service agent that made him laugh.

At the same time, Babette walked down the hall to the Oval Office reception area. With no one there to stop her, she entered Lee's office. Did Babette have time to find the DARPA file and compromise it?

I flip to the feed to see what she did. Yes, she went into the Oval Office, despite the door being shut.

A few minutes later, Eve returned. At first, she didn't notice that Lee's door was closed. When she did, she went to investigate. After talking to Babette for a few moments, she left to fetch Lee.

Maybe three or four minutes went by before Lee was seen following her back to his office. The feed showed her closing the Oval Office's door behind him.

A few moments later, the First Lady exited with Lee.

By then, the others had finished their desserts. Lee joined them, but skipped dessert. Ten minutes later, the whole group made its way to the Roosevelt Room.

When Lee joined them, he was carrying his folder.

Either he or Babette could have compromised it.

I send the security files to the Acme's cloud server, and text Arnie that he can access them there to do further analysis.

I walk back into the Oval Office reception area to say goodbye to Eve when I hear, "Donna Stone? What are you doing here?"

Ah, hell, it's Babette.

7

Black Widows

The term "black widow" is used to describe a species of spider that release a venom particularly harmful to humans, sometimes deadly. Like the majority of spiders, the black widow is dark in color. However, it does have one distinguishing mark on its abdomen, which resembles a red hourglass.

"Black widow" is also a slang term for a woman who is suspected of killing her husband.

Should you resemble the latter, here are a few tips:

1. *Don't leave clues of how you did him in. Here's where your obsession with spit-spot cleaning counts most!*
2. *Act bereaved. Alas, that means resisting the urge to flirt with the handsome detectives that show up to investigate. (And broad hint: If they refuse your offer of a cup of tea, it means they're on to you!)*
3. *Make sure he really, truly is dead. Why? Because you don't want him to quite literally come back to haunt you.*

Scorn drips from Babette's voice as she spits out my name. She can't—make that, won't—attempt any semblance of politeness.

I'm not the only one resisting the urge to blanch at her menacing tone. Unlike some who must tread these hallowed halls of power in her wake, those whose jobs don't tether them to her side quickly scurry from view.

In the couple of weeks since I last saw her, her barely-there baby bump can now be seen. And if her couture maternity frock is any indication, the announcement of a new addition to the First Family was made while we were out of the country.

I wonder how well the proud papa took the press corps' questions on the topic.

As if reading my mind, Babette's face turns crimson with shame. Instinctively, she raises her hand protectively, as if covering a scarlet A on her breast.

She should know by now that her secret is safe with me.

"I'm Donna *Craig* now, Babette," I declare with as much honeyed sweetness as I can fake. "Don't you remember? I was married a few weeks ago. You were at the wedding. In fact, you planned it—sort of...Ah, well, no matter." I smile brightly. "So glad I ran into you!"

"Really? Me and not Lee?" She sniffs the air, as if she smells a foul stench.

Babette's minions—Narcissa Belmont, her chief of staff; and Lucretia Suchoff, her press secretary—also raise their noses in disdain. This is certainly a change of venue from where they are more accustomed to having them: firmly up their boss's ass.

"Why, yes, of course," I assure her. "While Lee and Jack went to play golf, I asked Eve to point me in your direction so that we might have a little chat—"

The moment I say this, I catch the look in Eve's eyes. Bambi in headlights is putting it kindly. A sixteen-point buck at an NRA convention is more apt.

To Eve's credit, she's got a reason to sweat. Babette's head twists around quicker than Linda Blair's in an *Exorcist* reboot. "Is that so?" Her words are leavened with an acidic sweetness. "I didn't realize Eve knew I even existed, since *I'm always the last person to know my husband's schedule.*" She drills Eve with a deadly glare before swiveling so that I am now in her sights. "You, for example. Why wasn't I told my old friend Donna…let's see, what are you calling yourself this month? Oh yes—'*Craig*'—was coming?"

"It was a spur-of-the-moment trip. We're checking out colleges for our ward, Evan Martin."

"Poor Evan! First, his father is murdered by his mother, and then his mother meets her untimely demise, in prison no less!" Babette squeezes out an alligator tear. "Maybe it was for the best. Orange was never her best color."

Babette's cruelty never ceases to amaze me. I'm willing to guess she looks somewhat washed out in that same color. Maybe we'll soon find out.

With that in mind: "Babette, dear, do you have a few moments to meet with me?"

"Why?" Botox keeps Babette from frowning. Still, the trepidation in her voice is palpable.

Her pack of she-wolves picks up on it. Narcissa's surgically enhanced lips poise in a partially opened position, ready to object with some bogus excuse to steer clear of whatever turbulence I have in store for her boss. Lucretia's broad shoulders dip, as if she's ready to block or tackle me if I make some sort of desperate move toward the first lady.

Ha! Wishful thinking. So that they calm down, I take a step back. "A few words, about…a mutual friend."

The hard line of Babette's mouth goes soft. She thinks I mean Salem.

Good, exactly what I hoped. I really don't have anything to say about him, and I'm certainly not going to tell her about his unexpected resurrection—especially having been the one to put him back in a grave again.

She turns to her entourage. "Get lost. I'll text if I need you."

Narcissa and Lucretia don't have to be told twice. The pungent scent of *eau de I'm so outta here* fills the air. I am left alone with a woman whose beauty and position awes an admiring public, but whose inhumanity never ceases to stun those who know her too well.

I am in the latter group.

Babette knows this, which is why she closes the door to the Oval Office firmly behind us, blocking out any protests that Eve may have about us being in there without the great man himself.

Frankly, I can't think of a better place to interrogate the First Lady about any terrorists she may still know personally. Perhaps it will bring home all she has to lose: the pursuit of happiness, not to mention her liberty—

And if the crime merits it, even her life.

TO SOFTEN HER UP, I START WITH WHAT SHOULD BE A SOFT PITCH over home plate: "It's so kind of you to make time for me today."

Babette rolls her eyes. "Cut to the chase, Donna. You may have dropped off your new hubby to play golf with Lee, but you didn't expect to run into me before you took off back to whatever hole you crawled out of."

Is this the way she wants to play it? So be it. I don't get bitch-slapped without hitting back. "My, my, my! Was it that obvious?" I raise my hands to my face, in mock horror. "Look, I'll do my best to be civil if you will. Quite frankly, I'm here because I wanted to see how you were doing after…after the, er, accident."

"How am I? Lousy! The morning sickness is over, but I'm still in mourning." She sinks into one of the Oval Office's large wingback chairs, and massages her brow, as if rubbing away her grief. "You said you had something to tell me. What is it?"

"Frankly, I'd like to ask you a few questions."

She looks up, suspiciously. "No, no, no. That's not how this works. If you want to get something, first you have to give something." A smirk rises on her lips as a thought comes to her: "How about this? For each question you have, I get one too."

Hmmm. "Okay, Babette. Why don't you start?"

She blinks innocently as her lips curl into a smile. "Lee is under the impression that Salem was a terrorist. Did he get this ridiculous idea from you?"

"What did he tell you?"

"What do you think he said?" she sneers. "He told me it was classified, and that he can't tell me a damn thing. Only, in this case, he was angry enough about…this"—she looks down at her belly—"to call Salem a whoremonger. Even worse, he called him a *terrorist.* He indicated Salem died in some special ops mission. He said it was for the best; how I'd be hung for treason if the truth of our…our relationship got out." She sighs.

"Lee wasn't exactly on point. In truth, you'd be indicted for treason if you'd been caught passing classified intelligence to Salem. And for that matter, if Lee were subpoenaed and it was disclosed that he knew of your relationship, he could be impeached—or worse yet, convicted of a crime. As it's been proven in other administrations, the President of the United States is not above the law."

"Great dodge. I'll take that as a yes." She nods grudgingly. "It's your turn."

"Babette, are you still on Graffias International's board of directors?"

Her back stiffens. "I…I resigned when Lee was sworn in. It's the law, you know."

"Then why is your name still on its most recent corporation papers?" I counter.

She smiles slyly. "Is that a question?"

"No. It's a fact. And should anyone else discover it—"

"Merely a clerical error. I'll have someone take care of it immediately." She flicks her wrist in annoyance. "My next question to you is: what were the state secrets that Lee's previous secretary, Eileen Woodley, supposedly stole?"

"I can't answer that question for the same reason as Lee stated to you regarding Salem."

Babette rolls her eyes. "If that's the case, I get another turn."

"Sure, go for it."

She leans in, as if analyzing every pore in my face. "What exactly is it that Jack sees in you?"

I bite my tongue to stop myself from shouting out: You mean, besides the fact that I'm not a conniving gold digger? Instead, I tell her the truth: "That's easy: my husband knows I love him with all my heart, and that he can trust me with his life."

Proof that the concept is novel to her is that she reels back, like a demon sprinkled with holy water.

My turn: "Having established that Salem was involved in terrorism, what can you tell me about his business dealings, legitimate and otherwise?"

"I was his lover, not his accountant," she hisses. "Our meetings took place in a bedroom, not a boardroom."

"You've been on the board for quite some time, even before you knew Lee. Your first husband, Jonah Breck, was also on Graffias's board. Is that where you met?"

She wags a finger at me. "You aren't supposed to get two questions in a row, remember? But I'll give it to you, as a bonus. The answer is no. I met him around the same time he came on the board. And after Jonah's unfortunate demise, Salem asked me to take his place on the board."

I nod. Still, I'll have Emma pull together as much as she can on Babette's background, not the public relations fodder planted for reporters find for puff pieces in *Vanity Fair, Vogue,* or *Elle.* "Okay, now, what do you want to know?"

Her eyes glitter as she taps her OPI-glossed talons in

anticipation. "What's your opinion: was Carl a better lover than Jack?"

"Hardly," I growl.

"What?" She shakes her head in mock shock. "With those *long* fingers, and those bedroom eyes…not to mention all the not-so-subtle innuendos, I just thought Carl delivered mind-blowing sex! Oh, not that Jack's fingers are so short." She grins knowingly. "You've piqued my interest, Donna. So come on, give me *all* the juicy little details."

I shake my head primly. "That's a second question."

"Give it to me, and I'll do the same for you." She chuckles. "But just this once."

"He's a wonderful kisser. He likes to cuddle—"

She yawns—loudly.

"As I was saying before I was rudely interrupted with a view of the potential cavity in your Number 28 bicuspid, when Jack and I are intimate, he gives as well as takes. He is kind, loving, gentle, and—"

"You've got to be kidding me, right?" Her nose wrinkles in disgust. "Next you'll tell me that he only does it missionary."

I feel my face heat up, not out of shame, but anger at telling her anything at all about him.

Babette notices too. She giggles. "Oh, my God, I get it now! You're making him sound boring *on purpose*. You know, we were supposed to be honest with each other!" She clicks her tongue at me as she stands to leave. "I guess it lets me off the hook, and not a moment too soon. I'm getting bored."

"I still have two more questions, remember?"

She lets loose with an exasperated sigh, but sits down nonetheless.

"You stopped by the Oval Office on Thursday while Lee was in a meeting in the Roosevelt Room. You were in there by yourself for at least three or four minutes. What were you doing, Babette?"

Scorn lifts her brows. "Twiddling my thumbs. We're hosting Vice President Drucker and his wife, Tilly, at Lion's Lair this weekend. I wanted to go over the agenda to keep his boring wife busy. Apparently, he had something more important to do."

Gee, now what could that be…

Oh, yeah, I got it: *save the world from destruction.*

She shrugs. "She's gaga over celebrities, so I guess all I'll have to do is rustle up a few to hang poolside with us. At least there's one upside to this: considering the poor woman's girth, I should look practically svelte beside her, even in a maternity one-piece." She looks at her watch again, to let me know the clock is ticking. "You've got one more question, so you better make it a good one."

Oh lady, 'tis indeed. "Are you a Quorum operative?"

My question knocks the smirk off of her face. "How dare you!"

"That isn't an answer."

"I won't dignify that with another word!"

"I'll take your dodge as a yes, then."

Furious, she springs to her feet. "Get out of here! Get out of my life, once and for all! Why, I'll have you banned from stepping foot on one blade of grass on these grounds—"

"Calm down, Babette! I'm not going anywhere, but you're certainly free to leave."

"No—not until you answer one last question!" She grabs hold of my arm.

"Okay, shoot." If she had a gun, I'm sure she would.

"Did you…were you with Salem on the night he was killed?" Her voice cracks under the weight of her question.

"Me?" I'm flustered because I didn't see the question coming.

Hmmm. How much does she already know? I've got better than a fifty-fifty chance that she truly is clueless.

I'll take those odds. "Sorry, but no. I had better things to do *on the eve of my wedding.* And, even if I hadn't, I would never—repeat, *never*—be unfaithful to Jack."

Her face is a complete blank. Either too much Botox, or she's thinking this through.

Finally, she rises again. With head held high, she murmurs, "I'm glad we finally had this little chat and cleared the air, Donna. I always wondered if yours was the last face Salem saw. I can now sleep soundly without worrying that the woman my husband would so willingly fuck also killed the man I loved."

She opens the door and walks out.

Suddenly, I realize that she never even bothered to take this opportunity to ask me to confirm or deny her suspicions about her husband and me.

I guess she doesn't care.

I find myself with one more reason to pity Lee Chiffray.

"REALLY? THE GOLF GAME WAS THAT BAD?" I KICK OFF MY heels before plopping down on our hotel suite's sofa and draping my legs over Jack's.

"The game itself was fabulous—for one of us, anyway. Evan owned the back nine." He tugs at my toes, one by one. "This McIver guy would be an idiot to pass on adding Evan to his student body—if not for his grade point average, then because the university's golf team would lose out." He kisses my little toe. "Hey, the tub in the master bedroom is big enough for two."

"My feet smell that bad? Yeah, okay, I can take a hint." I pull my legs in under me. "But I'm not ruining a good soak by talking about my reconnaissance. We'll do it here and now."

"I'm all ears. I'd hate to think today was a complete waste of time."

"Really? You didn't have fun on the links?"

He rolls his eyes. "I could think of better things I could have been doing. Unlike you, I don't find hanging on Lee Chiffray's every utterance that enthralling."

That declaration earns him a kick. "No? Well, then, maybe you would have enjoyed answering Babette's questions instead—since they were mostly about you and your"—I glance down at his lap—"bedroom technique."

He's laughing so hard that he falls off the sofa. "And all this time I thought women never played kiss and tell."

I point to myself. "This woman did—sort of, in the hope that she'd give me pertinent intel in return."

"So, what did you ask her?"

"Everything: about Salem, the Quorum, even Jonah Breck."

He raises a brow. "Did you ask her about Lee?"

"You mean, how he is in the sack? Of course not!"

"That's not what I meant, my lascivious little arm

charm!" He shakes his head in wonder. "I mean, did she indicate he had ties to the Quorum?"

I grab his hands in order to pull him back up onto the couch with me. "I felt she'd be more willing to discuss Salem. She was, but only up to a point—that point being what I knew about his death. The last thing I was going to tell her was that I pulled the trigger—let alone that I somehow missed, but got a second chance at taking his life, with a set of pliers." I shrug. "It was all for naught. When it came to answering my questions about Salem, she turned on the dumb blonde routine." I bat my eyes, and with all of Babette's honeyed sweetness, I declare, "'Salem and I were just fuck buddies…The Quorum? What's that? …I was only put on Graffias's board because of Jonah's untimely demise.'"

Jack chuckles. "You fluffed her up by divulging the titillating details of my incomparable studliness for a few half-truths and dodges? What a waste."

"You're telling me. And for your sake, I thought it best to tone down the details of your, er, prowess. In hindsight, perhaps blabbing all the tantalizing details would have had her spilling her guts—to you, anyway." I nod toward the bathroom. "Speaking of your 'incomparable studliness,' actions speak louder than words."

He must agree because he picks me up in his arms and carries me toward it.

We make it as far as the door's threshold when my cell phone buzzes.

Arnie is calling.

Jack snatches the phone out of my hand, but puts the connection on speakerphone: "This better be good."

"I wish it were." Arnie sighs. He's on speakerphone as well, indicating that the rest of the mission team is also on the line. "We've viewed each security feed individually, to see if Donna missed something in her assessment: that no one other than Dr. Wells, Dr. Wollstonecraft, FLOTUS, and POTUS were alone with any of the files. Sadly, no."

"And worse news," Emma pipes up. "Except for the president's copy, all the Operation Hercules white papers were shredded after they were collected. The pieces were then incinerated."

"So, as of this moment, Lee's copy is the only one left," I deduce.

"There would be fingerprints on it other than Lee's," Abu points out. "For example, his new secretary's, and perhaps the Quorum asset."

"Lee insisted that he opened the secure pack himself before reading it. Before and after the meeting, he kept it under lock and key," Jack reminds him. "So if they're on it, she has to be the Quorum operative."

"The same goes for Babette, then," Emma counters. "You had quite an interesting conversation with her yesterday, Donna." I can tell Emma is trying to stifle a giggle.

"Yeah right, hardee-har-har." Obviously, everyone has read my summary brief of our conversation. "In any event, we've now got Lee's copy in hand, so that Acme can dust it for prints."

"If the West Wing security feeds are a dead-end, what's our next course of action?" Jack asks.

"Arnie has a suggestion," Ryan replies.

"More than likely, the white papers were compromised with a cell phone camera," Arnie reasons. "I'm sending you a phone app that releases a Trojan to the subjects' cell phone's WiFi and cellular signals. Once activated, it allows Acme to read their uploads, emails, and downloaded transmissions. When you go undercover, try to get your phones within a ten-foot range of the suspects' devices."

"As DARPA employees, can't we just plant the Trojan by sending an email, or a text?" I ask.

"We can't take the chance that the security measures on their cell phones can detect the source of the Trojan virus," Emma explains. "IP servers are the least secure point of entry."

"What if it's already been erased from their cell phones' memory archives?"

"We'll still know if it was there, and where it went afterward," Arnie replies. "Or, as a rapper would sing"—and sadly, Arnie actually croons—"'*Its vapor tail leaves an electronic paper trail...*'"

"Besides the fact that you sound like a scalded cat, no rapper in his right mind would sing about something like this," Abu mutters.

Ryan sighs loudly. "Keep on task, people."

"Lee mentioned he's headed to Lion's Lair this weekend with the family, for Janie's school orientation," I remind them. "Jack and I will come up with some excuse to get close enough to do the same with Lee and Babette's cell phones."

"Good, Craigs. Okay, we're signing off. Catch some shut-eye…or, er, whatever."

Jack waits for the click. "So, what do you say? Still feel like a little 'whatever'?"

"If you have to ask, you must scrub my back first."

"With pleasure."

We Craigs take our pleasures where we can. A marble tub in the Willard Hotel will do.

After all, tomorrow is another day.

"I don't think this is a good idea." Evan's declaration is made as he scrutinizes his image in the hotel suite's living room mirror. His brow is furrowed in a deep scowl.

He's been up since dawn. We weren't supposed to know it, but I heard him pacing in the bedroom on the far side of our hotel suite as he practiced some sound bites he hopes will convince Dean McIver that he has every right to take his place at his father and mother's alma mater.

"Are you kidding me? You look great." I'm not just saying this. His navy blazer, worn over a blue oxford shirt and gray slacks, fits him like a glove. I smile encouragingly as I motion toward the door. "And if we don't leave now, we're going to be late for your tour of Morgan Adams."

He winces. "I...well, frankly, I think it's a waste of time. Dean McIver was nice enough, but I could tell he wasn't very interested in discussing the school with me. Each time Jack brought it up, the man turned as white as a ghost."

"You're imagining it," Jack shouts from our bedroom. He saunters out, still knotting his tie. "The sooner we get there, the sooner you can take the tour, ask intelligent questions, make your pitch, and put him on the spot."

I point toward the door. "Shall we?"

Evan takes a deep breath, nods, and heads in the direction of his future.

A cell phone rings: Evan's. He pulls it from a pocket and

stares down at it. His eyes grow big. He looks over at us. "It's…it's Dean McIver."

Jack waves at the phone in his hand. "What are you waiting for? Take it."

Evan purses his lips before clicking onto it. "Yes, Dean McIver? We were just heading over…" His eyes grow large. His shoulders sag. "But…I don't understand! It wasn't my decision to…No, I guess you're right. I'd feel exactly the same way…I hope you don't think I…Thank you, sir. Good-bye." As he clicks off, stunned, he walks to a chair and sits down.

Jack and I walk over and kneel beside him. "What did the dean say?" Jack asks.

Still awed, Evan shakes his head. "He said I don't need to come on campus; that even if I apply for admission, he couldn't approve it in good conscience."

"Why not?" I ask.

"Because the scholarship program in my father's name was voided, and the funds committed to the new building were frozen by the trustee of my parents' estate."

"How could that be?" I ask. "It was part of your father's will!"

"I know!" As if summoning some thought about it, Evan closes his eyes.

"Something's not right about this!" Jack declares. "I'll look into it the moment we get home."

"Even if you can get the trustee to follow through on Dad's donations, I don't think the dean will change his mind about my acceptance."

"Why do you say that?" I ask.

Evan's eyes glass over with tears. "He also accused me of

using my connection with President Chiffray to influence him."

My face warms with guilt. "You did no such thing! The golf excursion was my idea—"

"That isn't the point," Jack growls. "If McIver was feeling so virtuous about the building and the scholarships, he should have passed on the golf invitation in the first place."

Reluctantly, I nod. "You're right. He seemed perfectly comfortable having his photo taken with the president."

"Until I got into the picture too," Evan murmurs. He buries his head in his hands.

"That's okay. We'll move up our trip to Boston by a day—"

Evan lifts his head. "No! Please, Donna! I'd…I'd rather not. I don't think I can go through this again."

"You can't let it shake your confidence," Jack warns him. "You've got so much to offer any university you apply to—"

"You may be right. But if I do get accepted somewhere, it should be on my own merit, not my parents' financial success." He rises unsteadily to his feet. "I better start packing. I'll take the rest of the summer to think about what to do…or not."

Jack nods at me—his way of telling me to back off and let Evan lick his wounds.

I have good reason to give it one more shot. "Listen, Jack and I have to meet with a few people in the San Francisco Bay Area. One of them happens to be on the Berkeley campus—and as it turns out, in the bioengineering department."

My declaration piques Evan's interest enough to lift his head out of his misery. "Who?"

"Dr. Shelley Wollstonecraft."

"I know that name." Evan thinks for a moment. "My dad funded her chair in the department."

"Would you like to tag along?" Jack asks nonchalantly.

Evan pauses. "Only if I can meet her incognito."

"Use your name, but don't bandy around those of your parents," I suggest.

Evan laughs. "You don't have to ask me twice."

Jack nods toward Evan's bedroom. "Grab your gear. We have a plane to catch."

Evan's glassy-eyed smile breaks my heart. I pray he won't let himself be waylaid by this bump on the road of his life's journey.

And wherever it takes him, Jack and I will make sure he'll always have a place to call home.

8

I See Dead People

It's okay to see dead people.

However, if you choose to interact with them, here are some do's and don't's:

- *Rule #1: Don't stick your hand through the ghost's ectoplasm. Besides being crude and offensive, as your mother would say, "You don't know where it's been, so don't touch it!"*
- *Rule #2: It's polite to act scared, even if you aren't. But don't over-act the role of horror victim. You're not going for an Academy Award, just a get-out-of-Hell-Free card.*
- *Rule #3: It's okay to communicate, but don't ask rude questions. Topics to avoid:*

- *How old the poltergeist may be. (No need to rile him up by reminding him how many years he's been gone, and therefore how old he really is.)*

- *How he died. (Possibly not the best memory he's held onto, considering it's his last one.)*
- *What he wants with you. If you're lucky, it's not to suck out your soul, or replace your soul in your body. Because, let's be honest: this wasn't exactly what you had in mind when you said you wanted a total makeover.*

WE'VE JUST LANDED AT SFO WITH EVAN AND TEXTED THE LIMO that will be taking us to the Four Seasons Palo Alto when my phone rings.

It's Trisha. "Mommy, guess what? Janie is in town! And she's hoping I can come for a sleepover. Please say yes because I'd rather not see the ghost again tonight–"

"Ghost?" My heart falls into my stomach. "Have you seen him again?"

Trisha sighs. "Yes."

"Don't worry, Mom, I'm on it," Jeff shouts from the background.

I'm almost afraid to ask, but I have to: "Trisha, honey, what does your brother mean by that?"

"He's trying to catch the ghost, but he keeps falling asleep on the job, and I'm tired of trying to keep the ghost occupied until he wakes up." She sighs deeply. "So, I'd like to sleep at Janie's tonight. Aunt Phyllis says she's okay with it if you are."

"Sure, okay. But wait until either Dad or I can take you over."

Curious, Jack looks over at me.

I mouth *Babette* to him. He rolls his eyes.

"You're coming home?" Trisha squeals.

"They're coming home?" Mary's hopeful wistfulness is the counterbalance of her sister's glee.

"Either Dad or me. I'll call you back."

"Thank you, Mommy!" Trisha kisses the phone ten times before clicking off.

"There's been a bit of a hitch," I explain to Jack.

He laughs. "That's obvious. What did you mean about Babette?"

"Apparently, Trisha just heard from Janie. She and her mother came in a few days early to Lion's Lair. The girls want to hang together."

He nods. "And, of course, we want them to, so that we can release the Trojan on Babette's phone."

"You'd have better luck with her." I bat my eyes. "You always do. Besides, Ryan has already set up my meeting with Rudy Brooks for this afternoon," I remind him. "Or, I should say, Marilyn Talbot's."

"And only one of us needs to take Evan to his interview tomorrow with Dr. Wollstonecraft, at Berkeley," Jack concedes. "I guess that settles it. He can hang at the hotel while you're with Rudy. As focused as Evan was on the plane with his college interview prepping, I think he'll be fine by himself for a few hours." He gives me a kiss. "Our Acme pilot, George, will be disappointed that we won't have a night to play in San Francisco, but if I'm to take Trisha on over, he and I better get hopping."

"If you talk POTUS into another golf game, I won't have to figure out a way to be within ten feet of his cell phone."

"I'm on it," he promises.

I don't have to ask twice. I already know he'd do anything to keep me away from Lee, with or without his phone.

He heads off to give George the bad news.

DNA 10Squared's president and Chief Technology Officer, Rudy Brooks, has his back to me as I enter his corporate sanctum: a corner office of the commodious three-story building at the edge of a verdant Silicon Valley start-up campus that was designed by the noted architect IM Pei.

A Picasso drawing in an elegant platinum frame adorns the wall next to his credenza. Rudy stares at it as he talks into his headset. His conversation is peppered with boasts of his firm's unicorn status, indicating it has a valuation of a billion dollars or more. He follows this up with other declarations that are sure to create a tent in the pants of whatever venture capitalist he's massaging. He ends the call by babbling, "Knowledge is in the end based on acknowledgement. Get with the program, Horace. The train is leaving the station, with or without you."

The best Rudy can do is one of Ludwig Wittgenstein's many illogical quotes, followed by a trite metaphor? *Meh.* I guess it's supposed to add credence to his carefully curated public persona.

And who the hell is Horace?... Ah! He's talking to Horace Levy, the elusive financier renowned for his innate ability to recognize the rare IPO-start-up unicorns amongst the herd of non-performing mules. Horace's reputation rises along with each tech firm's sky-high valuation. What all of them have in common: their products or services appeal to governmental agencies with big budgets to spend. And because he prefers walking the halls of power versus those of the tech campuses throughout Santa Clara County, meetings with the likes of a Rudy Brook are rare.

Hey, at least Rudy got him to come to the phone.

Rudy senses another presence in the room, and turns my way. Seeing me, he blanches. I can't say I blame him. Today, I'm not at my most beauteous by a long shot. As part of my cover, I've set up my interview as "Marilyn Talbot," supposedly a DARPA public information officer assigned to interview him for a magazine profile article. Once publicly disseminated, it should embellish his cred with other governmental agencies, as well as his stockholders—

Not to mention Horace Levy.

So, why would he risk it all for a treason rap?

We'll find out soon. Today, if I have my way.

Marilyn is supposed to be so innocuous that he'll soon forget her. With that in mind, I'm wearing a white turtleneck that would do a nun proud. My boxy navy suit hides any and all curves. To complete this frigid ensemble, I've crammed my feet into square-toed one-inch pumps, I wear square-framed glasses, and have my hair flattened into a severe women's-prison-matron's bun that sits heavily at the nape of my neck.

Even now, Rudy would prefer to inspect his well-manicured nails than look at me, as if doing so will burn his corneas.

So, mission accomplished—

Except for the fact that, in his shock, he's tossed his phone on his credenza, a full twenty feet from me.

"This is a treat," he mutters as he proffers his hand. In the nanosecond he allows for a handshake, our palms barely touch.

"Oh, Mr. Brooks, the pleasure is all mine," I gush. "This is a dream assignment for me! I'm all ears about Project Hercules."

He puffs up at my compliments, finally forcing his lips into a welcoming smile. "How about a little tour of the project's lab? It's where we make the magic."

"Super! Sounds like a plan! Mind if I record our conversation?" I pull out my cellphone and hold it up.

He shrugs. "Sure, why not?" He heads for the door.

"Um…don't you want to take your cell phone with you?"

"Nah. I want to give you my complete and undivided attention." He leers and adds, "You deserve it."

Yikes.

As I follow him out the door, he tells his assistant, "I'm letting my calls roll over to voice mail. Don't disturb me while I'm with Miss Talbot."

She nods vigorously, but smothers a sly grin. I take it I don't look like the typical woman for whom he holds calls. "If anyone calls to find out why you aren't picking up, when shall I say you'll be back?"

"This won't take more than twenty minutes." He drills me with his eyes, as if making that clear to me as well.

"Even if it's Mr. Ellison, or Mr. Andreessen?"

He sighs mournfully. "Yes, Chloe—*anyone.* I'll be back as soon as I walk Miss Talbot out."

If he escorts me out after the damn tour, the mission is screwed.

I try to think of some reason to change his mind, but he's already shepherding me down the hall, to the room where "the magic" takes place: Operation Hercules' lab.

Rudy talks a mile a minute, but nothing he tells me is more than the media sound bites he'll be spouting as soon as Operation Hercules is revealed to an unknowing public.

But, revealed by whom: the U.S. government? Or, the Quorum, while boasting it stole it from the U.S. Defense Department as it auctions off these so-called super soldiers to the highest bidding terrorist organizations?

Trust me, no DARPA public information officer would know how to spin that one.

Besides recording him on my cell phone's digital audio app, Emma is also monitoring the mission via my audio bud and security cam contact lenses.

So far, his answers barely touch the surface. Despite encouraging him to call me Marilyn, he keeps things formal to the point that he practically hisses the salutation "Miss."

I'm okay with that. He's not my type anyway. But because my goal is access to his cell phone, I am *not* okay with the fact that he doesn't have his cell on him.

I've got to get back into his office so that I can access it.

Up until now, I've been nodding benignly. Time to turn up the heat. Holding my hands behind my back, I slide off my wedding and engagement rings before slipping the engagement ring back on alone.

"Too bad all of this is top secret! It's such an interesting and worthwhile application for civilian use too. My fiancé would be all over financing something like this."

Rudy's eyes open, as if noticing me for the very first time—and this time he isn't forcing himself to be polite.

To validate my claim, I hold up my hand so that he can admire my engagement ring. "In fact, this is my last assignment at DARPA before my nuptials."

"Congratulations," Rudy's politeness is tempered by a doubtful smirk. "Who's the lucky guy?"

"He lives here in Silicon Valley." I shrug. "Horace Levy. He does a lot of work with…er, the Pentagon." To let him know I realize my *faux pas*, I tap my mouth with my palm. "You didn't hear that from me."

It takes a few moments before Rudy realizes his jaw has dropped open. If only he knew he was salivating too. "Horace? Yes, I know Horace!...Of course not, Mum's the word!" He's telling the truth. The sole purpose of his call to Horace is because of his governmental connections. "Oh, and listen, Marilyn: feel free to mention DNA 10Squared to him."

I put a finger to my lips to remind him that we share a secret. "Can't! At least, not now that your project is top secret. I guess it's why your company isn't already on his radar." I snap off my audio app. "But who knows what the future holds?" I pucker my lips suggestively. "I should be going. Horace and I are going into the city for dinner. Traffic between Palo Alto and the city is awful in the early evening!"

"I'm surprised he doesn't just helicopter in," Rudy mutters.

I stare at him until he's uncomfortable, but then I burst

out laughing, stymying him to no end. "Oh, but we are! I *was* referring to San Francisco's *copter* traffic." I look down at my watch. "As soon as Mark and Priscilla reach Horace's helipad, we'll take off. They're both standing up for us"—I duck my head shyly—"you know, during the nuptials." I wave off the hopeful look in his eye, "It'll be just a small wedding party at Horace's Mendocino lodge. He's a very shy person."

Rudy frowns. "So I've been told."

I smile hopefully. "Rudy, I noticed you have what looked like an authentic Picasso in your office. Before I head out, would you mind if I took a closer look at it? He's one of my favorite artists." I duck my head shyly. "I was an art history major until I realized it wouldn't pay the bills. It'll be a joy living among Horace's wonderful collection."

Rudy's eyes flicker with jealousy. Still, he's able to keep it at bay in order to exclaim, "By all means."

"You should be just as proud of your part in Operation Hercules," I whisper reverently. "I'm sure it'll pay off in spades."

"That's the plan," he declares.

When we walk back, he's got his hand firmly on my back.

"IT'S...JUST...BEAUTIFUL," I SIGH, AS I WIPE AWAY AN imaginary crocodile tear. I don't know how long I've stood in front of the Picasso—certainly the four minutes and thirty seconds needed for Arnie's Trojan app to do its thing.

"Transmitting," Emma assures me.

Just at that moment, Rudy's face lights up along with a grand notion: "Take it."

"Say *what*?" Emma practically shouts in my ear.

I shake my head, and not just to get her voice out of my head. "No…no! I couldn't!"

"I insist. Consider it my wedding present to you and Horace." To prove that he won't hear no for an answer, he plucks it from the wall and holds it out to me.

"Mr. Brooks, I—"

"Call me Rudy, please. And may I call you Marilyn? … Good! Marilyn, I mean it. If you don't take it, I'll be insulted! Horace is a saint of our industry. If this makes you happy, then I'm happy too."

"Oh…shit!" Emma squeals in my ear. "A *Picasso*!"

I back out toward the door. "He'll be as speechless as I am."

He waves me out. "It's only a painting, after all. I'm sure Horace will be the first to say, 'the world is the totality of facts, not things'."

Yet again with the Wittgenstein witticisms? The dude needs new material. "You're probably right," I murmur. I smile as I wave goodbye—

And hightail it out of there.

"What will you say to Ryan?" Emma asks when I'm safely down the road.

"Oh, hell, I don't know!" I sigh. "One thing for sure: I won't be quoting Wittgenstein."

BECAUSE EVAN IS WORRIED ABOUT BEING LATE FOR HIS

appointment on the Berkeley campus with Dr. Wollstonecraft, he begs me to drop him off in front of the building while I search out a nearby parking spot.

There aren't any.

By the time I find one and hustle to the Bioengineering building, he's already been introduced to her.

Worse yet, they've started the tour without me.

I won't be able to plant the Trojan until they get back. Even then, it may be a long shot, based on what the department's administrative assistant says. "The professor appreciated his promptness, considering how full her agenda is today." She nods at the roomful of teens and their parents who squirm anxiously in their seats beside me.

"Perhaps if you call her to find out where they are, I can join them," I suggest brightly.

The assistant leans in and whispers, "To tell you the truth, Professor Wollstonecraft prefers having one-on-one time with prospective students. She feels they're more candid in sharing the goals they have for their futures."

In other words, there's nothing I can do but cool my heels.

I take my seat beside the assistant, and wait. And wonder how to explain to Ryan that I blew it.

Twenty minutes later, I hear Evan's voice from down the hallway, thanking Dr. Wollstonecraft for "agreeing to meet with me on such short notice." By the time they come into view, he adds, "Berkeley is very high on my wish list. But I guess you hear that from everyone."

"Yes," Shelley admits. Still, she's smiling as she adds, "But not everyone has your GPA combined with your stellar extracurricular record, and such extensive knowledge of what Berkeley's bioengineering department has to offer."

She sounds sincere. Considering my reason for being here, I wonder how much of it is an act?

I also wonder what coerced her to sell intel to the Quorum. The intel gathered from her cell phone would have given Acme those answers. I'll have to figure out a different way to get to it.

I think I have my answer when Dr. Wollstonecraft hands Evan her business card. "This is my private email. I'd be interested in the experiment you mentioned, on the memory games you performed on the dogs."

Hearing this, Evan's smile broadens. "It was a blast to do. Of course, it scared the heck out of my dad. He didn't understand why I built such an extensive kennel in the backyard."

She looks around at the room. "Is he here with you today?"

Evan's face loses all color. "Um…no. He's no longer with us. Nor is my mother. I'm here with one of my guardians." He beckons me over. "Professor Wollstonecraft, this is Donna Stone…I mean, Craig! Donna, this is Shelley Wollstonecraft."

As I hold out my right hand, I initiate the app that releases the Trojan.

Now, all I need to do is keep her talking for the next four and a half minutes…

"It's a true pleasure to meet you," I exclaim fervently. "I have to apologize for missing the tour, but if it gave the two of you a chance to know each other better—"

"Excuse me, Dr. Wollstonecraft," her assistant interrupts loudly. "Mr. Courtland is on the phone for you. He says he's called your cell phone several times already. He insists on talking."

Is it Todd Courtland? I wonder.

Shelley frowns. "Oh! ...I'm so sorry, Mrs. Craig. If you'll excuse me. Evan again, a pleasure." She hurries off.

I look down at my watch: less than two minutes, darn it.

Evan chatters happily all the way to the car: about the department's state-of-the-art lab, its most recent grants, and its cutting-edge research in neuroscience.

"What was that about some science project with the dogs?" I ask him.

"It was something I tried the summer of ninth grade—before Mom got the bug to run for the presidency." He frowns at the thought. "I trained the three dogs to play with a toy mouse. Afterward, I trained them to attack it."

"Interesting concept. What was the purpose in it?"

He shrugs. "I was trying to understand hate."

"Were you successful?"

"In making the dogs hate the mouse? Unfortunately, yes—with two of them, anyway. The third dog refused to hate his. Before I could figure out why, Mom had made her decision to run for the presidency—and to give the dogs away. She said I wouldn't have time for them once the campaign season started."

Evan has so much to forgive Catherine for.

I wonder if he'll ever quit hating her.

When we land at LAX, Mary, Jeff and Jack are already waiting for us in the passenger pick-up zone. They jump out of my van, and in no time we are enveloped in a group hug.

When I lift my head, I realize someone is missing: Trisha. "Where is the little one?"

"Still at her sleepover. *You'll* want to pick her up later this afternoon." His emphasis on the word "you'll" is delivered with a smirk.

"Sure I will," I respond coolly. "Care to go with me?"

As the kids jump into the car, he shakes his head adamantly. "Been there, done that. I've got the emotional scars to prove it. Her double-entendres and lascivious suggestions bordered on sexual abuse."

"I'm sure you sidestepped it admirably. What I'd like to know is how close you had to get in order to upload the Trojan virus."

He shudders. "Too close. Since when does crying on someone's shoulder include a quick squeeze of his junk?"

"You're telling me she had the nerve to—"

"I kid you not." He raises his hand in a pledge. "I had half a mind to ask her to share her prognosis with my proctologist so that I can skip this year's physical."

I'm still laughing as I get into the front passenger seat.

From the rear-view mirror, I notice that Mary is holding Evan's hand. Even before we hit the 405, they are in deep conversation regarding his take on the Berkeley tour.

Hearing Dr. Wollstonecraft's name, Jack's eyes shift to. "All is not lost," he murmurs.

"Pray tell," I implore him.

His shake of the head indicates I'll get my answer later.

Instead, he glances in the rearview mirror. His eyes fall

on Jeff, who is deep in thought. "You're awfully quiet, young man. Is all this the talk about college admissions giving you food for thought?"

Jeff looks up. "What? …Oh! No. I'm just…" He shrugs. "I'll tell you tomorrow."

Jack smiles. "After we drop you kids at home, we've got to swing by the office, but we'll certainly be home by late afternoon if you want to bare your soul to me then."

Jeff shakes his head. "I'll need another day on my, er, analysis." Whatever is on his mind, it's no joking matter.

"Will you be able to follow up with Dr. Wollstonecraft on your experiment?" Mary asks Evan.

"Yes. It's somewhere in my boxes of things stored in your garage. I can dig it out."

"Better sooner than later, so that you're fresh in her mind," Jack warns him.

"I've only got a print version. Should I send a copy by mail?" Evan asks.

"No, via email," Jack suggests. "We've got a scanner at the house. Give it to us before we leave, and we'll turn it into a PDF file and drop it onto a thumb drive, so that you can email it to her."

Twenty minutes later we are home. Another twenty and Jack and I are scanning Evan's report and the accompanying photos while he writes his cover letter thanking Dr. Wollstonecraft for her time, and summarizing the attachments.

"Fingers crossed," Evan declares, as he hits the send button on his email program.

I wait until we're back in the car before leaning over with a thank-you kiss for Jack. "It was kind of you to help him with his follow-up message to Shelley."

"It's not all altruistic. I have an ulterior motive, which you'll hear when we join Ryan and the others."

"As long as it helps Evan's cause, I'm game."

Given the grimace on Jack's face, I may be asking too much.

9

Funeral Arrangements

It is said that one of the saddest days in your life is when you have to make funeral arrangements for a loved one.

However, if your feelings for the departed are at best "meh," here are some shortcuts you should feel free to take:

First, don't let the funeral director talk you into an expensive casket. Suggest cremation, and tell him you're passing on the expensive urn. To make your point, take a mason jar with you and leave it there.

Next, keep the eulogy short and sweet. The deceased's name, rank, and serial number will do. If his crime toward anyone is part of the public record, feel free to read it out loud, so that if the victim is in attendance, they'll feel vindicated. In fact, expect him to break out into a happy dance.

And finally, don't invite everyone the deceased may have known. Just a few close friends and family will do. If you're lucky, they'll feel the way you do about him, and will conveniently have something more important to do that day—like spend the day with someone who made them laugh instead of grit their teeth.

~

RYAN, EMMA, ARNIE, AND ABU ARE ALREADY IN ACME'S conference room when we arrive.

We barely have time to take our seats before Ryan tersely declares, "We've got clearance on FLOTUS and Rudy Wells."

"We still have to clear POTUS," Abu points out.

"I have to pick up Trisha from Lion's Lair. In fact, I plan on doing so when we leave here." I sigh. "Sorry, Ryan, that I didn't get to upload the Trojan on Shelley Wollstonecraft's cell."

Ryan tilts his head, stymied. "Sure you did. It was just activated."

I shake my head in wonder. "But…how?"

"When you mentioned you missed your opportunity with Shelley's phone, I attached the Trojan to Evan's email to her," Jack admits.

"Apparently she opened it, because we now have access to her photo archive, which is linked to her cell phone as well," Arnie explains.

I glare at Jack. "Look, I certainly understand what's at stake here, but if it rings any alarms with the school's cyber-security support, it will affect Evan's application for admission to Berkeley."

Arnie waves my fear away. "Donna, come on already! Heck, I've cracked the White House. I can certainly slip by a few academic coders."

Jack takes hold of my hand. "Donna, I know I should

have discussed it with you first, but the opportunity fell into our laps. As our mission leader, I had to take it."

"Great, then. Considering that Dr. Wollstonecraft is now in the clear, I'll let you explain it to Evan if it blows up in his face." I rise. "I need to pick up my daughter."

"Don't you mean *our* daughter?" Jack mutters.

"You're right. She is our daughter. And once again, we are using her childhood close friendship to promote a mission. I get it, Jack: it's a necessary evil. Still, it doesn't make it any easier." I walk away so that the others can't see my tears.

Ryan follows me out. "Donna, I know you've always hoped to separate your personal and professional lives. I'm sorry it hasn't always worked out that way. But I also know you'll never jeopardize the success of a mission because of it."

He's not just saying this to appease me. Only recently I learned that Ryan was once married. When he revealed his government-sanctioned double life to her, the thought so repulsed her that she put herself in danger, and paid the ultimate price: her life.

When I learned of Carl's duplicity, I had the same response, with a different result: I joined Acme to avenge him.

Still, on a daily basis I play hide-and-seek with death.

He knows I'll get what Acme needs, one way or another.

THE SECURITY DETAIL AT LION'S LAIR ARE SO ACCUSTOMED TO seeing the Donna-mobile that they never look twice when I hand them my ID, and in fact reward me with the shadow of a smile. They know me as a friend of POTUS.

In reality, I've been on both sides of that particular coin so many times that I'm no longer sure of this myself. I have to admit I'd prefer he turn out to be the man I hope he is—if not for our friendship, then certainly for the sake of our country. I guess clearing him of the treason committed in the Oval Office is the best way to show my friendship to him.

I just hope he doesn't catch me in the act.

He is there to greet me at Lion's Lair's grand entrance. He smiles warmly, and his posture is relaxed. As he helps me out of the car, he also pulls me in for a chaste kiss on the cheek.

"California agrees with you," I reply.

He chuckles. "If only I could move the West Wing permanently to Hilldale."

I shake my head. "You'd only be transferring DC's issues with it. Lion's Lair would quickly lose its charm."

He stares, stymied, if only for a moment. "It's not this stucco monstrosity I find so charming. You know that."

Yes, I do.

In his eyes, I am a friend—to his chagrin, with only one, albeit very important benefit:

I can save his presidency.

Or break it.

He places his hand on my arm in order to lead me in.

I am assured his cell phone is on him because he pulls it out in order to ring Janie's new au pair. "Sally, please let Trisha know that her mom and I are on our way up to fetch her. And tell Janie no tantrums, or else Trisha won't be allowed over during the rest of the time we're here at home." He clicks off, shaking his head in annoyance.

I look forward to meeting Sally. She's got to be better than Janie's last au pair, Frannie, who turned out to be a Quorum operative. The White House has had a hell of a time getting good help.

After texting Arnie the code phrase that warns him to look for the Trojan going live (*"Leaving soon to pick up groceries"*), I slip my hand into the pocket of my jacket to engage the app that may end Lee's and my friendship once and for all.

I then count down the seconds until this may happen: *two-hundred seventy, two-hundred sixty-nine, two-hundred sixty-eight, two-hundred sixty-seven…*

LEE WALKS AT A LEISURELY PACE: UP THE STEPS INTO THE GRAND foyer, and toward the elevator that will take us to the top floor, where Janie's bedroom suite is located.

Once the door closes, and he's assured we're away from prying eyes and perked ears, he mutters, "I wish Babette were half as strict with Janie as I am. It would make life easier. Instead, she encourages Janie to pit us against each other so that she can be viewed as the 'good parent'."

"That's a shame," I reply. "Although, I do understand her desire to stay close as Janie grows older."

"You've got it all wrong. Babette's fear isn't about Janie growing older, but about her own aging. She doesn't want to be the parent. She wants to be the indulgent older sister."

Ouch. But, yeah, he's got Babette pegged.

One-hundred forty-three, one-hundred forty-two, one-hundred forty-one…

"Under any circumstances, it's hard to bring up a child," I point out. "With considerable wealth and all the trappings of the White House, it's got to be nearly impossible to keep a child's feet on the ground."

"Please don't make excuses for Babette. We both know she's self-centered. I'd hoped another child in her life would change her for the better, but who am I kidding? She'll always put herself first. It's just…it's just who she is."

"Is Babette home?" I ask—a safe topic, I hope, but I doubt it.

"No. We're hosting Drucker and his wife, Tilly. She took them to the Reagan Presidential Library. Drucker wanted to pay his respects graveside." Lee's eyes roll skyward. "It's a great photo op for him, as you can imagine."

I have to purse my lips to keep from laughing.

Lee's not. He's frowning. He turns to stare at the door again.

No better time to change the subject. "I'm so happy that Janie called Trisha. She hasn't been sleeping well lately."

Lee reaches for my hand and squeezes it sympathetically. "Really? Why is that?"

"She claims a ghost has been visiting her at night. Sadly, the ghost is Carl."

"That's not a dream. It's a nightmare."

How do I respond to that?

I can't. We've both learned the hard way that what he said is the truth.

We make the rest of the trip in silence.

He doesn't let got of my hand until the elevator door opens.

"Trisha doesn't really want to go home." This is Janie's way of greeting me. "She's afraid of her ghost dad."

Trisha ducks her head over her friend's indiscretion.

I take hold of my daughter's hand. "If you want, I'll sleep with you tonight. If he shows up again, I'll tell him to go away, once and for all."

Hearing this, Lee's eyes open wide. I guess I wasn't as successful as I'd hoped in keeping the hard edge out of my voice.

At least my declaration puts a hopeful smile on my daughter's face. Grateful, she hugs my waist.

Lee puts a hand on Janie's shoulder. "Let's walk our guests to the front door."

"No! I won't have anyone to play with tonight—so I won't come down to eat with our boring old guests! Sally can bring my food up here to me," Janie shouts. As if it will help her make her point, she crosses her arms and turns her back on him.

Trisha's eyes open in shock.

She isn't the only one taken aback by Janie's pout. Anger flashes across Lee's face. "No, Janie, unless you join us—and behave yourself—there will be no dinner tonight." He motions us toward the door. "Ladies, shall we leave Janie to enjoy her pouting session in peace?"

As we reach the hallway, my instinct is the same as Trisha's: to look back at Janie.

Suddenly realizing Lee meant business, Janie turns around at that very moment. Fear has dampened her eyes with tears. Seeing that we are staring back at her, she drops her head in shame, but is too proud to take back her threat.

While I nudge Trisha down the hall and toward the elevator, my cell phone buzzes with a text message from Arnie.

His coded message—*We have no milk*—is a bit of good news—for Lee anyway, if not our mission: There is no evidence that his phone took the leaked photos of the Operation Hercules white papers, or that he sent anything at all to Salem's email address.

Once again, we're back to square one.

WHEN THE ELEVATOR OPENS ON THE GROUND FLOOR, EVE IS waiting for us.

After shaking my hand, she turns to her boss. "The first lady is running a half-hour late, Mr. President. The vice president wanted to take his time at the museum. Also, Mr. Reynolds and Mr. Courtland are waiting for you in your office. They say it's a matter of utmost urgency."

Lee frowns. He turns to me. "If you'll excuse me, Donna. Eve will walk you out."

"But of course, Mr. President."

He parts with a wistful smile. Maybe it'll broaden when he gets the news from Ryan that all the suspects have been cleared—including himself.

Ironically, it'll also mean we're back to square one: no suspects in the theft of the Operation Hercules research.

Eve waits until he's further down the hall before turning to me. "Mrs. Craig, when we last met, you asked me to be on the lookout for any suspicious activity in the West Wing."

She's piqued my curiosity enough that I nod slightly.

She hesitates before finally murmuring, "I don't know if what I found relates to your investigation, but I know the president feels he can trust you with his life, which is enough for me to hand it off to you."

"What is it, exactly?"

"I didn't find it in the West Wing, but here at Lion's Lair, in my private quarters. Previously, they belonged to Eileen Woodley. If you follow me, you can see it for yourself." She leads Trisha and I back into the elevator then pushes the button for the third floor, which holds Lion's Lair's guest quarters.

THE SUITE OVERLOOKS THE CHIFFRAYS' PRIVATE GOLF COURSE. It's done up in a sunny yellow, and its furnishings are less formal than the museum pieces throughout the downstairs. It has its own living room, dining room, a bedroom, a bathroom, and a galley kitchen.

Eve walks over to a floor-to-ceiling bookcase. Not all of its shelves are filled with tomes. Some contain curios. She pulls out one of the books: a John Le Carre novel: *The Night Manager*.

"I was looking for something to read," she continues. "Instead, I found this."

When she opens the novel, I see that the pages are

centered out. The gap is square, and just large enough to hold something:

An iPad.

Yes, this is interesting.

Eve takes it out and hands it to me. "It needs a password to open it."

"Do you know anything about Eileen Woodley's departure from the president's staff?"

"Before taking her place, I'd previously worked for the secretary of state, so I wasn't part of the West Wing staff when…when Eileen passed. But I'd heard scuttlebutt: something to do with a breach of protocol, despite the fact that she'd been with him for years, even during his time in the private sector." She looks down at the iPad. "I presume it was hidden in this manner for a reason that may jeopardize POTUS, should it be revealed in anything other than your investigation. As you requested, I want to ensure his hands are clean."

"I'm sure the president would appreciate your actions in this regard. My hope is that once we break the password and determine what and why it was left in this manner, he'll be able to thank you in person."

I slip the iPad into my purse. "I guess you should walk us out."

Eve looks down at her watch. "And the sooner the better. We want to get you down the hill before the others get back from Simi Valley."

I get it. The last thing Eve needs is to be blamed yet again for my presence.

We reach Hilldale Avenue just as the first lady's motorcade is pulling onto it from our gated community's secure main gate.

Trisha slumps down in her seat. "Whew! That was close, Mommy!"

She's telling *me*.

10

Dead Man Walking

In prison parlance, "dead man walking" is the term for a condemned prisoner making his last walk to the death chamber.

Popular culture also uses it as a way to indicate an unavoidable loss that is about to occur to an unsuspecting victim. You could use it as well, to describe:

- *An employee who doesn't know he's about to get fired, despite the fact that the rest of his office has been clued in;*
- *A presidential candidate who goes through the motions of campaigning after Super Tuesday, in spite of the fact that poll results show he doesn't have a snowball's chance in hell; and*
- *Someone with no inkling that he has a target on his back.*

Whereas the first two examples are metaphorical, the last one could be literal. Word to the wise: If it's you who pulls the trigger, don't miss.

And if you succeed, don't get caught. Lethal injection is far worse than Botox.

WE COME HOME TO A FULL HOUSE.

Jack is in the backyard, grilling burgers in an apron that proclaims MR. GOOD LOOKING IS COOKING, while Abu butters buns and lays them on the warming rack. Ryan and Arnie nurse beers on two of our outdoor chaise lounges. Emma sits with them on a third chaise, but she's sipping bottled water.

Out on our grassy lawn, Evan and Mary each hold a chubby little palm of Emma and Arnie's toddler son, Nicky, as he attempts a few unsteady steps.

This doesn't look like any traditional family gathering, but I have to ask anyway: "Where are Aunt Phyllis and Jeff?"

"Aunt Phyllis is at her meditation class," Jack informs us. "And Jeff is upstairs, in his bedroom."

"Oh...I forgot! He may need me for our 'speriment!" Trisha bounds into the house.

I open my purse in order to toss the iPad on Arnie's lap. "Do you think you can break the password on this?"

Smiling, he lifts it up. "Is that a dare?"

"Yes. And the sooner the better. It once belonged to Eileen Woodley."

Arnie's smile fades. "I'm on it." He leaps up and heads to the kitchen.

I take his chaise.

"Where did you get it?" Ryan asks.

"Eve found it within a book in Eileen's old quarters at Lion's Lair. POTUS doesn't even know about it yet."

Ryan sits up.

Emma, "Oh, my god!"

Hearing her, Nicky squeals too, before plopping down on the grass.

"Phew!" Evan mutters. "I think he sat in his…you know…"

Jack's reaction to the news is to freeze. But the burger he flips in mid-air is still subject to gravitational pull. It falls on the ground.

One of our dogs, Rin Tin Tin, scarfs it up. The other, Lassie, chases after him, whining all the way.

"Get in here—*now!*" Arnie yells. "*You've got to see this!*"

He doesn't have to ask twice. Ryan, Jack, Abu, Emma, and I run into the house.

"Wait!" Mary shouts. "What about Nicky's, er, poo?"

Emma runs back to her chaise. Underneath it is a diaper bag. She tosses it at Evan. "It's never too early to learn! Remember, after you use a baby wipe, powder him!"

The teens stand there in shock.

I brace myself for a similar reaction to what my Acme team is about to see.

"THEY USED DRONES." ARNIE STABS A STUBBY FINGER AT THE far left third of his laptop's triple-split screen.

He has zoomed in as close as possible so that we can see

them: three, perhaps the size of gnats, and possibly made of a clear plastic so that they are all but invisible to the naked eye.

"I don't get it," I murmur.

"You will," he assures us. "Just watch. The portion of the screen on the far left is the feed from the White House's hallway security cameras."

I recognize the location: it's the anteroom next to the Roosevelt Room.

"I'm going to back it up, so that you see where this little critter comes from." He reverses the feed just a few seconds—

So that we see them fly out from under the catering cart being wheeled into the Roosevelt room.

Well, what do you know?

"Now, watch the middle section of the screen. It's from one of several feeds I just pulled off Eileen's iPad. Somehow, she rigged a camera in the ceiling of the Roosevelt Room, and another in the Oval Office. Both must still be live. Otherwise, they wouldn't have captured last week's meeting, or what happened when everyone broke for lunch."

"Holy shit," Ryan mutters.

In the feed, the caterers set up the coffee and tea service, while the drones, which are never within peripheral vision, move very quickly toward a far corner of the ceiling.

Arnie freezes the feed. "The drones wait there, even after the meeting starts. Here we go."

He runs the feed without sound so that we can't hear the discussion that is for the attendees only.

"Now, I'll fast-forward, so that you see what happened during the lunch break. Just watch the middle feed and you'll see how the white papers were compromised," he adds.

Suddenly, the attendees leave the room at warp speed. When the doors shut behind them, the drones swoop down over the table, scanning it for what they need: white paper left on the table.

They find one: in front of the chair where Rudy Brooks sat.

One of the drones hovers for a moment, possibly taking a photo of the cover sheet. Next, another drone works as a paperweight while another flips to the next page. This goes on until all the pages have been photographed.

The drones freeze when the door opens and someone enters: Shelley. She goes to her seat in order to take her pocketbook off the table, where she left it: on top of a white paper.

After she leaves, the drones move toward it. The same covert ballet occurs: scanning, shooting, and moving papers.

When finished, the drones look for the final paper, but all the rest are in briefcases, or covered by dossier folders.

Finally, a door opens: Rudy enters.

He doesn't notice the drones leaving in his wake while he picks up his cell phone. A second later, he startles the caterers, who return with fresh coffee urns.

Whereas Rudy goes back to the dining room, the drones hover in a corner of the Oval Office reception room's ceiling.

Babette's entrance into the Oval Office itself gives them their chance to enter with her.

Arnie switches the feed in Eileen's iPad to the Oval Office. The drones have already taken their positions in a ceiling corner, waiting for the perfect time to scan the last white paper. They get it after Lee enters, has an agitated discussion with Babette, and then escorts her out the door.

When he comes back to grab his copies of the white papers, they head out the door with him—

Only they head down the hall, flying high over the heads of unsuspecting staffers.

"Where did they go?" Jack asks.

Arnie shrugs. "Great question. I'll know after further examination of the footage. But I do have one last gem."

The screen now goes to a single still shot: it's the cover of one of the white papers. In quick succession, we see each page.

"The drone's feed was also sent to the iPad," Arnie explains.

"Does its IP address match up to the device that sent the email to Salem?"

"No. It came from elsewhere. I'm tracing it now, but it's been masked. I should have it in a couple of hours, though." He smiles encouragingly. "Maybe after we eat? Speaking of which, I'm getting sort of hungry."

"Oh, hell! I left the burgers on the grill!" Jack runs out the kitchen door.

From here, his cursing is unintelligible. Finally, we hear him slam a platter onto the kitchen counter. He comes into the great room, followed by Mary and Evan, who holds Nicky as if he's a keg of dynamite.

"Okay, who's up for pizza?" Jack growls.

"Only if you order from the artisan pizzeria on Hilldale Avenue. The cornmeal crust is divine! Can we get at least one with sun-dried tomatoes on it? And perhaps broccolini?

I'm willing to share, of course—especially if it's an Acme expense…"

As if the pronunciation to-*mah*-toes wasn't already a dead giveaway, we look up to find Dominic standing in the front door.

He's brought a guest with him: Jean-Pierre.

The handsome young man waves tentatively at me. He looks paler, and thinner. Despite his grin, there is a deep sadness in his eyes. His smile broadens, however, when he sees Mary.

Evan frowns when she smiles back.

I run over to Jean-Pierre for a hug. "It's so good to see you up and about, Jean-Pierre!"

"Thank you, Madame Craig. It is an honor to be in your home. I wish it were under better circumstances."

"By the time I got to Biarritz, this young chap was already hot on the trail of our old friend, Pinky Ring." Dominic slaps him on the back.

Embarrassed, Jean-Pierre shrugs. "I was lucky. The bullet was a flesh wound. No need to nurse my pain. It is much more important that I find Gigi before she suffers the same fate as Nicolette and Suzette. I have a few clues to share, but I told Monsieur Fleming only if I am allowed to keep searching as well."

"You're in," Ryan assures him. "What do you have?"

"When I was released from the hospital, I went to Gigi's home, to inquire of her parents anything that they may know of her. They say she called them the day after the yacht incident, claiming she'd found work abroad, as an *au pair*, here in the United States. I asked to access their phone bill online.

The call came from Chicago. I then sought out others who may have had contact with Monsieur Pinky Ring. The limo driver who helped load the man's bags into a private jet says Pinky Ring had two women with him. One was not feeling so well. Her face was wrapped in a scarf. It could have been Gigi, and she could have been drugged." He frowns. "The driver took them to the airport, and on to the tarmac. He also remembered the plane's identifying number. Monsieur Fleming suggests its route can be traced from that."

"I'm on it," Emma assures him.

"Dad, when are we going to eat something?" Jeff yells from upstairs, just as Ryan's phone buzzes with an incoming call.

Noting the Caller ID, Ryan's eyes grow big. He walks quickly toward the dining room, closing the door behind him.

By the time he returns, he has the pizzas we ordered in hand: three extra large, with sausage and extra cheese, regular crust; and one mini-pizza with sun-dried to-*mah*-toes and broccolini, on a cornmeal crust.

"I tipped the delivery kid a buck. From the look on his face, I guess he thought I was stiffing him." He shrugs as he plops the boxes down on the center of the kitchen island.

The way the boxes are torn open, it looks like a fumble on the five-yard line.

Ryan lets loose with a taxi whistle. Everyone freezes. "The rest of you can chow down, but Donna and Jack, you're coming with me. You too, Arnie."

Arnie's mouth, which was already open wide for his first bite, sags into a frown. "But…can we at least take one of these with us?"

Ryan shakes his head. "I don't think POTUS would appreciate it. I know for a fact that he's lactose-intolerant." He's out the door.

Of course, Jack and I follow.

Arnie sighs, tosses down the pizza, then lumbers out after us.

EVE MEETS US AT LION'S LAIR'S FRONT DOOR AND USHERS US into the conference room.

It's practically a full house already. Lee sits at one end of the table, Vice President Drucker at the other. On one side of the table, Todd Courtland, Blake Reynolds, and Intelligence Director Branham face us.

This does not bode well.

"Let me do the talking," Ryan hisses to Jack, Arnie, and me. "Lips zipped."

Lee nods, but he doesn't stand up. Instead, he turns toward Drucker. "Mr. Vice President, gentlemen: many of you are already familiar with Ryan Clancy, head of the security firm Acme Industries, as well as two of his key assets, Jack Craig, and Donna Craig. They are joined by Acme's IT director, Arnie Locklear."

We round the table to shake hands. When I reach for Blake's, it is limp and clammy. "Congratulations on finding a way to drop the ignominious surname of Stone," he declares with a smirk.

Director of Intelligence Branham looks over sharply. He gets the message loud and clear: I was related to *that* Stone— the former DOI, and the traitor.

As I hold out my hand to Branham, I resist the urge to wipe Blake's sweat off my hand first. "Yes, Director, if you didn't already know, your predecessor was my ex-husband."

He nods. "I'm quite aware of it. I'm also aware of your role in exposing his deceptions, and in his extermination." Smiling broadly, he takes my hand in a firm grasp.

I stifle the urge to stick my tongue out at Blake.

When I shake Todd's hand, he murmurs, "Sweet."

I tamp down the desire to curtsey at the compliment.

Vice President Drucker watches all of these exchanges carefully. When it's my turn to, I say hello. Instead of answering me, he scrutinizes me, head to toe.

You'd think someone in his position would have better manners, right? Well, don't presume anything. Actions always speak louder than words.

Ryan takes the seat closest to Lee, and across from DI Branham. Jack lets me sit next to Ryan, which puts me across from Blake. Jack nudges Arnie to take the seat next to me— that is, directly across from Todd. This way, if we need him to keep his mouth shut, he'll feel two kicks as opposed to just one.

"Thanks for coming over on such short notice," Lee says to Ryan. "There is a crisis taking place in the intelligence community." He nods toward Marcus. "DI Branham will explain."

"For the past few months we've lost contact with at least seventeen of our deep-cover assets, and five FBI agents who had infiltrated known terrorist cells here." The looks on our faces give Branham reason to pause a moment, in order to let this news sink in. "Our operatives were positioned all over the world: cities such as Moscow, St. Petersburg, Beijing,

Dubai, Lisbon, Istanbul, Ankara, and Cairo, as well as in Argentina, Brazil, Venezuela, South Africa, India, Pakistan, Kazakhstan, Sudan, Angola, and Ethiopia. We aren't the only ones. CIA Director Bradley Lance would have been here to brief you as well. Instead, he is meeting with his UK, Australian, Canadian, French, German, and Japanese counterparts secretly in London, to get a handle on the situation. They too have lost operatives, in similar numbers."

"Have we recovered any bodies?" Todd asks.

"No, not as of yet, which indicates to us that any and all may still be alive," Lee replies. "At least, that is the hope."

"Well, then is it possible that these missing operatives could have been turned by, say, the Russians, or the Chinese—or the Islamic State, for that matter?" Drucker asks. "Such assets are poorly paid. With all the money our enemies have at their disposal to throw at them—"

Branham shakes his head adamantly. "Vice President, I assure you that these are all highly-decorated men and women who risk their lives every day to protect their country. No offense to the highly paid consultants here at the table, but as you just pointed out, money has nothing to do with it."

Drucker's nod comes with an unconvinced shrug. *I guess he feels everyone has his price.*

Carl did. Again, actions speak louder than words.

"All the more reason I feel it wise to inform the vice president and DI Branham of the security breach Acme stumbled upon a few days ago, regarding a Quorum operative who was previously thought deceased." Lee turns to Ryan. "It may shed light on why this may be happening."

Do you really want to do this—like, now?

I give a sidelong glance to Ryan, then to Jack. In both cases, I'm met with imperceptible headshakes that tell me they feel the same way.

In other words, shut up, and let Ryan do all the talking.

Ryan starts by clearing his throat. "In fact, Donna and Jack had sightings with two such Quorum assets. They were able to exterminate one—again—but the other got away."

"What do you mean, 'again'?" Blake asks.

"A previous extermination of the first Quorum asset was verified by, er, two Acme operatives. A second extermination took care of the matter once and for all."

Ryan neglects to mention that the agents in question are actually sitting here, at the table. And to Lee's obvious relief, he doesn't mention that the Quorum operative in question was one of the Chiffrays' oldest and dearest friends.

"Acme failed the first time," Blake sneers. "How do you know it didn't happen again?"

"The target was taken out in an explosion. What was left of the corpse was verified via DNA analysis," Ryan retorts. "We're not talking about a cat with nine lives here." No need to mention that the only thing left of Salem was a finger.

"What does any of this have to do with the missing CIA and FBI agents?" Drucker asks.

"If what Acme suspects is correct—that the Quorum is behind it—the abductions may be tied to a new top secret program at DARPA," Lee admits.

Drucker frowns. "What does the program entail?"

Lee shows his hesitation with a shrug. "Super soldiers."

Arnie leans over me in order to tap Ryan on the arm. "Isn't now a good time to tell them how the breaches to Operation Hercules were committed?"

When Jack and I kick him simultaneously, he yelps. But it's Ryan's glare that sends Arnie ducking behind me again.

"What?...Breaches have taken place in this DARPA program?" Drucker turns white. "Why wasn't I told of...of any of this?"

"You mean, about the project? Because you don't have clearance, Mr. Vice President," Lee retorts.

Anger puts color back into the vice president's face. "I'll be sure to point that out to the Senate Investigations Committee when they come for your scalp."

"Your loyalty is always appreciated," Lee growls.

He stares down his vice president. When the other man finally shrugs, the steam seems to go out of Lee's anger. He leans back in his chair. "You're overreacting, Tom, " he counters. "The breach was internal, and therefore called for unbiased outside investigators who had no previous knowledge of the program. Since it was Acme who discovered the breach in the first place, I felt it was the organization for the job."

"Admit it! Your attraction to this rogue organization is its 'loyalty' to you." Drucker drills each of us with a caustic gaze.

It stops pointedly at me.

I dare not blink, let alone move a muscle.

Drucker faces Ryan. "So, despite knowing how it happened, you haven't yet discovered the culprit?"

This time, Arnie is smart enough to keep his mouth shut.

"In all honesty, Mr. Vice President, the investigation is far from complete," Ryan explains. "This new information just came to light not even an hour ago."

"I'll immediately recommend to the Senate Ethics

Committee that the Department of Justice begin its own 'unbiased' investigation. I have no doubt my recommendation will get enough votes on both sides of the aisle." Drucker's voice shakes with rage. "Acme should be prepared to turn over all of its files on the matter—and to lose its government-sanctioned status."

Blake looks over at me. I want to slap the smile off his face.

I turn to find Lee staring at me too. Why is there pity in his eyes?

Shit.

Drucker rises. "Do you know what this will mean to your administration, Mr. President—and for that matter, the party? No matter. You'll find out soon enough."

He stalks out of the room.

Reynolds is on his heels.

Arnie drops his head onto his chest. "Well, this didn't go well," he mutters.

He stifles his pain from our kicks.

———————————————

11

Ghostbusters

———————————————

When you see a spook, who 'ya gonna call?

I doubt you'll find it funny the first time you see a spirit from the netherworld staring back at you in the bathroom mirror while you're flossing (yes, I know how you love to floss), so here's why having a local team of ghostbusters on speed-dial is important:

- *Reason #1: No matter how polite you try to be, you don't want to be the one to ask the ghost to leave the premises. Why? Simple. His response may come with a tsunami of bile, a flaming ball of fire, or spitting a mouthful of nails. In any regard, them's fightin' words, so better let someone else take the heat in this existential battle.*
- *Reason #2: They won't crap their pants at the various and sundry antics used by your ghost in the hope of getting you out. You may be able to sleep through a few shrieks in the middle of the night, or worse yet, some bed shaking, but what are you going to do when your*

spook starts to drag you into a hellmouth? Don't ruin a good manicure by clawing at your bedposts. Better to leave the ghost chasing to the pros.

- *Reason #3: The ghost was possibly there before you. If so, its occupancy in the property is valid if he never gave notice of termination and remained on the premises. The ideal solution: make sure your ghostbusters have earned their law degrees, and are members of the local bar association, because nothing is scarier than a long, drawn out legal battle.*

"WHAT PART OF 'KEEP YOUR MOUTH SHUT' DO YOU NOT understand?" Ryan's shout, directed at Arnie, reverberates through the car. "Who told you to offer up anything unless specifically requested by me?"

I'm glad Jack is at the wheel. As angry as Ryan is, he could easily drive us off the road.

"But...but Vice President Drucker was staring right at me! If he already knew something I thought it would look bad if we didn't say anything."

"Who told you to *think*?" Ryan retorts.

As Jack veers onto the shoulder of the road, I realize I should have taken the wheel instead. "Wait...Arnie, what did you just say?"

"I said the veep didn't seem surprised about the super soldier program—just that a breach was discovered."

"You're right," Ryan muses. "Which would indicate he already knew about the program, whether the president wanted him to, or not."

"If so, who told him about it?" Jack asks. "Branham?"

"He doesn't like Drucker any more than Lee does," I reply. "And Blake and Todd aren't good enough actors to pull off those stunned looks on their faces when they heard of Operation Hercules."

"As for awareness of the program itself, perhaps each of the lead scientists knew the name of the operation, but they had no idea of the roles of their counterparts," Jack reasons. "And from what we can tell, none were in communication prior to the meeting."

"Is it possible that Drucker may have known the scientists?" I ask.

"It's something we should investigate—and the sooner the better. He's out to sink POTUS. And since our lifeboat is tethered to him, if he goes down so do we." Ryan looks at Arnie. "When we reach Donna and Jack's place, we'll grab our cars and head over to the office. I'll need you to go through Eileen's secure cloud and search for any whisper of knowledge that Drucker knew of Operation Hercules before today, or had contact with the project's scientists."

Arnie nods solemnly. "Got it, Chief."

"While he does that, I think I'll check in with Bosworth Hobart to see what kind of chatter the Spooks Anonymous members are hearing, if any, on the missing agents," I suggest.

"Great idea," Ryan says.

I joined Bosworth's chapter of the international support organization known as Spooks Anonymous to help with my own transition out of a covert life. A lot of good it did me. Instead, it convinced me to stay in the game. I met too many others who, like me, could never get over the thrill of the kill.

Ah, well, we all have our little addictions. At least mine is government-sanctioned. Hopefully, it will stay that way.

I text Bosworth's telephone number with the coded message that requests admission into the next meeting: WANT TO MEET FOR A BAGEL?

Ten minutes later, he writes back: SURE. TOMORROW MORNING 9AM IF U GET THERE FIRST, ORDER ME A RAISIN.

Decoded, that means, to meet him at the meeting tonight at nine. "Raisin" indicates its location: the smallest ballroom in the Beverly Hilton: a large, anonymous hotel with lots of hallways, doorways, and escape hatches.

Perfect for people who spend their lives looking over their shoulders.

"THE GAME AGREES WITH YOU," BOSWORTH HOBART, MY former sponsor in Spooks Anonymous, admits wistfully.

I shrug. "Yeah, well, lesser of all evils." I poke my finger through the hole in the halo of haze from his vapor cigarette. "And how have you been?"

"Busy, both in a good way, and a bad one."

I laugh. "Make my day and start with the good stuff."

"Fair enough. I'm learning origami. It'll go far if I have to run to Japan."

"You'd be much better off if you learned to manage a cat café. They're big there, you know."

He frowns. "Nah, wouldn't work for me. I'm allergic to the critters."

"Oh." I wait to see if he can add to his picture of current bliss. When he can't, I sigh. "Okay, what's the bad news?"

"We should have a full house tonight. All of the disappearances are making people antsy."

"Great. I'll keep my head down and my ear to the ground." I look at my watch. It's a quarter after nine. I nod toward the door to the meeting room labeled, *Wilshire Gallery*: "Should we go in?"

He rolls his eyes. "The lapsed! How soon they forget." He points to a closed door marked BROOM CLOSET.

We walk over. He looks around to see if anyone is watching. Noting we're all alone, he raps his knuckles in some sort of convoluted knock-knock game.

Slowly the door opens, but no one is on the other side. In fact, it's not a meeting room at all but a darkened corridor.

"After you," he says.

I wince. "Should I crawl through?"

"Nah. But I'd suggest ducking if you hear gun shots."

Some things never change.

BOSWORTH IS RIGHT; THE ROOM IS FILLED TO CAPACITY. THANK goodness it's not truly a broom closet. In fact, it's the same auditorium where they hold the Golden Globe nominations.

Unlike the well-juiced lighthearted revelry of that more celebrated event, this one is akin to the last passengers on the *RMS Titanic,* all arguing at once as to who gets in the last few lifeboats.

They are of both genders, all ages, and nationalities. I recognize a few of them: Ursula, the swallow-turned-nun; Jasper, a grizzled hitman whose now shaky hand saves him in his daily game of Russian Roulette; Lydia, a retired CIA Bureau Betty with too much knowledge of the game, and too much time on her hands; Frank-slash-Ivan, who boasts so much about his hits that no one really knows how many are real and how many are imagined; and then there's the Castilian spymistress who carries a stiletto between her heaving breasts.

These people don't just need a life. They yearn for the lives they once had.

In other words, the life I lead. I'm still not totally convinced that I should count my lucky stars.

Bosworth shouts above the hysterical din, "Calm down, everyone, or someone may send management to investigate!"

His threat has the desired effect. You could drop a pin on the carpeted floor and probably hear it.

"That's better," he growls. "Now, only when I point to you is it your turn to speak."

They nod obediently. Lydia raises her hand. "The disappearances are all over the spook loops! I know at least ten of the missing personally! If they're being tortured, a few may fold! In fact, two of my contacts squeal like little piggies if you waterboard them longer than ten seconds. Think of what they'll give away!"

"You read the spook loops?" Ursula looks at her aghast. "But it's against our group's bylaws—"

"Give away, to who?" Ivan interrupts with a shout. He

stares around the room, wild-eyed. "Whom are they taking to? My contacts in Moscow swear it isn't the GRU!"

"And you trust those drunken Cossacks?" the Castilian spymistress smirks. "They chortle whenever they feed you this misinformation! Had Stalin known you were ever hired there, he'd be turning in his grave!"

"Why is Ivan still talking to Moscow?" Ursula asks indignantly. "It's not fair! He's out of the business, just like the rest of us!"

Bosworth throws up his hands. "Enough already! Enough! It's Jasper's turn! He actually sighted one of the missing spooks, right here in Los Angeles."

His declaration shuts them up. The wave of faces turns to Jasper.

Their stares cause him to shake. Even his voice trembles as he murmurs, "It's…it's true! I saw him. Short and bald, with those round-frame glasses—a former Stasi. 'Heinried Müller' is what he called himself."

Ah, so Pinky Ring's name is Heinried Müller! Finally, Jack has the answer to the riddle of his nemesis's identity.

"Müller? That sniveling little bastard?" This time Lydia's spittle fans out, drenching three others in the face. "They put a revolving door in the Berlin Wall just for him. I prayed he'd be crossing when it came down, so that he'd die in the rubble."

"That is what I'm trying to tell you! He did die—albeit not so poetically. In London, some six or seven years back." Wild-eyed, Jasper shakes the man beside him "Please, you must listen to me! There are others too! I know, because he wasn't the only one! He was there for a rendezvous with another who was long presumed dead. A woman with an exceptional figure. She was known as a mistress of disguises. I remember her as having ravishing red hair—a true beauty! Last night her head was covered in a turban, so I cannot swear it was she, since this woman also had a scar on her face. It made me gasp! They turned and saw me! I ran as if my life depended on it—"

Scarred woman.

Tatyana Zakharov.

When she first came up against Jack, she was the victor in their struggle for a thumb drive containing a list of bank accounts holding funds from Russian oil bribes to the Russian president. I ran into her when she tried to abduct Lee during a peace summit held here in Los Angeles. Jeff was taken in his stead.

Guess who killed her? Yep, you got it. I am the ultimate tiger mom.

But it was Jack who tortured her in Acme's Club Dread. The facial scars were the most obvious result.

Could Tatyana have been the woman with Pinky Ring? On the Biarritz hotel's security camera footage, her face was always covered, so it was hard to tell.

"Another man joined them, also long dead." He points to Lydia. "You women used to swoon for him. He was a hand-some double agent. No, make that a triple! He was always changing alliances—"

"That is *so* like a man," Lydia spits on the floor in disgust.

Yes, I'm disgusted too. Doesn't she know how dirty that is?

Wait…what's this about a triple agent?…

"You couldn't have seen this Heinried fellow, or the good-looking one, or for that matter the slut, Tatyana," the

Castilian spymistress scoffs. "All three are dead, remember? We are talking about spooks, not *ghosts*."

"I did, I tell you! This, I swear on my handler's grave!" Jasper insists.

"You ungrateful son of a bitch!" someone yells from the back of the room. "I'm still alive! Are you trying to put a curse on me?"

"That's just my point!" Jasper howls. "We are all cursed! The living are being taken, while the dead walk amongst us!"

"Bah!" Frank-slash-Ivan throws up his hands. "I'm alive, and I may as well be dead."

Suddenly, the room goes black. The speakers roar with a man's voice, obviously altered mechanically: "I'm happy to accommodate you, Ivan."

The streak of bullets from assault rifles flare from two directions.

Bosworth body-slams me to the floor. We fall deep within one of the stage's voluminous velvet curtains.

His timing couldn't be better. A spray of gunshot puckers the curtain over our heads, ripping it off its rod. It falls on us. It is so thick that I can barely breathe, and I dare not move.

Just as quickly as it started, the gunshots stop. Its silence only amplifies the chorus of moans from the injured.

Eventually, the lights come back on. I push aside the curtain. Not many are left standing—Jasper and Frank-slash-Ivan included. They lay in pools of their own blood.

Lydia sobs over their bodies. Ursula whispers a prayer in their memory.

Humbled and awestruck, the Castilian spymistress

shakes her head, mumbling, *"Aye, Dios mio*! He was right! They have come back to haunt us!"

The shooters are nowhere in sight.

I suddenly realize Bosworth is still buried somewhere in the curtain. I find him from the circle of blood that blackens one panel of it. Furiously, I dig through it until I hold him in my arms. His eyes are closed. I reach down to his neck for a pulse—

Yes, he is still alive.

Slowly, he opens his eyes. He flinches as he touches the wound on his arm. "Just a scratch," he mutters.

With my help, he sits up. He pulls out a cigarette—not vapor, but a real one. He shrugs at me.

I bend down beside him. "Those things will kill you." I hold out my hand to his good arm. "Come on; let's get you patched up."

When we're in the car, I call Ryan on speaker to tell him what just went down, and to ask if Acme's resident physician, Dr. Friedman, can patch up Bosworth.

"Yes, of course, bring him in," Ryan replies.

"How should we handle the rest of the carnage?" I ask him. "All those dead bodies..." I shiver at the memory.

Bosworth snorts. "It's already taken care of. Our cleaners are meticulous."

"How do you know any were still alive?" I ask incredulously.

He glares at me. "We take care of our own."

Enough said.

"Donna, Emma is pulling footage now from the hotel's security audio and video feeds, as well as the Beverly Hills

PD's street cameras. By the time you get here, we may have a clue as to who did the hit."

"The bullet grazed Mr. Hobart, but he will be bandaged up in no time," Dr. Friedman, assures me.

"Thanks, Doc. Hey, would you mind giving him a ride back into the city? Ryan needs to see me."

"Sure, no problem," Friedman agrees.

I give Bosworth a peck on the cheek. "Stick to the vapor cigs," I warn him.

Bosworth acquiesces with a sly grin. "You know as well as I that this isn't going to be what kills me."

"Maybe not, but let's not tempt fate, shall we?"

He whistles appreciatively as I walk down the hall.

Arnie is in Ryan's office. However, Jack is not. "Is the illustrious Mr. Craig taking the night off?" I ask.

Ryan shakes his head. "Not quite. He's on his way to DC to apprehend a suspect. We've had a break in the case."

"I'm all ears." I plop down on his couch next to Arnie.

"Arnie was right—in regard to one thing, anyway," Ryan explains. "Drucker knew about Operation Hercules since its inception. Show her, Arnie."

Arnie's shaky smile indicates his knowledge that he's still in the doghouse for his diarrhea of the mouth this afternoon at Lee's little shindig. He clicks a button on his computer screen. It shows Drucker and Gordon Soames talking in the West Wing hallway, outside Drucker's office. "Our audio scanning software went back as far as eighteen months, looking for any word recognition on the phrase, 'Operation Hercules'. We were concerned because Eileen never set up security feeds, either video or audio, in Vice President Drucker's West Wing office."

"Isn't it odd that she did it to every room in which POTUS might have had some meeting except for Drucker's?" I ask.

"Not necessarily. She knew of the animus between the two men. Knowing Lee would rarely set foot in there, perhaps she thought it wasn't worth the hassle."

"Another reason could be that he's Quorum," I counter.

Ryan shakes his head at the thought. "Jesus, Mary, and Joseph, I hope not! I really don't want to go there. I'm hoping this is a simple case of political ambition. In any event, we lucked out. Such a conversation happened right outside his door."

"With whom?" I ask.

"Just watch." Arnie clicks the button.

On the screen, Drucker is coming out of a meeting in the Roosevelt Room. The halls are bustling, but when he passes Gordon Soames, the White House photographer, he nods and smiles. They stop to exchange small talk—something about the Washington Nationals' losing streak. But then you hear Gordon say, "They're meeting now."

Drucker softly asks: "On Hercules?"

Gordon gives barely a nod.

"Is it in place?" Drucker asks.

Gordon gives another imperceptible nod.

They then go their separate ways.

"By 'it,' do you think they meant a drone?"

"We don't think it; we know it," Ryan declares. "Eileen's cloud has a file with the drone's footage of Lee and Marcus Barnham's meeting in the Oval Office. Its timestamp matches the date of this audio feed."

"When will you break the news to Lee?"

"First thing tomorrow. By then, Jack will have gotten the unadulterated verification we need from the suspect." He rubs his face wearily. "That is to say, Gordon. If need be, Jack will detain him, or bring him here to Los Angeles. I'm sure the president has a few questions for him as well."

"It's going to be interesting to see what Lee wants to do about Drucker."

"My guess is nothing—at least at first. But it's a card he can play when the right time comes: either with the party bosses, or against Drucker himself, criminally—if you're right and he's Quorum."

"We may never know." Emma's voice comes from the doorway. Her face looks strained. Nicky sleeps in her arms. "Drucker is in a coma."

"What?" Ryan and I shout in unison.

Emma lays her son in his father's arms. "It happened twenty minutes ago. His motorcade was hit after he left Hilldale to go back to LAX. Mrs. Drucker is confirmed dead, as are the security detail who were in her car with her. The media is reporting it as terrorism, but no one has claimed the hit, so we don't know if it's a domestic or international cell that caused the chaos. The president and his family are now in lockdown, in Lion's Lair."

"That means all of Hilldale will be secured as well! I should get home! Mary, Evan, Jeff, and Jean-Pierre are still awake, and they'll have so many questions—"

"Donna, wait! I think you'll want to know about the hit on the Spooks Anonymous group at the Hilton."

Emma's words stop me short. "Yes, of course."

"As you suspected, there were two attackers. Frankly, I'm surprised there weren't more dead and injured in the melee, but they seemed to have targeted just the man talking."

"They could have taken him out after the meeting," Ryan points out. "They also used this opportunity to send a message to the spook community."

"Who exactly is 'they'?" Arnie wonders aloud.

"Hard to say," Emma replies. "They dodged security well enough. The only thing I know for sure is that one is a woman and one is a man. Both were dressed casually. She had on a sunhat and glasses. He wore a baseball cap, false facial hair, and dark glasses." Emma scans through the camera footage for us to make her point. "I tracked them to their vehicle, and then picked them up via satellite surveillance."

She fast-forwards to Acme's SatCom feed as it follows the car—

Which hits the 405 and goes south, into Orange County.

It gets off a few exits before Hilldale, taking a two-lane back road instead. It's on one of the less traveled routes used by Lee's security detail to deliver him and other dignitaries to Lion's Lair.

The suspects pull the car off the road, behind a shed that keeps it from being seen from either direction. The car is close enough that they can climb onto the shed from the car's roof. When they jump out, they are both wearing ski masks. They leap up there with a couple of big boy toys—in this case, MANPADs: shoulder-launch surface-to-air missiles.

Half an hour later, their target comes into sight: the convoy of limousines and SUVs that made up Vice President Drucker's motorcade.

They allow the first few cars to go by before taking out one of the limos. When the missile makes impact, the explosion sends metal, glass, and carnage in all directions including toward other cars.

"That must have been the one with Mrs. Drucker," I whisper.

The other limos swerve at the sight in front of them. The larger security cars make a half-moon around the other three limos in an attempt to shield them.

They succeed, but at the expense of yet more brave agents.

A second blast from one of the terrorist's MANPADs tosses an SUV in the air; when it lands, debris shatters the glass in one of the limousines as it attempts a U-turn.

Still, the limo screeches away.

The others speed off after it.

The terrorists must know an SOS went out because they leap off the shed.

Their SUV detours around the disabled vehicles and the fire-ravaged debris, taking them in the opposite direction from where they came.

"If they wanted to assure themselves of the kill, why didn't they wait until Drucker was safely ensconced on Air Force Two?" I ask. "One of the missiles would have had no problem taking it down."

"Perhaps they felt a closer proximity would guarantee a hit," Ryan muses.

"Or maybe it brought back too many memories of the last failure," Emma replies.

"What do you mean by that?"

"Keep watching," she warns me.

We see the terrorists' SUV zig and zag through Orange County's catacomb of neighborhoods.

Suddenly, I realize it's headed toward Hilldale.

They change their mind when they see the lineup of law enforcement waiting at the entry. Instead, they turn around and head back toward the 405. When they get to the exit, they pull over into a strip mall, where they ditch their vehicle for two others.

The woman, back in her disguise, jumps out of the car first, from the passenger side. She grabs both MANPADs, stuffs them in the trunk of a station wagon, and drives off.

The bearded man jumps into a sports car: the Jaguar F-type. Before he peels off, we watch by his side view mirror as he pulls off his beard:

It's Carl.

But...*how?*

"I've...I've got to get home!" I stumble out the door.

There is no time to lose.

THE POLICE BLOCKADES ON THE WAY TO HILLDALE ADD another hour to what is usually just a half-hour commute. All the while, I hit a round robin of telephone numbers on my speed dial, hoping to reach Mary, Jeff, or Evan, but no luck. The lines are jammed. I'm sure this is part of the security measures Homeland Security has taken in response to this crisis. When I hit the barricades at Hilldale's entry gate, I use my security clearance to get inside.

I pull into my drive to find a dark house. I run inside, shouting, "Mary? Jeff? Evan?"

Mary runs out, a finger to her lips to silence me. "Mom! Shhhh! Trisha is still asleep! What's wrong?"

I collapse in relief. "I couldn't get through to anyone's cell phone! There was an attack on the vice president. All of Southern California is in lock-down, specifically Hilldale." I'm talking so fast that my words come out in fits and stops.

By now, Jeff, Evan, and Jean-Paul are hovering over me. I stare back, incredulous at their silence to this news. "Weren't you aware of any of this?"

They exchange shamed glances. "Um…no! We were too busy trying to solve the issue with the ghost," Evan explains.

"The *ghost*?" I squeal. "What the heck are you talking about?"

Jeff grabs my hand. "Come here! You have to see it!"

He's got his laptop set up in the great room. The screen shows Trisha, asleep in her bedroom. "While you were out of town, I set up a few security cameras in Trisha's room," Jeff explains. "I've been monitoring her sleep, just like I promised. Well, tonight, *he came*."

Jeff hits the fast forward button.

Carl walks into Trisha's room. He moves toward her bed, staring down and watching as she sleeps. He's about to lean down to kiss her cheek when he looks over to the door as if he heard a noise.

The next minute, he's gone.

As awestruck as I am, all I can mutter is, "She was right!"

"What do we tell Trisha?" Mary asks.

"I…I don't know. Your father will be home tomorrow morning. I want to wait until he's here and discuss it with him."

I wish he were home now. I hate the thought of sleeping alone.

Then again, it's not as if Carl comes to me. It took him long enough, but he finally realized he wouldn't find me eager to see him in any form he takes.

I head for the stairs, but not for the master bedroom.

Tonight, I'm bunking with Trisha.

———————————————

12

Haunted House

———————————————

How do you know you live in a haunted house? That's easy!

- *When you pass mirrors and you catch glimpses of wraiths that dissipate, like a fine mist, before you get a second glance. (Thankfully, they don't look like anyone you buried in the backyard.)*
- *You hear whispers and crying and pleading coming through the walls, at all hours of the night—and it's not coming from your dungeon's guests. (That's what a good ball gag is for…)*
- *Doors open and shut, and stairs creak, even when no one else is there. (Most certainly not the cops! Why would anyone suspect little ol' you of murder, torture, and mayhem?)*

If you can't shake the feeling of dread, ask yourself: "Is it time I sell my house?"

Well now, that depends. Is it in an appreciating neighborhood?

Is it in an excellent school district? Can you at least recoup the cash you've already put into it? Then, by all means, do it!

As for potential buyers who oooh and ahhhh over the vibrant colors of your legacy peonies, no need to point out the reason: bone meal and organ mulch.

Oh—and, don't worry about the dungeon. Some buyers consider it an ideal entertainment space.

I feel an eerie presence in the room.

It's not Trisha. Her little arm hugs my waist.

Which begs the question: Can I smash in the head of a ghost with the baseball bat that now lies under Trisha's bed? Doubtful. Despite what we're led to believe in movies, ectoplasm doesn't really splatter. If it did, more ghosts would duck out of the way when we run into them—or *through* them, for that matter.

The head of my very live ex is another thing. What I saw on the satellite feed was a very real, very alive Carl—

So how can it be he was also in Trisha's room at exactly the same time?

Better to take my chances that he's back from the dead.

I drop to the floor, grab the bat, and swing—

My assailant grunts as he kicks something: apparently, it's my daughter's Furby, which declares, "Trisha is so much fun to play with!"

I'm about to swing again when I hear Jack hiss, "Damn, Donna! What the... *You almost broke my knee cap!*"

The flashlight app on his cell phone goes on.

"Don't put that thing under your head," I grumble. "You look like a ghost. Speaking of which—"

Trisha grumbles in her sleep.

Jack puts his fingers to his lips to shush me. Then he puts out his hand to help me up.

I take it, along with the kiss he offers. I'm sure he'd like me to take much more, but we've got too much to talk about. I lead him downstairs instead.

Frankly, I don't think he's going to want to hear that Carl has returned from the dead.

JACK IS STARVING. HE WOLFS DOWN THE SCRAMBLED EGGS AND toast I set down in front of him as if he hasn't had a meal in a week.

It seems as if we haven't seen each other in that long a period of time, but in reality it's only been sixteen hours, tops—long enough for George to fly him to Washington, DC, and back.

After taking a long sip of his coffee, finally sated, he asks, "Who goes first?"

"I think you should. Mine is…well, it's a bit more complicated."

Shaking his head, he lets loose with a mirthless chuckle. "Sure, if you say so. So here's the scoop. I went to Gordon's home. He didn't answer the door, but I saw he was in there because the curtain was sheer enough that anyone could see him sitting in an armchair, watching television. So, why wasn't he answering the door?"

"Um…I give up." I'm still rubbing the sleep from my eyes.

"Yeah, I know, it's too early for this line of questioning." He kisses the palm of my hand. "Long story short, I tap the window. Still, he doesn't answer. When I break down the door, he still doesn't move. Turns out his throat has been slashed."

"Shit." My palm goes limp in his hand.

"That was my reaction too." He shakes his head at his luck, or lack thereof. "Now, here's the clincher. He had the whole place wired with hidden security cameras."

"I can see why. He certainly had a reason to be paranoid. Can we access the feed?"

"I hope so. It was wireless. I took Gordon's computer with me so that Arnie could hack it."

"In doing so, we may find his killer. Smart move."

"Ryan hopes so. It's allowed us to get back into Lee's good graces again. The attack on Drucker has him shook up."

"I don't doubt it." I pause, then add: "Then I presume he told you about Emma's reconnaissance regarding the attack."

"Yes, of course." He frowns. "I thought you'd call me with your two cents about it."

I laugh. "You mean with my sixth sense, don't you?"

He looks at me strangely. "You sensed he might still be alive?"

"No, nothing like that. I guess…I've just wanted closure on his passing. We—you, me, and the children—have never known for sure." I shrug. "Jack, something else happened last night. Jeff set up a couple of web cams in Trisha's room. He caught...the ghost."

Jack spews his coffee, choking. "Come again?"

"Yes, a ghost. He captured it on the camera's feed. It...was Carl." I can't stand that my voice is cracking. "How could he have been at two places at one time—running for cover, and standing over Trisha?"

"The simple answer is that he wasn't. Either he was here, or out there somewhere, or in neither place." He takes a sip of coffee as he thinks this through. His hands are so big that the mug looks tiny with his fingers wrapped around it. Finally, he sighs. "Donna, how will you feel if he's alive?"

"I thought we'd put it all behind us. If that's the case, it'll be a living hell—not just for you and me. My God, think of the children..." I'm stuttering now.

Jack puts his hand on mine to stop my shaking. "If he is alive, Carl can't hurt them. They have us."

He's right.

That's all I need to know.

Dawn is breaking over the horizon for yet another summer morning. If we're lucky, the children won't stir for another couple of hours, so that I can forget what faces us when I awaken in his arms all too soon.

"I'm going to ask Jean-Pierre to teach me French," Trisha declares.

Evan frowns at the thought, but then a devious grin rises on his lips. "I can teach you even better," he offers. "In fact, if you want to impress Jean-Pierre, tell him—"

He bends down in order to whisper something in Trisha's ear.

"Let me try! *'Ren-tray chay-twah, con-nard!'*" Her eyes open big. "Did I say it right?"

Jack looks up from his computer. "*No.* And don't say it again."

He mouths the English translation of *rentre chez toi, connard* to me: *Go home, asshole.*

Trisha frowns as she heads for the great room. Thank goodness only I hear her repeating the phrase as she walks off.

"Hey, I just looked it up on my cell phone!" Jeff shouts from the great room. "Guess what it means?"

"Don't say it!" Jack and I shout back in unison.

Jack's gaze drills into Evan. "Really? You're teaching her to curse—*in French*? I'd expect this from Cheever—that is, if he spoke anything other than Pig Latin. Maybe Jeff. But you?"

Evan hangs his head.

Jack is antsy. I can't blame him. We've put in several calls to Ryan, to see if he has any updates on the status of Drucker's condition, or on the manhunt for Carl and Heinried. He hasn't been able to return them because he's been escorted to Lion's Lair. I'd love to be a fly on the wall there—or for that matter a drone.

By tousling Evan's hair, I let him know as far as I'm concerned he's off the hook, but he wants to be much more than that. He stares out the kitchen window into the back-yard, where Jean-Pierre is testing Mary on her French.

Thank goodness, not the kissing kind.

In all honesty, he's been a perfect gentleman. I don't know why Evan is getting so hot under the collar—

Okay, maybe I do. He's not used to seeing her enthralled with anyone but him.

In Evan's defense, he's never taken advantage of it—at least, not that I know of.

Has Jean-Pierre shown my daughter the same respect?

The buzz of Evan's cell phone and his cautious hello to Dr. Wollstonecraft snaps me out of my natural state of parental paranoia. "A malware virus…from my email?" The dread in Evan's voice reflects his fear.

Oh no…

So much for Arnie's insistence that Berkeley's IT security team wouldn't detect it.

"No…Yes, I appreciate you saying so." Evan's eyes open wide. His anxiety causes him to tighten his mouth into a frown and curl his free hand into a fist. "Dr. Wollstonecraft, I couldn't be more sorry. Is there anything I can do? …Oh." His shoulders sag in frustration. "Yes, okay…thank you."

He hangs up, defeated.

"What did she say?" Jack and I ask simultaneously.

"Apparently, my email contained a virus of some sort. She asked me if I knew about it, and how it might have gotten there."

"What did you tell her?"

"I said I knew nothing about it, of course." Evan throws me a wary glance. "Why do you ask? Is something wrong?"

Jack jumps in. "No…not at all! Did she mention anything about, say, its effect on her work?"

"They didn't discover it until it had already released itself in her computer, so she's concerned that she may get in trouble, since some of her research is done for the government." Evan looks from Jack, to me, and back again. "Do you know her?"

I say, "Just met her the other day, with you," at the same time Jack states: "Our paths may have crossed."

Evan catches my glare at Jack. He turns to Jack. Warily, he asks, "How? Is she under investigation?"

"No…but…she was. She's been cleared," Jack explains.

Evan frowns. "Cleared how? Did the malware virus have anything to do with it?" He flips around to face me. "Is that why you insisted that I send my research paper to her as soon as possible?"

I can't help it, I'm too ashamed to look him in the eye.

He has his answer.

Evan doesn't have to say anything, either. I see his accusation in his eyes: *You used me.*

Without a word, he goes upstairs to his room and shuts the door.

It doesn't help that Jean-Pierre is making Mary laugh: a normal event in a far-from-normal house.

I start to go after him.

Jack holds me back. "Let him cool off."

"Shouldn't I explain? If he loses his chance at Berkeley, he'll know it was because of us, and that isn't fair!"

"Dr. Wollstonecraft wasn't accusing him," he points out. "She was making him aware that malware was attached to the file. People unwittingly send malware to friends or family or coworkers all the time."

"True, but in this case, Evan now knows the source: us. More to the point, he knows we did it deliberately, and without his knowledge or consent."

"My point exactly. *He didn't know it*. Had he known our plan, he wouldn't have given his consent. Therefore, he has clean hands."

"He doesn't see it that way. Nor should he." I start up the stairs.

"No, Donna...not now. Give him time to cool off first. Yes, I had no right doing it. At the same time, he's lived in our world long enough to realize the priorities."

Jack is right; still, Evan looked up to us. Evan trusted us.

I guess he doesn't anymore.

Jack looks down at his phone. "Arnie just texted me—and everyone else in Acme. There have been a series of attacks: Lisbon, Geneva, St. Petersburg, Rome, Chicago, and Tokyo."

"It's happening," I murmur.

"Yes." He shakes his head angrily. "Where the hell is Ryan?"

He taps out a text on his cell, at first oblivious to the sound of sirens coming up the block, and then the screeching of cars out front.

Mary's laughter has stopped. "Mom?" she calls frantically. *"Mom! What's happening?"*

I run to the back door, only to find it blocked by a SWAT team. They shove Mary and Jean-Pierre into a van waiting in the driveway, all the while shouting for us to get down on our hands and knees.

Another team has already swarmed through the front door. One of the agents corners me. His Glock is pointed at my chest. He motions for me to get on my knees. "Hands behind your head, lady!"

I shout through the madness, "What the hell is happening?"

Trisha screams as she's carried downstairs by a female SWAT officer, and out the front door. Right behind her, Jeff is being nudged outside by another.

"Is there anyone else here in the house?" the SWAT leader barks.

"No, of course not," Jack mutters from where he lies on the floor. One of the officers has his M4 semiautomatic on Jack's neck. He slams it against Jack's head.

I shouldn't, but I flip around so that I can grab my assailant's groin. Grunting, he bends over. I punch his knees out from under him so that he's now the one on the floor, and I'm the one holding his Glock—

And circled by six others, all with their guns pointed at my chest.

"Don't shoot my mommy!" Trisha screams from the doorway.

They don't. Instead, one of them knocks me out cold.

13

Wake Up!

Instead of the usual staid funeral parlor service or morose graveside ceremony, why not throw a wake? It is the best way to put the F-U-N in funeral! Here's how:

- *Step 1: Find a great bar in which to hold it. Ideally, it will be some place that won't mind an unending round of toasts in the deceased's memory, off-key singing of the deceased's favorite ditties, and the bereaved-albeit-drunk jumping up on the bar to eulogize him.*
- *Step 2: If it becomes a cry fest, do your best to cheer up the crowd. However, if you're not naturally funny, take the time to practice your comedy routine. Why? Because nothing sucks the energy out of a room quicker than a joke that's deader than the corpse.*
- *Step 3: Leave the best speakers for last. By this, I mean the ones who won't slur their words because of too much tippling. It also helps if they can still stumble to*

their feet. Gives apt meaning to the phrase, "Last man standing," doesn't it?

WORST. HANGOVER. EVER.

I open one eye to find myself staring at Ryan. Jack is sprawled on the other side of the couch. Trisha holds an ice pack to the back of his head.

Jeff, Mary, Evan, and Jean-Pierre hover over me. Seeing my second eye open, their faces flash from concern to relief.

When I try to jump up, one of my ankles feels leaden—

For good reason: I'm wearing an ankle monitor.

That's when I notice: so is Jack.

"It was the best I could do," Ryan explains. He holds little Nicky in his arms. The toddler is smacking him on the head. Ryan is pretending to frown, but Nicky knows better. Giggles squeak out of him.

Someone is coming in through the back door. I'm relieved to see it's only Arnie and Emma, with boxes of pizza. "Come and get it, kids," she commands them.

Reluctantly, Evan and my children head in her direction. When Jeff passes, Ryan hands him Nicky. Jeff stutters, "But…I mean, what if he—"

Ryan stuffs the diaper bag under Jeff's arm. "You're not a man until you've changed one, trust me."

Noting that Jean-Pierre stays put, Mary says, "I think they mean all of us."

Jean-Pierre, stone-faced, shakes his head. "My place is here, with Madame Craig."

Hearing this, Jack raises a brow.

Mary looks warily at me.

Steamed, Evan pulls Mary into the kitchen with him, letting the door shut behind them.

Ah, jealousy. If I weren't so angry myself about this absurd situation, I'd revel in it.

Instead, I lean back onto the couch. "Does someone want to tell me what the heck is going on?"

Ryan sighs. "Apparently, you're a person of interest in the bombing of Vice President Drucker's motorcade."

I leap up. "But…but how can that be? Didn't you show Lee the Acme SatCom footage of the actual killers? Didn't they see that it was Carl and some…some woman?"

"Yes, I showed it to POTUS, Branham, Todd and Blake Reynolds. But it's Reynolds' supposition that you and Jack are allied with the newly resurrected Carl."

"Ha! Really?" I roll my eyes. "Now, that's rich! And how did he come up with this little bit of malarkey? Has he forgotten that Jack and I discovered the breaches in the first place?"

"He's hanging his premise on the fact that it was you and Jack who confirmed Carl's supposed death in the first place," Ryan points out. "He also claims that the Acme SatCom footage bears this out: that you're the woman with Carl who attacked the vice president's motorcade; and that you did so because Drucker was pushing for an investigation into the leaks on the super soldier project"—he clears his throat—"which would have revealed that Carl now walks among the living, and that he is the true leader of the Quorum, as well as the mastermind behind the Operation Hercules theft and these terrorist assaults."

"Carl, maybe," I concede, "But I have proof I was elsewhere: the Spooks Anonymous meeting! There were witnesses, including Bosworth—"

Ryan shakes his head. "Bosworth is on the run. And for that matter, we can't find anyone else, either. They've all disappeared."

"The hotel's security footage will bear it out," I counter. "I entered before the carnage started, and left after the shooters—"

Emma shakes her head. "Sadly, all of the hotel's footage of the ingress and egress into its parking lot has been erased as well. However, the NSA's own SatCom footage of cars coming and going from the hotel matches ours—including that of the suspects' car, upon leaving the Hilton to make the hit. It also matches ours as to where the suspects went, after they split up." Her blush comes with a pitying look toward me. "Here's what happened to the female suspect."

She starts another video.

The woman's car goes south on 405, but only a few exits before it takes the one to Hilldale. But before it reaches my gated community, she pulls onto a narrow residential street studded with leafy oak trees. Her final turn is into the large circular driveway of a large ranch home with a three-car garage.

When she backs out again, it's in a car that is the twin of mine.

She stops it when she reaches the street in order to get out and check the mailbox. She is no longer wearing the hat or sunglasses.

In fact she makes it a point to look around, and then up at the sky, as if she knows all eyes are on her.

The woman is me.

"But…It…I was at Acme! So was the real Donna-mobile! It's how I got Bosworth to Dr. Friedman!"

"As always, your comings and goings from Acme are done via the company's tunnel into our underground parking lot…" Ryan doesn't have to spell it out:

Only my Acme colleagues can vouch that I was there during the time in question.

And, if they aren't now under suspicion, standing up for me will certainly cast a shadow of doubt over the whole organization.

"Why is Jack shackled as well?" I ask.

"It's also Reynolds' contention that Carl sent Jack to kill Gordon."

"Proof positive that the man is an idiot," Jack grouses.

Ryan frowns, but chooses to ignore him. "Gordon's body was discovered within twenty minutes of Jack leaving his place. Had the police arrived earlier, he might have been arrested on the spot, and held in some DC jail. At least he got this far."

"Let me guess: there is no exterior footage of anyone else around the property, leaving Jack as the fall guy," I retort.

"Bingo," Jack mutters.

"In Lee's defense, he doesn't buy into Reynolds' allegations. In fact, it was POTUS's directive that you're not to be taken into custody. Instead, you're to stay under house arrest until Branham's people can do a side-by-side analysis of our SatCom footage along with the current evidence. If it disproves Reynolds' theory, you'll be free to go." He stands up. "In the meantime, there is to be no contact with anyone after this meeting—including anyone from Acme."

"How much do you want to bet that Lee wanted Acme to handle the breach—in order to set us up?" Jack growls.

Ryan shrugs. "Maybe it's to give you time to prove your own innocence before the super soldiers have a chance to create more chaos."

"I don't get it. What are you trying not to say here?" I ask.

Ryan rolls his eyes. "What I'm trying very hard not to say is that these things fit around anyone's ankle—even Arnie's and Emma's."

Jack frowns. "Do you mean…"

"I think Ryan is also trying to say that I'm jonesing to beat my record for how quickly I can divert the signal on a couple of ankle monitor locks so that you can prove your innocence," Arnie cuts in.

I wave toward the window. "The Feds have us under surveillance, don't they? Didn't they see you enter with Ryan?"

"Arnie and Emma used the secret tunnel," Ryan explains.

When we rebuilt our house, we recreated the tunnel Carl had built under our original Hilldale home—sadly, something we had to blow up the last time we went on the lam.

Ah, well. On the upside, the entertainment flow in this newer house on the same lot is much nicer, and the tunnel is now even longer. Renovations add so much to a home's resale value.

I gave Ryan the tunnel's coordinates and the code to enter on the other side, in case there was an emergency. This certainly qualifies as one.

"Why leave? All the leads are cold," I point out.

"Acme now knows where the super soldier encampment

is based, thanks to Emma's sharp eyes in following Carl's trail," Ryan counters.

"Where is it?" Jack asks.

"Santa Monica. They've taken over an abandoned hotel property on the south side of the Promenade Mall," Ryan replies.

"Doesn't it help make our case to the DOJ that we aren't involved by staying put?" I ask. "If Reynolds finds out we're gone, things only get worse. I can't take care of my family while I'm serving a life sentence for murder."

"Donna, the Quorum neutralized you so that you wouldn't stand in its way." Emma takes my hand. "Something is going down in the next twenty-four hours. And if it does, you'll still be implicated unless you can prove your innocence."

Jack nods. She makes a good point.

"What do we know about it?" I ask.

"Some of our field agents doing deep cover in some of the domestic hate groups have reconnaissance of a big powwow going down today. The Quorum is leading—and I use this term lightly—a 'conference' on how to use social media to recruit emotionally isolated lone wolves to their cause." Ryan frowns. "Even more importantly, it's offering financial aid to any and all cash-strapped terrorist cells. I'm sure there is a bigger ulterior motive—some quid pro quo that we don't yet know"—his eyes move to me—"until we go in and find out. Better yet, we could stop it in its tracks."

"It won't be easy to infiltrate the convention," I warn them. "What if I run into my doppelganger while she's with others who can vouch for her?"

"If you're alone with her, ideally, you'll apprehend her. In any regard, she won't recognize you. If they can create a fake Donna, we can create a couple of fake terrorists." Ryan reaches for the briefcase at his feet. He pulls out two dossiers, opening them to the pictures inside. "These two less-than-upstanding citizens are on the FBI's Most Wanted list. They are also around the same height and weight of you and Jack."

"Abu and Dominic apprehended them a couple of hours ago as they were on their way to the Quorum's Terror-Con," Emma adds.

The man has sharper features than Jack's, a scar on his right cheek, and light brown hair. I stare down at the face of a woman with high cheekbones and striking brown eyes, with an aquiline nose. She could be Middle Eastern in descent, despite the fact that her dark hair has gold highlights; she is in fashionable Prada and heels, and isn't wearing a scarf or hijab. "What's her story?"

"Rima Kouhri is American born, and of Syrian descent. She recruits teen girls to join jihadist camps," Emma explains. "Jack's cover is that of an Neo-Confederate extremist named Clem Odum."

Ryan pulls something else out of his briefcase: a clear acrylic box containing a latex mask of Rima's face. He tosses it to me, then Clem's facemask at Jack.

I laugh. "Talk about old school!"

Arnie hands us each a another, but smaller acrylic box. "There are also fingerprint tips that will verify your new identities. We've added their cornea scans to your WiFi contact lenses. And par for the course, you'll be on audio bud. You'll also find a dozen GPS disks in there. If you get close enough to a prime target, tag them with it. That way, if we lose their trail, we can pick it up again."

Jack laughs. "You've thought of everything. For the first time in my life, I pray the Feds don't raid the joint, or we'll all end up in some black site."

"All the more reason this mission must succeed. With a possible mole in the West Wing, if you fail, POTUS must disavow knowledge of your disappearance."

"In other words, ghost protocol. No surprise there." Jack shrugs. "Always thinking of his own skin, first and foremost."

"On the other hand, if you succeed, you save Operation Hercules, redeeming your reputations and that of Acme's."

"Not to mention Lee Chiffray's," Jack mutters.

Emma catches me wincing. Realizing it's time to change the subject, she adds, "You'll be joining Abu and Dominic, who are already in at Terror-Con." Saying the name puts a smirk on her face. "I've put the hotel security cams on a benign loop. All morning long, while the conventioneers listen to Carl and Company's song and dance, I've been leading them through conventioneers' rooms with no hot spots in order to tag suitcases with these disks. That way, the Feds will be able track them to their home bases for further reconnaissance that will put them behind bars."

"However, the moment you're inside the hotel, they'll be put on alert to provide any necessary backup." Ryan hands us two more photos. "Memorize these faces too, so you know what Dominic and Abu look like now. They're disguised as brothers who run an Aryan supremacy cell in Manhattan."

He hands us photos of our teammates. They could pass

for twins: both blue-eyed, with white-blond hair. The look isn't much of a stretch for Dominic, but for Abu, the transformation is striking.

I smirk, "Talk about brothers from another mother."

Ryan nods toward Jean-Pierre. "You'll need someone on the outside. Jean-Pierre will be your getaway driver."

Jack shakes his head. "No way! If he's implicated in our escape, he'll get deported!"

"Worse yet, if the Quorum gets suspicious of him, he'll get killed," I add.

Jean-Pierre shakes his head. "I insist on helping! It is my only chance to find Gigi, and help her escape. It's why I came here. Monsieur Clancy understands."

I've no doubt Jean-Pierre is right. Ryan suffered the loss of his wife and spent a lifetime regretting it. He'd do what he could to help Jean-Pierre avoid the loss of another dear friend at all costs.

"So that Jean-Pierre will be where you need him at all times, he's also been given field gear, including undetectable earbuds and WiFi lenses," Ryan adds. "In the meantime, Arnie will hack Gordon's computer for his security feed, which should provide us with the identity of his real killer, and clear Jack of any wrongdoing. Emma and I will handle the mission from this end. Once we locate and exfiltrate Donna's twin, she'll be in the clear."

"Got it." I turn to Arnie. "I need your help on another matter."

He declares, "Sure, name it."

"Trisha claims she's seeing a ghost—Carl's in fact. To see if she's imagining it, Jeff set up a webcam in her room. Well guess what? He caught him—at least, we think it's him."

Arnie opens his mouth, but before he can ask, I interject, "Don't go there. Sure, it looked like a ghost, but something was off. I just can't believe it's real! Are you up to proving me right"—I wince—"or wrong?"

"You bet!" Arnie heads toward the kitchen "Let me talk with my little ghost-busting partner—"

"Hey, aren't you forgetting something?" Jack points to his ankle monitor.

"Oh…sorry." Arnie heads back.

Emma sighs.

Blocking the signal is old school for Arnie and only takes a few minutes. He hacks Jack's monitor first. Jack is quick to place it on Arnie's ankle.

Then it's my turn to swap with Emma. In no time, we're done.

"Now, get out of here, you two—before we all end up in these things permanently," Emma huffs.

She doesn't have to ask twice.

____

14

Death Becomes Her
____

What becomes a legend-in-the-making most? Her funeral couture! So that you look your best on the day of your big sendoff, here's what you do:

First, pick out the perfect dress that will knock them dead! Tips: stay away from black (since everyone else will be wearing it), and keep to a style with classic lines. You don't want to show up in the afterlife in something that looks dated after a few millennia.

Second, set up a practice session with your funeral director, to go over your hair and makeup requirements. If you're lucky, he'll make you look better dead than alive!

Third, ask that they set your face in a smile, but that your teeth don't show. Nothing is worse than having everyone remember you with lipstick on them!

Finally: Consider dying young. You might miss out on a lot of fun stuff, like having kids, a fiftieth wedding anniversary, and playing grandma, but remember: looking your best always means making sacrifices.

R YAN IS RIGHT. S ECURITY AT THE Q UORUM'S CONFERENCE IS tighter than a gnat's ass. A workshop minion pats us down before we go through a gauntlet of ID measures, all of which we pass, no problem.

The hotel's lobby holds sixty or so people. "It's as if the *Star Wars* bar scene was reshot with every hate group stereotype," I murmur.

All of them are making their way toward the hotel's meeting room. I watch as a group of tatted-up skin-headed Neo-Nazis walk warily around a cluster of black-clad Muslim extremists. Nothing brings people together like a thirst for knowledge: in this case, seeking ways to tear each other apart, literally.

We are handed a badge, but there is no name on it, just a bar code. "My guess is that it has a GPS tracker as well," Emma warns us. "Dump it if you wander into what is clearly an off-limits area. And by the way, we're tracking at least two hundred hot spots."

"Are there any large clusters of hot spots in some of the bedroom suites, or some that are in the same large room, but look isolated from each other? Perhaps lining the walls, or in rows?" Jack asks.

"What you've just described fits one of the ground floor conference rooms, all the way in the rear of the hotel," Emma replies. "It seems to hold about fifty, maybe sixty people. They are in straight rows. None are moving."

"It may be a holding pen for the missing agents," Jack suggests.

"Jack, check it out," Ryan commands. "If it's what you

suspect, Abu and Dominic will join you, and I'll inform Branham. He'll send out the Cavalry."

"Roger," Abu murmurs.

"There seems to be a digital lock on the door," Emma notes. "I'll try to hack it. Wait until you get my high sign. When you reach it, I'll open it from this end, so that it doesn't set off a silent alarm."

"Will do," Dominic promises.

"In the meantime, Donna, keep your eyes on the prize: Carl, Gigi, Heinried, the Biarritz mystery woman, and Fake Donna," Ryan says. "If you see any of them, call for back up."

"On it," I whisper.

As I round a lobby corner, I notice a door placard that reads:

TRIED AND TRUE INDOCTRINATION THROUGH MEMORY MODIFICATION

SPEAKER: Dr. X – PROGRAM RESEARCHER

Ryan and Emma see the same thing through my eyes. I know this because Ryan exclaims, "Damn it! Lee will be livid."

"No shit. Imagine the backlash should it ever be known that DARPA taught them all they needed to know to create homegrown jihadists," Emma adds.

"I'm going to go and check it out," I say. "I guess we'll know if Dr. Wollstonecraft was turned after all." I pray not, for her sake and Evan's.

"Hey, I've just passed the finance pitch room," Jack says.

"It's empty, but there's a brochure on the table. I've pocketed it. Should be interesting to see what terms the Quorum offers these days."

"I wonder if the interest is lower than the mortgage on our condo?" Emma muses out loud.

I'd laugh along with the rest of them, but I've just walked into the Memory Modification workshop.

My eyes move to the podium, where Dr. X stands—

Or in this case, Dr. Norbert Welles, the researcher from the start-up MesmerMind, who headed up DARPA's research on neural implants.

Well, what do you know…

"—THAT MIND NO LONGER HAS TO BE OVER MATTER," NORBERT Welles explains to the ballroom's crowd, which is standing room only. "Instead, it can now work in tandem with the physical enhancements that will be taking place in your super soldiers."

I squeeze in between a bow-tied Louis Farrakhan wannabe and someone who's ignoring the dress code notice that KKK robes can be warn only during cocktail hour.

Both seem happy to have me as a buffer. In fact, Mr. KKK taps his hat in my honor. Bowtie blows me a kiss. Suddenly, both of them are too close for comfort. Yuck! I've never thought I'd be the meat in a hate group sandwich. Honestly, this job comes with so few perks. I'm going to talk to Human Resources about that.

"This short video shows you our process in its entirety," Welles declares. "Let's watch it, shall we?"

The lights go dark so that all can clearly see the wall-sized monitor behind the podium. A second later, the screen is filled with the image of a beautiful young woman:

Gigi.

"*Oh, mon Dieu!*" Jean-Pierre shouts so loudly that I cover my ear.

She is seen lying on the beach with her friends, Nicolette and Suzette. "As you see, this potential recruit has no direction in her life," Welles says. "When taken in by us—under no duress, mind you, and that is *very* important—she gives us a full dossier in personal intel: family members, friends, intimates, as well as her memories at every age. From that, we are able to discern her greatest fear, and turn it into her greatest loss—a post-traumatic stress, if you will." He pauses grandly. "With loss comes grief. With grief comes resolve. Our goal is to turn her resolve into *revenge*."

The video now shows her strapped down on a laboratory table. Electrodes protrude from her head. Next to it are three monitors, each attached to a different machine: a PET scan, an MRI scanner, and a digital infrared camera for thermographic imaging.

"The human brain has millions of neurons, each covered in tiny filaments known as dendrites. While they never touch, they communicate via the synapses—or spaces—between them. Our emotional memories, say fear or hate, or for that matter, love—are stored in a group of neurons called the amygdala, which is located here"—he points to the spot between Gigi's eyes—"in the temporal lobe." He gazes around the room. In answer to some of the awestruck faces he sees, he chuckles. "Bored, perhaps, with this science lesson? Here's where it becomes interesting. You see, we plant *a false memory*—in this case, the death of a dear intimate at the hands of a militant government agency. First, you'll see the memory itself."

The next scene is a video of a SWAT team surrounding Jean-Pierre. Despite kneeling with his hands behind his head, despite the fact that he's begging for his life, they riddle his body with bullets.

The last thing he's heard shouting is, "Gigi—Donna! Save me!"

Why me too?

"Once the memory is planted, we embellish it with others. The recruit is now open to ways in which she can seek revenge in order to right the wrong. To accomplish her goal, she will even consent to changes in her physicality." The video now shows quick scene cuts of Gigi working out through the course of each day since we last saw her. By the last shot she is toned and muscular.

The screen goes black.

In his next sentence, Dr. Welles explains why: "For us to see the extreme lengths to which she is now willing to go, you'll follow me. We have buses set up to take us on a little field trip."

The crowd drones excitedly as it eagerly moves out of the room and into the lobby.

"That fantasy—it was *not* me!" Jean-Pierre insists. "I swear on…on Nicolette's grave!"

"We don't doubt you," Ryan declares. "Jean-Pierre, you must focus on the task at hand."

"*Oui*, Monsieur." The resolve in Jean-Pierre's voice is clear and resolute.

As I fall into line, I hear Ryan say, "Jack, turn around and get on that bus with Donna! She may need backup."

"On it," Jack whispers.

As one of the last people on the bus, I end up near the front of it.

Norbert Welles comes up behind me.

I take the only seat available—

Next to my ex-husband Carl.

No. Oh…no.

"What are the odds?" Emma squeals into my ear.

You're telling me.

"Excuse me, Madame, but you're sitting in my seat." Welles is clearly annoyed that he can't sit near his fearless leader.

Carl looks me over appraisingly. "Where are your manners, doctor? A gentleman always gives a lady the last seat."

As we pull away from the curb, I see Jack, running for the bus.

He is too late.

I don't look at Carl. Instead, I look out the window at the car in the next lane.

Oh, my God, it's Jean-Pierre.

To keep from drawing attention to him, I look front and

center instead. I'm glad I'm wearing sunglasses. Otherwise, Carl might see the dread so obviously in my eyes.

Suddenly, he lays his hand over mine.

Yes, it is quite real. So real, in fact, that when I try to slip out from under it, he holds tightly to it, willing me to look his way.

When I acquiesce, he declares, "Trust me; you'll enjoy our little field trip."

I pray my lips aren't quivering as I reward him with a shy smile.

"That's better," he murmurs.

Ryan implores, "Jean-Pierre, move in front of the bus—now!"

Jean-Pierre slides over, causing our bus to stop short.

Instinctively, Carl's hand reaches for the safety rail on the seat in front of us.

I reach for his jacket pocket instead, dropping one of the tiny slim GPS disks into it.

We don't go far, just a half-mile north to Wilshire Boulevard, and then west.

The bus stops two blocks from Santa Monica's open-air mall, the Third Street Promenade.

I don't like the feel of this.

One of the Quorum's convention monitors comes our way. She's frowning. I hold my breath to see if she stops to say something to Carl—or worse, to me.

But no, she stops at the seat in front of us, where Mr. KKK sits next to a dude whose whole head is covered with a tattoo of a coiled rattlesnake. Mr. KKK is told in no uncertain terms that he is to take off his robe and stash it under his seat.

He does so, meekly. Without it, he could pass for a mild-mannered accountant: khakis and a golf shirt, and a baseball cap over snowy white hair.

Everyone rises to get off the bus. I move in behind Dr. Welles, and Carl moves in behind me. As I slip another of my GPS disks into Welles's coat pocket, I feel my bum being patted by Carl's very real hand.

How dare he!

As we leave the bus, the convention moderator warns us, "Stay in groups of two or four. In no more than ten minutes, gather on the top floor of the Barnes & Noble, on the east side of the promenade. You'll have a great view of our little event from there. Look south, on the west side of the promenade, toward the store called Haute Hipster. Take note of where the bus is located, because after the event you'll want to reserve a few memory modification slots for your new recruits. The slots are offered on a first come-first serve basis. Remember, we offer very reasonable payment terms…"

Oh. Shit.

I walk quickly so that I'm in the thickest part of the crowd, which is already entering the bookstore.

I pray Carl isn't following.

As if reading my mind, Emma murmurs, "Don't worry, he's talking to the bitchy convention monitor…Oh, my God, can you believe it? He's putting the moves on her too—"

"Yeah, I believe it," I mutter. Once a man-whore, always a man-whore.

While the hate-mongers eagerly make their way up the escalator to the top floor of the bookstore, I duck out and head toward the restroom, in the back of the store.

On my way in, I slip my badge into the pocket of a store

employee. At the same time, I snatch a pair of reading glasses from a rack.

I enter into the restroom, where I take off my jacket, stuffing it into the trash can. I yank my hair out of its chignon so that it falls to my shoulders, and put on the reading glasses.

When I walk out of the bathroom, I pile a stack of books in my arms, as if I'm an employee.

The Quorum monitor is herding the last of the conventioneers toward the escalator. She doesn't notice me as I pass her because I've ducked behind my stack.

Carl isn't on the escalator. Where did he go? Hopefully, far away from me. Maybe he's already on the top floor.

With that in mind, I drop my books at the front desk and rush out of the store.

As quickly as I can, I move toward the Haute Hipster, staying flush to the storefronts on the east side of promenade so that I can't be spotted from the Barnes & Noble's window.

I am almost there when I see her.

Only she is no longer Gigi.

She is me.

She moves slowly toward the Haute Hipster. She is still four storefronts away. Although it's a clear and cloudless mid-summer day, she is wearing a bulky raincoat. Despite the warmth of the hot lazy afternoon, she is shivering.

Passersby ignore the woman whose eyes are filled with tears. She puts her hands over her ears, as if she's trying to shut out the voices in her head.

I can imagine what they tell her, "Do it! Go ahead, do *it*!"

"It" is the unimaginable.

"It" is supposed to even the score.

In truth, "it" never does.

But Gigi no longer knows right from wrong. She has lost the ability to reason. To remember. To care.

Maybe I can bring these feelings back to her.

As I run toward her through the thick throng of shoppers, I notice someone else is coming up to her as well:

Heinried Müller.

To get her attention, he waves at her. Once he has it, he mouths *Jean—Pierre*.

It does the trick: she finds her resolve.

She reaches under her coat and pulls out a placard. It reads:

TERRORISTS ARE ALL AROUND YOU

She holds it up in the air for all to see.

Passing shoppers take notice. Half of them shake their heads at what they think is yet another crazy homeless woman in paradise. The other half pull out their cell phones to take her picture.

Just another day in America.

She walks the final few steps that put her in front of the store. Just as she turns to go in, she places her hand in the pocket of her coat and pulls out a cell phone.

She looks around once more—

And sees him, running toward her:

Jean-Pierre.

His scream—"Gigi! No, no, no"—comes too late.

Yes, she hears him shout her name. Yes, she turns around to see him. And yes, the memory of him puts a look of sheer joy in her eyes, and a smile on her lips—

Until she is no more.

Just as she reaches for the vest bomb beneath her raincoat, I duck into a tavern and hold on tight to its metal door's handle.

Through the door's porthole window, I watch as glass and steel and body parts fly in all directions. Even hanging on for dear life, my body is pulled sideways. Everything and everyone else in the tavern is blown toward the back door.

It seems like forever, but it's only a few seconds until gravity drops my feet toward the floor again. The silence immediately after the blast seems to go on forever, until I realize my eardrums have been blown out. Then suddenly, the moans of fear and screams from pain fill the void left by our shock and disbelief.

I run out to find Jean-Pierre. Like everyone else, he was thrown off his feet. Luckily, he was tossed against a vendor's tent that was filled with tables of folded shawls and scarves. He has already crawled out, dazed. I make my way over to him, but my staggering steps can't compete with the adrenaline rush he feels when he sees Heinried, dazed, walking away from the debris field.

Jean-Pierre runs after the older man.

Sensing him, Heinried turns around. At the sight of Jean-Pierre, Heinried sprints right, down Arizona Avenue.

I run after them.

I've just about caught up to Jean-Pierre when I see it all: the light, changing to red. The pedestrian crossing sign is flashing a big red hand, the universal language to stop, and a

Santa Monica Big Blue Bus is charging north on Ocean Avenue.

Heinried doesn't notice it because he's looking back in order to see if Jean-Pierre is still following him.

Noting the look of fear in Heinried's eyes, Jean-Pierre, still a block away, sprints even faster—

But stops short when Heinried finally looks forward—

As opposed to his left. Otherwise, he would have seen the bus that is moving too fast to stop.

When he's hit, he goes flying onto a car. As he hits its windshield, the car swerves in a circle. He's flung off onto the road. Every ambulance or police car that whizzes around the bus on its way to the scene of the explosion pummels Heinried's corpse.

By the time the last one rolls over him, I've caught up to Jean-Pierre at the street corner.

Jean-Pierre laughs hysterically. It is the only way he can keep from crying over Gigi.

When Jack finds us, I am still holding our dear friend in my arms.

15

Four Pardons and a Funeral

At a memorial service, one must be on one's best behavior. Here are some definite don'ts, especially if the departed was less friend than enemy:

1. *Just because the deceased is lying in an open casket and has your undivided attention, curb your natural tendency to eulogize her with smack. No doubt others will agree with you, but there is a time and a place for everything.*
2. *It is truly very bad form to steal her funeral flowers. Despite your fondness for ranunculus, walking off with a horseshoe wreath touting the deceased's name is a petty act, unworthy of you. And, besides, where would you hang it?*
3. *Don't be the only person wearing bright pink. It may suit your skin tone much better than black, but there are less obvious ways of demonstrating that you didn't really give a damn about her. For example, you can*

show up with her now ex-boyfriend, explaining that
you had hoped to comfort him during his time of grief.
You'll know just what to do to have him smiling in
no time.

"UNTIL YOU ARRIVE HOME, I'VE CREATED A MEDIA BLACK-OUT here at your house," Arnie informs us. "Other than Emma and my connections with Acme's SatCom, no WiFi, cellular, or land line, or other communication devices of any kind can penetrate the blackout field. That way, your children can't be informed about your, er, 'imminent demise' until they see you're alive and well, no matter what else they hear or see to the contrary."

I breathe a sigh of relief. "Thank you for that, Arnie—because what they'll hear won't be pretty by any means."

That their mother is a known terrorist who has maimed or killed innocent people who just want to live their lives in peace…

That, once again, they will be the neighborhood pariahs…

That doing my job means making hard choices—none of which allow us to be "normal."

I sigh mightily. I'm still stunned, and exhausted.

I'm not the only one. Jack is driving us home while Jean-Pierre sits in the back seat, staring out the window. Gigi was his mission: his quest. Getting so near to her only to lose her again seems to have broken his spirit. He too will never know "normal."

He must regret he ever met us. This is one of those situations in life when not knowing an outcome is better, if only to allow one to hold onto some glimmer of hope.

"Great news! Abu and Dominic rescued the missing agents," Emma announces in our ears.

"So…so they were the hot spots in the big conference room after all?" I'm still so dazed myself that I'm only partially focused on what Jack is saying.

"Yes! And Dominic and Abu were in luck. Since all of the conventioneers were at the mind modification demonstration, only a skeleton crew was left to guard the kidnapped agents. Before they eliminated the guards, I put the hotel's security cams on a loop so that anyone monitoring the hotel via long distance wouldn't be alerted to it. Then I unlocked the doors." She sighs. "The agents were tethered to hospital beds, and hooked up to machines that were monitoring their brains. They were dazed, but they were able to go out a fire exit. They are now safely in the custody of the FBI."

Jack laughs. "I would have loved to have seen the look on Carl's face when he came back to that empty room."

"How about the fact that Heinried Müller, a.k.a., Pinky Ring—gets killed by a bus—twice!" Emma marvels. "Talk about bad karma."

"Hey, and guess what?" Arnie exclaims. "Dominic and Abu are sitting in on the kidnapped agents' debriefings. We did the FBI another solid, too: Emma pulled archival webcam footage of the convention's registration, then cross-referenced it with our facial recognition software. Bingo! Almost sixty domestic terrorist leaders! You'd think that would soften up the Feds toward us."

"Yeah, you think?" I lean my head back on the headrest of my seat and close my eyes.

Jack pats my hand. "Donna, are you okay?"

"Am I...okay? No, Jack! *I'm dead.* Remember? And I'm a terrorist! I blew up innocent people—"

He shakes his head. "You did nothing of the sort! A brainwashed young woman whose features were altered to look like you did it. And she fought the urge to do it up until the very last second of her life. Her DNA will prove it."

"It doesn't stop the world from thinking otherwise," I reason. "The act was captured on the mall's security cameras, and quite a few cell phones too. I'm sure it's all over social media. If they aren't already, any moment now the FBI will be storming the house again, but this time they'll be looking for you—who now looks like Number Fourteen on their Most Wanted list. We're quite a pair, aren't we?" My eyes open wide at my next thought: "Oh, my God! How do you think our children will react when their friends show them replays of me, blowing myself up?"

"Some friends," Emma grumbles.

"This may cheer you up," Arnie declares. "I had a chance to look at Gordon's webcam footage. Müller is the one who slit his throat."

"So you hacked the feed? Great!" Jack exclaims. "I'm in the clear."

"Well, that makes one of us," I mutter.

Emma hushes me with a warning: "Ryan has briefed POTUS on the mission by phone! He wants me to patch you in, too."

"'Bout damn time," I grumble. "A pardon can't come soon enough."

We hear a couple of clicks on the line, then: "Donna, and Jack? It's Ryan, with President Chiffray."

"Hello, Mr. President," Jack and I say in unison. Guess which one of us is rolling his eyes? Oops, did I just give it away? So sorry.

"I want to thank you for alerting the FBI in the surveillance of these known terrorists, and the discovery of the missing covert operatives," Lee says. "It was truly an awesome assist."

"*Awesome assist*?" Jack hisses. "The nerve of this guy!"

I pinch him so that he shuts his yap.

"Needless to say, I've commanded Assistant Attorney Reynolds to drop all allegations," Lee continues. "However, we still have the issue of finding a mole in the West Wing. I hope you'll agree to help us do so."

"I thought we'd proven it was Vice President Drucker," I reply. "I assume Ryan shared with you the video of the conversation he had with Gordon Soames. It occurred at least a year prior to when the researchers' results were breached."

"Ryan did. And although this recently discovered intel proves Vice President Drucker knew of Operation Hercules, it doesn't make the case that he caused the breach with the drones, and then turned around and gave information to the Quorum. Remember, he was ambushed only after Arnie revealed the breach two days ago, and the vice president's wife was killed in the attempt on his life. In any event, we won't be able to interrogate him until he comes out of his coma."

Lee has a good point.

"What about Soames?" Jack asks. "He could have easily released the drones."

"We don't have the proof we need to verify it," Lee replies.

"Okay, then, what is it that you're asking of us now?" Jack's wary growl is meant to warn Lee to tread lightly.

"The mission is more Donna's call than yours," Lee responds blithely. "It will put her in deep cover." He pauses. Finally: "Donna, will you agree to stay 'dead'?"

"What?" I can't believe my ears. "For God's sake, why?"

"Because Carl thinks he's just ruined your reputation—and Jack's too, unless Jack agrees to stay under house arrest for Gordon's murder," Lee explains. "Carl thinks you're now on the run, alone, and that you're less likely to track him down. Of course, you'll do the opposite—with Jack and the rest of the Acme team as back-up."

"Emma, are the GPS trackers Donna planted on Carl and Dr. Welles live yet?" Ryan asks.

"Yes, sir. Live and well. It looks as if the men are together—and, unfortunately, over the border, in Mexico."

Hasta la vista, baby.

"It's our chance, Donna," Lee pleads, "to put him behind bars permanently."

Somehow my worst nightmare was resurrected. He's got a point: time to put it to rest once and for all.

"Under one condition: Jack has to be allowed to tell my children the truth–that I'm alive, and that it wasn't me who was killed."

Lee thinks for an eternity. "Even one little slip up on their parts puts your safety at risk. Do you trust them?"

"With my life." Always, and forever. Just as they trust me with theirs.

"I'll honor your condition," Lee promises.

"Okay, then—I'll do it."

Jack smacks his forehead as if I'm crazy.

Maybe I am.

But the way I see it, I've got nothing to lose and a lot to gain—another chance to kill Carl.

Bring. It. On.

Trisha shakes her head adamantly. "I don't think it's a good idea."

I haven't asked my children for their permission, or even their approval. It is not their place to give it. Instead, I'm living up to my promise to them: that I will always be as honest as my job allows.

I've explained why I need to keep playing possum. I've asked that they play along too.

Without saying a word, Jeff agreed immediately. His own personal experience with terrorism gives him a perspective on trust and self-sacrifice that makes him far wiser than most.

Mary's acknowledgement was just as stoic. She'll ignore the snickers. She's learned the hard way that peer approval isn't always right, or just. Jack and I may not always be forthcoming about our missions, but she realizes everything we do has our family's best interests at heart.

I nod at Trisha, but then I ask, "Explain why."

My youngest wrinkles her nose in thought. "God may take it wrong. He may think you'd rather be with Him than with us."

"He knows that's not true," I explain. "He knows I'm doing this so that the bad men don't win."

She crosses her arms at her chest. "You mean, like…Carl Stone?"

It's the first time she's called her biological father by his given name. Why? I wonder. "Yes, Trisha, like him. What brought him to mind?"

"He wants me to hurt you."

"Hurt me?" I ask. "How?"

"He told me to put the cleansing powder from under the kitchen sink in your coffee." Disgusted, she wrinkles her nose. "He thinks I'm just a little kid, but I know that's wrong! My real father would never want that."

She's right. Carl's mind games are bad enough, but I never thought he'd stoop so low as to ask one of our children to physically hurt me. He's gotten meaner in the next life.

Finally, Trisha nods. "I won't like it, but I can pretend."

"Thank you." I hug her tightly before turning to Evan. "Think you can carry this off?"

Evan is tall enough that he can put both hands on my shoulders. Gazing into my eyes, he declares, "Whatever you need, Mom."

I'm so relieved that I burst into tears—of joy.

Sheesh. I am *such* a sap.

"Group hug?" Jack suggests.

My God, he's a bigger sap than me.

Yet another of the many reasons I love him.

～

My funeral is a glorious affair.

It has something to do with the *joie de vivre* of its planner: the first lady, Babette Chiffray—who revels at the chance to put her enemies in the ground, this time literally as opposed to figuratively.

Trust me, if it were up to her, she'd have let me rot in a hole in the backyard. But since Janie insisted on supporting her best friend and threatened to run away if she couldn't, Babette had no recourse but to join her—with one condition: that her posse was allowed to control the event.

Even Babette realizes that the funeral of a terrorist isn't the best photo op for a first lady. Still, she was determined to make the most of it. Narcissa and Lucretia rallied every news network to show up.

Besides, Babette always looks fabulous in black.

Despite his daughter's insistence that she attend and his wife's hunger for any spotlight, Ryan back-channeled my request to Lee that the president stay away. No need to suffer the political backlash that an appearance will garner, especially since DNA testing on one of Gigi's body parts found at the scene—a foot—proves that she was me.

How the hell can that be?

I'm relieved to see Lee honored my wish. When my pardon comes through, we'll celebrate a better kind of home-coming: Carl's, to a maximum security jail cell.

As distraught as Aunt Phyllis is, maybe it's a good thing Babette talked my aunt into letting her make the arrange-ments. I guess my aunt will jump for joy when she discovers I'm really alive. Or else she'll brain me with a frying pan for playing such a mean trick on her.

Many were injured, but to everyone's relief, only one

person died: the bomber herself. The Quorum's planning didn't account for the fact that Haute Hipster was closed for inventory. The clerks doing it were in the back storeroom. Still, the sensationalism of yet another major domestic terrorist attack—this one involving a suicide bomber—has taken its psychological toll on America.

My service is taking place the day after the event. Our feeling about it: the sooner, the better, we reason, so that the world can forget my supposed culpability and we can get all get on with our lives.

I have to give credit to Babette's posse, Narcissa and Lucretia. They took care of every niggling detail at warp speed—including the most important one: getting every major network to cover it live.

As always, Babette has at least one ulterior motive: making sure she is front and center when the cameras and microphones are pointed her way.

I watch it via satellite feed on Arnie's computer, from the privacy of my great room. The drapes are drawn to guard against the NSA agents' prying eyes. Although Jack is supposedly still under house arrest, he has special dispensation to go to my funeral with my children; so as far as the Feds know, the house is empty. I entered through the basement tunnel.

At the cemetery, the paparazzi jockey around each other at curbside, but they know better than to trample those who are pushing up daisies. The wall-to-wall Secret Service detail has no other problems with crowd control because the only ones to show up besides Babette, Janie, and my family are my Acme co-workers.

Most of our neighbors chose not to pay their respects.

They prefer to make their feelings known via the picket signs in front of our lawn that proclaim:

TERRORISTS AREN'T WELCOME IN HILLDALE!

Cheever Bing's mother, Penelope, is leading the lynch mob. According to what I can catch via her bullhorn, owning a home in the same neighborhood as a known terrorist—even a dead one—is killing their property values.

To that extent, they're probably right.

Still, when the facts are finally released, will they show up at my doorstep with Bundt cakes? I hope not. Because no matter how delicious they look, I'll still put them through a metal detector—

As I requested, Ryan gives my eulogy. His insights on me are spot on. So is his obvious love for me. When he calls me "the daughter I never had," I tear up.

Jack stands on the other side of Babette. Her slim hand tucked into the arm of the bereaved widower. He pats it so often and looks so soulfully into her eyes that you'd think it were him consoling her, and not the other way around.

Bravo, Jack, *Bravo!* The Oscar for "Best Performance by a Covert Operative" is yours hands down.

My children should also be up for Academy Awards. Jeff looks stoically straight ahead, never down at the casket. He's not just pretending that he is burdened by the horror of terrorism.

On the other hand, Mary uses it as performance art. She sheds enough crocodile tears to rival Babette. And while Evan gives Aunt Phyllis a broad shoulder to lean on, to his dismay Mary uses Jean-Pierre's to comfort her.

In truth, it is she who is comforting *him*. What little of Gigi's remains is left is already on a plane to Biarritz. May she finally rest in peace.

Trisha chooses not to act. But at least she's not acting out either—that is, until she can't stand Janie's sobs. At that point, she jerks her friend to her side and whispers in her ear.

Oh, no. What did Trisha say to her?

It's enough to make Janie sob even harder and shake her head in awe.

Babette notices this. She sends Janie's *au pair*, Sally, to quiet her little girl. Instead, Janie whispers agitatedly in Sally's ear, but Sally firmly shakes her head *NO*.

Ryan winces, but continues with his last words to and about me in a voice loud enough so that others can hear above Janie's drama.

A curt head thrust indicates Babette's desire to question her daughter herself. The little girl runs over to her and whispers something in her mother's ear.

Babette turns white.

She holds tight to Janie.

As soon as Ryan's last words are spoken and my body is lowered into the ground, Babette is walking off with Janie— practically running, in fact.

The others ignore her. They are here for all the right reasons: to pay their respects—or, at least look as if they are.

My children throw flowers into my grave.

For Jack, it's a clod of dirt.

He tosses it for Gigi, not me.

He then looks skyward—to me—and winks.

IT'LL TAKE HALF AN HOUR BEFORE THEY'RE HOME FROM THE cemetery. I decide to busy myself by cleaning up the house. I grab my vacuum and head upstairs.

Trisha's room, in its typical disarray, is as good of a place to start as any.

She no longer likes to sleep in it. She even dresses in Mary's room now, running in to grab clothes out of her closet or bureau, which is why half her clothes are now on the closet floor.

I raise my head in silent prayer that her nightmare—and mine—will soon be over, when I see it, hovering in the corner of the ceiling:

An iridescent insect?

No. A drone.

I take the long arm of the vacuum and swat it down.

Did I break it? I pick it up. Thank goodness, no.

I can't wait to get ahold of Arnie and see what he makes of it.

I've just picked it up when I hear his voice whisper in my ear: "Honey, I'm home…"

Before I can turn around, I feel the sting: of a needle, filled with some knock-out drug.

Catching me as I fall, Carl murmurs, "Miss me, babe?"

The drone falls out of my hand as I black out.

16

Dead on Arrival

"Dead on Arrival," or "DOA," is a term used by first responders and other trained emergency personnel to indicate a body has clinically expired before they came on the scene.

This phrase has been co-opted in the English language in regard to other incidents in everyday life that fail even before they begin: a missed opportunity, for example; equipment that arrives broken; or, say, an idea that pops into one's head, but upon further cognitive processing, is considered a non-starter.

Sometimes, personal relationships are DOA.

Telltale signs that your current paramour sees it in a similar light will reveal themselves in other phrases he may use to describe the status of your coupledom, like "friends with benefits," or (quelle horreur!) "just...a friend."

At that point, "dead on arrival" may take on a new, literal meaning: one that describes what (or in this case, who) is planted under your backyard flowerbed.

Should a neighbor inquire, "Um...is that your boyfriend in the wood chipper?" You can honestly answer, "Nope, just…a friend."

❧

"I SO ENJOYED KILLING YOU." CARL'S VOICE SOUNDS SO FAR away. And yet, his hot breath wafts in my direction. "And now, I get to do it all over again. What fun!"

His warm lips nuzzle my cheek.

I'm too tired to open my eyes. Instead, I lift my arm a few inches, only to discover that my wrists are bound together by some kind of restraint.

Ah, okay. No matter. I swing my legs straight up, where he should be—

But I hit nothing but air.

Carl chuckles at my feeble attempt to harm him. "You've got it all wrong, wifey! I said I'll be killing *you*—not the other way around. Again! What are the odds, eh?" He shrugs. "But hey, I understand. It's not easy to let go. You've seen it on the face of your twin. She had a hell of a time letting go, didn't she?" He stops as a memory strikes him. "Granted, your father had no issue with it. As I remember, he drank himself to death. Ah well, at least he enjoyed himself on the way out."

Finally, I'm able to force my leaden eyelids open, only to find myself staring at my ex-husband.

I resist the urge to touch him. Make that, to punch him. I already know he is all too real.

Maybe that's a good thing; I've got so many questions to ask—and for that matter, so much to say to him. I've got yet another chance to give my ex a piece of my mind.

It would help if I weren't shackled, naked, to this operating room table.

I guess the reason why when I realize Norbert Welles stands a few feet away, tinkering with his mind-melding machinery. And since it looks as if I'll only have time for one or the other, I think it best that I skip the tirade and go for the questions. Turning to Carl, I ask, "Why aren't you in Mexico?"

"Did you think I wouldn't find the GPS tracker?" He shakes his head at the thought. "It did its job: let you and your keepers think you were safe."

"Where am I, anyway?"

"Our mad scientist's laboratory." He nods toward Norbert. "In other words, nowhere you'll be found."

I shiver at the dark tone in his voice. "How did you get into my house?"

"The same way you got out after breaking off your ankle monitor—the tunnel in the basement. It was a great idea of mine, wasn't it? I'm sure you'll think of an appropriate way to thank me." Carl smiles. He's in a chatty mood because he thinks he's holding all the cards.

"How is it that you're alive at all?" I ask.

Carl takes his time before answering me, as if weighing the value of the secret to his resurrection against my odds of death, here at his hands. Apparently he thinks I've already lost. I pray he's wrong. "I almost didn't live. When the Quorum found me, I was near death. They nursed me back to health—body, mind and soul. The Super Soldier research was instrumental." He lifts his arms, as if performing a magic trick. "Without it, I wouldn't be standing here today."

"Was Drucker your leak regarding the fact that we were on to you?"

"Nope. It was your hacker-slash-clown, Arnie." Noting that my eyes are growing wide, he taunts, "*Tsk, tsk*, someone forgot to sweep Lion's Lair for Eileen's security bugs! They were live during your meeting there, with Lee and his government goon squad. If Arnie had kept his yap shut, we would have never known you were on to us." Carl chuckles. "Hitting Drucker's motorcade took a thorn out of our side—and Lee's for that matter. Lee now has a reason to rally the troops against domestic terrorism. Even if Drucker survives, he'll assume it was Lee who tried to take him out, if only to keep him from making a political stink about the breach."

"Was it Soames who released the drones in the West Wing?"

"Good call—although now that your new hubby is the prime suspect in his murder, you'll never be able to prove it."

"Was the 'demonstration' at your little terror convention really necessary?" I ask.

"Bread and circuses, baby. You see, domestic terrorism is a growing market segment, and the Quorum wants to own it. The anger and helplessness people feel against their government isn't just happening overseas. It's here too—and it has been since a band of patriots became our Founding Fathers." He puts his hand over his heart in mock salute. "But with the domestic cells, there's always a loose end—the still live bomber, who's usually stupid enough to get caught. Sadly, domestic ideology isn't as strong as that of the radical jihadists. They seem to have forgotten the homegrown motto, 'Give me liberty, or give me death.' Our little demonstration gave them the nudge needed to get off their haunches." He shrugs. "No one says it has to be a game of follow the leader. Recruiting the young and impressionable—who seek immortality through heroism—is much more appealing. That's where Dr. Wollstonecraft's research—"

Norbert sighs loudly in offense.

"Excuse me, I should say Dr. *Welles*'s memory modification research is the most impressive tool in the Quorum's super soldier shed."

"Of all your captives, why use Gigi?" I ask. "She didn't really look anything like me."

"In height and build, she was passable. But what made her truly plausible was her DNA. The match was close enough for us to fake it. Rudy Brooks' research gave us the key to creating a good enough fake, should the Feds find anything left to ID her—that is, you."

"Gigi couldn't have been the 'Donna' who hit Drucker's motorcade with you," I counter. "She was too conflicted to be a reliable asset."

He shrugs. "You're right. And from the look on your face, I see you're now wondering how many other Donnas are really out there. Not to worry, wifey! I'm not out to build a harem—although the thought is tantalizing." To prove it, he tweaks my nipple between his fingers. "For that little mission, Tatyana fit the bill. She wore a face mask—just as you did when you infiltrated our convention…Yes, we figured it out when you neglected to return with the rest of the group."

He flips me onto my side in order to graze the base of my spine with his palm. "We had a hell of a time getting that tattoo off the base of Gigi's spine. It was so painful! She cried for hours. All the while I thought how much easier it would have been if you'd had one too." His hand roams to my left bum cheek. He grabs it, weighing in his hand. "I like the idea of branding you," he proclaims. "But none of that hearts-and-flowers crap. It's got to make a statement—say, my name, here"—he taps the cheek hard—"and again, here." He smacks the other cheek even harder. "Like branding a cow. Hey, now that's a great idea! I'll use a branding iron!"

"Save it for the next victim," I retort blithely. "I'm no longer your wife. Even before you died, I'd divorced you. Remember? If anything, it would be Jack's initials with mine."

He scowls at me, but his growl is meant for Norbert. "Get out. I'll call when I'm finished here."

"But…but we don't have much time! Tatyana will be here any moment. She'll hit the roof if she finds you with your wife—"

"Too bad. This job has so few perks as it is." Carl whips around so that he's facing Norbert. "Beat it, Dr. Frankenstein."

He picks Norbert up by the collar and goose-steps him out the door, slamming it behind him.

So that's it. Carl isn't a ghost after all. *He's a super soldier.* Like Salem, does Carl now possess super-human strength? It gives him the chance at his long-lived fantasy: he can rape me, and there's nothing I can do about it.

Not without a fight.

As I attempt to rise up on my elbows, Carl slaps me so hard that my head hits the table. Before I have a chance to gather my thoughts, he's leaped onto the table and is straddling me.

He sits on his haunches, right over my thighs, so that my knees can't bend. He bends over me. His tongue takes a slow, lazy path over my face. The damp trail it leaves behind tingles my skin. When he gets to my left breast, he circles it with his tongue. As his saliva hits the laboratory's cold air, my nipple goes taut.

"Let go of me," I growl.

"From what I remember, you like this kind of foreplay."

"I draw the line at making whoopee with laboratory rats."

His next slap is harder than the last.

My skin feels inflamed, but I bite my tongue as opposed to shouting out in pain.

"Beg me to stop," he taunts. "Go ahead, Donna. All it takes is one word from you."

"How…about…two? *FUCK. OFF.*"

"Oh, yeah, baby, I plan to do just that." He fumbles with his belt. In no time, his pants are around his knees.

I see his fifth appendage…

Oh, my God—*really*?

It's…*TINY.*

Let's be clear here: I'm not talking short and stout, or just a mouthful. I mean maybe a thimbleful—*and that is a really big maybe.*

But his hands are *so huge.* Go figure.

My stare moves from it to his face. "What the hell happened? Do those things shrink in the afterlife?"

He slaps my face again.

I'd cry if I weren't laughing so hard. "No, no, seriously, tell me: was it the ounce of flesh you gave when you made your pact with the Devil to come back?"

He hits me again.

I roll my eyes. "Well, now at least you finally have a reason for your Napoleon complex."

The next time he strikes me, it's with a full palm. "You don't get it. *I am Carl*." There is no doubt in his voice.

But the giveaway is his anger.

"Sorry, Whomever You Are, but the Quorum chose the wrong dude to play Carl. I knew Carl better than anyone. If you can't convince me, you'll never be able to convince anyone else." I look up at him and smile. "Who are you? And why give up your life and take over that of a known terrorist's? I mean, let's face it: if you're going to go through all that plastic surgery, why not get them to go the extra mile?"

Three slaps follow: openhanded, back and front.

Norbert runs in, screaming. Tatyana is at his side. "Stop it!" Norbert pleads. "If you keep bruising her, you'll ruin the project."

Fake Carl quakes with anger.

Tatyana moves in closer to assess the damage. "Not too bad," she pronounces grandly. "I'm sure she deserved it." As our eyes meet, she grins wickedly at me. "Ah, my twin! So happy to see you."

"*Your* twin?" I glare at Carl. "What the hell does she mean by that?"

Carl shrugs. "Oh…didn't I mention? Tatyana needs to disappear. For that matter, we all do. As for how it's accomplished, well, the most public way to do so has already been demonstrated."

"I'm to be a suicide bomber?" *Like hell*. "Sorry, I don't do vests. Not very slimming."

Tatyana giggles. "Not to worry. My one stipulation to using you of all people was that you'd undergo liposuction too." She pats my belly. "I don't know why some women let themselves go."

She got too close. When my spittle hits her eye, she screams as if she's been burned.

It can be arranged.

Carl sighs loudly. "Seriously, wifey, what does it matter what face stares back at you in the mirror? You won't be wearing it long, anyway." He picks up a syringe, tests the tip with a short squirt, then adds, "Look at the upside: you'll be avenging my death yet again."

What the hell does he mean by that?

As he heads my way, Tatyana blocks him. Seductively, she puts her hand over his—the one holding the syringe. "Why don't you let me do the honors? After all, she's mine now."

He smiles lovingly at her as he hands it over. "If you insist, my love."

Talk about a perfect couple.

But that's just it: they aren't perfect. They aren't even honest facsimiles.

To test this theory, I taunt, "Hey, Tatyana, what happened to all your ugly facial scars? You know, the ones Jack gave you?"

Tatyana's hands go to both sides of her face. "I…I never had scars!" Her eyes move frantically to Norbert. "What is she talking about?"

He takes her in his arms. "She's just being cruel. You've always been perfect, darling."

This bucks her up. In three strides, she is next to my table.

As she stabs my arm, she whispers, "Sweet dreams, bitch."

MY LIFE FLASHES BEFORE MY MIND—

Or is it truly my life?

Yes, I remember how Carl and I met: at the shooting range. Falling in love came somewhere between allowing him to help me with my supposedly poor aim (he didn't realize I'd faltered my shots to get his attention) followed by a heartfelt conversation about lives, goals, and dreams over a diner's late-night special of eggs and fries; and ended with a walk back to my place, letting him undress me, then touch me; making love.

To me, it seemed as natural to me as breathing.

No, he wasn't my first love, but as his wife, I always thought he'd be my last.

The many joys we shared now play out in my brain:

He is at my side at the birth of our first two children, patting down my feverish brow, holding my trembling hand, and cajoling me to push through the pain so that we can get to the fun part: raising them together.

What a great father he was. All those hours spent in the backyard, teaching our young son how to throw a baseball. Pushing our daughter on her swing set. Wearing them out with games of hide and seek.

After they'd fallen into bed, we'd do the same—not to sleep, but to make love. His passion, hardened inside of me, never disappointed. Afterward, when he curled up around me, I never felt safer.

I remember his anguished kiss when I told him I was pregnant with Trisha—and his final words to me before he walked out of the hospital on the day of her birth in order to retrieve the maternity bag we'd forgotten: "Don't worry, honey, I'll be back in no time."

Only he didn't come back.

Suddenly, another memory comes to me: Carl's car, driven at a breakneck speed explodes: a fireball, lighting up an inky desert sky.

Where was I? Not there. So, how do I know this?

No matter. I know what I must do now: *avenge his death.*

I am a killing machine. A swallow who slits throats. A femme fatale who totes the most daring of all fashion statements: a semi-automatic.

All for the love of Carl.

How I miss my Carl.

How dare another man enter my bedroom and presume he can take Carl's place: *Jack.*

I see the memories so clearly in my head:

How my children are wary of him—as they should be.

How he chides me with derisive taunts, and attempts to bully me into submission.

He doesn't trust me. Well, tit for tat. *I don't trust him either.*

Until…

When I am sick with a spiking fever, he is there, cooling me off, steadfastly at my side until I am well.

And when my children need a father, he is with them:

making Trisha laugh, checking their homework, coaching Jeff's games, taking Mary to the Father-Daughter dance…

He lives to hold me. To kiss me. To adore me.

He is always there for me, catching me when I fall. Pulling me out of harm's way. Taking bullets for me…

Carl's bullets.

Carl wants me to die.

For Tatyana. For his own glory.

Well, to hell with that.

I hear myself moan.

So does he. "She's coming to," Carl says to the others. "Time for the test. Leave me alone with her."

"Some test," Tatyana growls.

"The first of many, sweetheart. Hey, we're doing it for you, right?"

The pause in the conversation is followed with a giggle.

Obviously, size doesn't matter to her.

Me neither. But if I'm going to give it up, the guy has to at least want me to live afterward.

I wait until the door shuts tight and his footsteps bring him to my side before I fake a groggy groan, and then slowly open my eyes.

He waits until my gaze finds him and moves toward his face.

Seeing it, I blink once. Then once again.

And then I smile. "Oh…Carl…*my angel!*" As if unaware of my restraints, I try to rise. My eyes plead with him to explain. "Am I ill?"

Carl honors me with an ear-to-ear grin. "No, my love. Not anymore."

He reaches over to unleash me.

Payback time.

"You came back to me." Even as I gently touch the contours of his face, my teary eyes never leave his.

"Hush, baby, hush," he coos. "We're back together again."

As if convincing myself that he's right, I murmur, "How…why?" I look around. The operating cart is right beside us, bearing a mallet, forceps, ear wax excavator, surgical mouth gag, eye speculum…

Yeah, all good.

He sighs, as if our tale is sadder than that of *A Dog of Flanders*. "It's a long story. You were taken in by a Quorum agent: Jack Craig." He frowns. "Donna, I won't lie to you. He made you do some truly awful things. I'm sure it was your way of living with his abuse."

"Yes! I remember…" I shut my eyes, as if in pain. "The cruel words! The…*the beatings*!" I curl up in his arms, sobbing.

"He has our children, Donna! He took them away from you! But now that I'm here with you again, I'll help you get them back."

"Oh, Carl! Would you?" I lift my mouth, parting my lips just slightly.

He takes the hint. The kiss is chaste.

I sigh blissfully. "I've waited so long for that."

My eyes sweep his face with my desire.

This time, his kiss goes deep.

My tongue moves through his mouth, inviting him to

take a chance at something a bit bolder.

To appease me, he takes a breast in each hand, cupping them together so that his mouth easily moves from one to another.

My hands are busy too. The left one grabs the ear wax excavator: a tiny metal pick. The right one grasps the mallet. With my hands behind me, I lean back onto the operating table, as if enjoying all the sensations from his touch.

I doubt he'll think the same of mine.

As he bends down in front of me, his mouth roams over my body in anticipation of my sweetness.

But before delivering, he looks up at me. Is he gauging my veracity?

He cannot doubt the look of ecstatic desire in my glistening eyes.

Finally, I whisper, "Yes...*please.*"

He bows his head to accommodate.

The first strike comes as he kisses me gently below the waist: the steel pick to the neck.

Blood gushes out one side as he falls to the other.

The beating, with the mallet, isn't wasted on his face, but on the back of his head, easily crushing the motor nerves that allow him to breathe; and on the back of his neck, severing his head from his spine.

He is left face down, paralyzed and gasping.

But only for a few moments. As soon as his heart stops pumping, the blood stops seeping from his head and his neck.

Still, I feel his pulse, to make sure.

No need to say goodbye to Carl yet again.

While I'm at it, I take his gun.

I see my clothes, tossed on a chair in the corner. I slip them on and head for the door.

I open it slowly…

To a darkened hallway. No one is there.

I hear gunshots, coming from far off, down another hallway.

I duck when Norbert comes into view, wild-eyed and scared for his life.

One shot, right between the eyes, puts him out of his misery.

"That was for Gigi," I murmur as I pass his body.

Two down, one to go.

TATYANA DOESN'T KNOW TO LOOK OUT FOR ME. IF SHE'D TRULY had any past experience with me, she would have known better.

From what I can tell, this is an abandoned office building. The halls create confusing mazes.

I use the sound of gunfire to find my way around.

I don't have to go far. I find her with her back to me, peering around a corner. As a bullet goes whizzing over her head, I whisper, "Do you even remember your real name?"

Her head whips around.

Then it explodes.

Silence.

I hear footsteps: quick but cautious.

I'd know them anywhere.

Jack pauses before peeking around the corner. He's crouched low, his gun held high, but ready to draw—

Until he sees me.

He runs to me.

There will never be a sweeter kiss.

As Ryan, Abu, and Dominic rush by us down the hall to the lab, Ryan shouts back to us, "Jeez, you two—get a room."

Gladly.

But first things first: tying up a few loose ends.

17

Dead End

At some point, each of us discovers—and sometimes, much too late—that the route you took is really a dead end.

Should you should find yourself in the middle of nowhere, do this—immediately:

1. *Turn around. Don't be hard-headed about it. Here's the reality: you can't get there from here.*
2. *Just don't back up. Going the wrong way on a one-way street will get you hit in the rear end every time. Think of the damage. Yes, it will cost you.*
3. *Start over. No one else has the right to plot your course. Just because someone else "got there from here" doesn't mean you will too. Time to throw away someone else's road map, and take a road never traveled.*

Starting to see a pattern here? Good for you!

And if you think I've only been talking about a failure in your GPS system, you're wrong. We're discussing your life.

Remember, you only live once. Don't spend it in some dead end. There is always a way out.

"A DRONE CREATED ALL THE NIGHTMARES FOR TRISHA? WHY didn't I think of that?" Arnie is so angry with himself that he smacks his head with his palm. "I'll bet it has a projector—you know like a hologram."

"Only one way to find out." I toss it to him.

Like a child with a new toy, he shouts, grabs his bag of tiny screwdrivers. and gleefully runs off to his cubicle down the hall in Acme's vast offices.

Emma sighs. "He will have dissected the damn thing in no time, and all will be right in the world again. Seriously, I don't know who's a bigger baby: him, or Nicky."

"Let's not digress to the obvious, people! We all want to get out of here before sundown." The thought of a decent night's sleep brings a smile to Ryan's lips. "Any more loose ends to clear up so that we can close the case file on Operation Hercules?"

A thought hits me. "I've got one. How did you guys find me?"

"You can thank your penchant for slovenliness," Dominic replies. "I presume it's why you wore the same pants in which you put the GPS tags, is it not?"

The way in which I stab the table with my pen between his open index and middle fingers warns him against presuming anything.

"Donna!" Ryan warns.

I put my hands in my lap and smile prettily at him.

He shakes his head. "Anything else?"

I turn to Jack. "What did Trisha say to Janie that got her so upset?"

Jack laughs. "It's my fault. You see, I told her that should she have the urge to tell someone where you really were, she should simply reply that you are watching from Heaven. Unfortunately, Janie then let it be known that her mother had already informed her that you were burning in hell instead. Your daughter—being a chip off of your very luscious block—replied, in no uncertain terms, that if that were the case, Babette would most likely join her there, since Babette was, and I quote, 'the worst mother in the world.' Needless to say, Janie didn't take it too well. Apparently, neither did Babette. I think the Craigs have finally been banished from Lion's Lair."

"Oh, I seriously doubt that," Ryan retorts. "Speaking of the Chiffrays, Lee wanted to show his appreciation to the Craigs with a little quid pro quo: he asked Assistant Attorney Reynolds to send a letter to the trustee of the Martin family, warning of an investigation if Evan's funds weren't released to him, or to the organizations who were also beneficiaries of the Martin Family largesse. Evan should be hearing from the trustee within twenty-four hours."

Good for Lee. Other than a pardon, it's the best way he could repay me for initiating ghost protocol on this operation. I'm sure Reynolds balked, but too bad.

"Which leads us to one other bit of cleanup. I feel it will answer a lot of the questions we still have outstanding as to why Operation Hercules failed so miserably in its application." Ryan turns to Emma. "Want to give them the news?"

"It was really Abu's great idea." She nods in his direction.

Abu shrugs "As Donna so pointedly discovered"—he smothers his grin—"this Carl—as well as Tatyana, Salem, and Heinried—were imposters, and the real ones are dead after all. But who were the fakes? And, for that matter, who put them up to it, and why? I found it hard to believe that Fake Carl was the mastermind. So I got to thinking: what if it were something Eric Weber set into motion? I thought it worth mentioning to Ryan."

Ryan nods. "And I asked Emma to tap into the visitor logs at Eric's, er, 'hotel'." He means the dark site where Eric is being held until he takes his last breath. "There's been only one visitor."

He taps the screen, showing time-stamped webcam footage of it:

Dr. Norbert Welles appears on the screen.

"My God," Jack murmurs. "How did he get access?"

"Apparently, he used his research with Operation Hercules as the reason for need."

I zoom in to the name he writes when he signs in:

Frank N. Stein

"Clever," I murmur.

Ryan shrugs. "What do you say, Donna, are you up for a visit to your biggest fan?"

"Yes," I reply.

But only because I need closure on this anecdote.

～

"YOU LOOK DISAPPOINTED, MY DEAR! WERE YOU EXPECTING A straight jacket and metal mask?" Eric Weber clucks his tongue. "How cliché."

Frankly, I didn't know what to expect. His cell—at Magic Mountain—a state-of-the-art maximum-security prison high on a sheer butte somewhere deep in a Utah mountain range —could be on the set of a James Bond movie. Even seeing that he is tethered by his wrists and ankles to a metal chair that is bolted into the steel floor of a cage made of impenetrable glass, I ask myself: Can even this place hold back the wrath of the titular head of the Quorum?

With what I've just been through, I give it a fifty-fifty chance.

When I don't answer him, he stares me down. There may be a smirk on his face, but there is adoration in his eyes.

A psychopath who is in love with the one who got away? Now, *that's* a cliché.

Finally, Eric sighs. "I presume you're here to talk about my little army of phantoms."

"Yes." I lower myself onto the chair that has been placed five feet from the glass cage. My strategy: act dumb. With so many still unanswered questions, it's easy to do. "Eric, how did you do it? How did you bring them back to life?"

He laughs joyously, as if we're sharing a joke at a cocktail party. "You've got it backwards, my dear! *We never did.*"

"But…but I was with him: *Carl.* He knew things only Carl would know. And his DNA analysis confirmed it. For that matter, so did that of my…twin, or whatever—"

"Good, good! The authorities must cover all aspects of verification, eh? And that of Salem as well?" His grin is as wide as a jack-o-lantern's. "And what of Tatyana? How is she?" He shakes his head at his gaffe. "I meant to say, how *was* she? She is now dead again, I presume?"

"Yes. Jack killed her—this time around."

"Don't be so jealous. You got her the first time. Maybe it was an act of transference on his part. She was so much like you—a natural. Did he strangle her? Such a pretty little neck!" He tilts his head and smiles, as if envisioning the deed.

I stifle my urge to shiver. "Nah. Bullet to the head." I mimic the act, pointing to his as I pull an imaginary trigger.

Apparently, he doesn't like my little joke. His jack-o-lantern grin fades. "You should ask your questions," he demands crisply. "Otherwise, you'll lose your window of opportunity to leave. At dusk, the winds are so wicked that one cannot fly off this godforsaken rock."

"Eric, level with me. Were they clones, or"—okay, I don't believe I'm saying this—"Zombies?"

"*Zombies*? No! Clones are closer to the truth. We called them 'twins' because their genetic make-up is almost identical to that of the original subject—the 'immortal,' if you will. But the goal was to simply satisfy any DNA test that would validate the twin as the immortal."

"How did you accomplish this?"

He's all smiles again. "Whereas it is true that each snippet of DNA contains common variants, the code found in all organisms can be laid out in a simple chart bearing sixty-four amino acids. God gave us a wonderful head start, and Dr. Brooks' research took advantage of it." He laughs. "The good doctor created a database that identifies tens of thousands of these commonalities in the genetic code. Like Acme and other covert agencies and governments, the Quorum keeps samples of our operatives' DNA on hand. Dr. Welles took it from there. An acceptable twin's profile had to have somewhat more than four hundred matching variants." He preens at the beauty of it all.

So that's why Salem's and Carl's evil twins passed Acme's DNA analysis—and Gigi too, for that matter.

"Obviously, a twin's external features weren't always the same as the original's," I counter. "Even identical twins have mirror features."

"When enhancements were needed, it was done the old fashioned way: with dye, make-up, or sometimes a vocal chord was altered," Eric concedes. "And of course, plastic surgery—you know, a nip here, a tuck there." He taps the middle and index fingers together, as if they are scissors.

"Speaking of which, there was one very important feature you got wrong on Fake Carl." I hold up a pinky finger then let it droop.

He chuckles at the sarcasm in my voice. "The rumors of Carl's manhood were so often exaggerated that I doubt *any* twin could have lived up to it! I suppose we should have tried harder. If it is any consolation, he was a disappointment to me, too…Oh! Not in *that* way." He chuckles knowingly. "The audacity of the man—to think he could run this scheme without me! Such arrogance! In that way, too, he was exactly like the original. And it was he who convinced the others that they didn't need me."

"Who was he, anyway?"

"A Russian, of course. Undercover here, in the United States." Eric sighs. "SVR agents—bah! There isn't a loyal one among them. I blame Putin for that." He shrugs. "No matter.

I knew *you* could stop him, my dear Donna. My little super soldier girl!"

I yawn to show him I am immune to his flattery. "Why attempt to fake an 'immortal' in the first place?" I ask.

His smile fades. "Isn't the reason obvious? All facets of Operation Hercules—regenerative bodies, strengthened bodies, perfected bodies—and full access to everything your mind holds, including every memory—is one way in which the Quorum lives forever."

Noting my stare, he sighs at my lack of awareness of the obvious. "How did you feel, my pretty, when you saw Salem, whom you'd only killed a few weeks prior? I'm sure Jack did a double-take at the sight of Heinried. Just the thought of an organization made of humans who'll never die strikes terror in the hearts and minds of men!" My slight nod is the acknowledgement he needs. "Oh, how I wish I could have been there when you set eyes on Carl! Did you faint? Were there tears? ...No? Of course not. You're made of stronger stuff than that. It's why we had such a hard time finding a perfect match for you." He sighs. "I'm sure you don't want to hear this, my pet, but in full disclosure we encouraged your twin, little Gigi, to put on a bit more weight."

"Thanks for your honesty," I say dryly. "The brain-washing portion of your little experiment must have taken forever. And where did you get all the juicy little details that only the original or an intimate would know?"

"Every Quorum member goes through hypnosis. Their memories are documented in a dossier." He leans in, conspiratorially. "Traditionally, it is used as a way in which to ensure our members' loyalties. No one wants her naughty little secrets aired in public, am I right? But last year, when we first saw Eileen's intel on Operation Hercules, we realized how it might be better used: as a means to *immortality.*"

I shake my head in disbelief. "You're quite mad."

"Ten years ago, I would have agreed with you. Ten years from now—had you not interfered, that is—I'd be recognized as the genius who discovered the fountain of youth!" His eyes open wide with his passion. "What others would pay for a sip! And, as with everything humankind does, it all begins with the hunger for war. Blame your government, my dear Donna, not little old me. If it wasn't trying so hard to create the perfect soldier, you wouldn't be sitting here with me today." He chuckles. "For that alone, the stealth of Operation Hercules was worth it." A sudden thought darkens his eyes. "Poor Eileen! I'd hoped she'd live to see this day." He shakes his head sadly. "Still, she has achieved a sense of immortality. Her work continued even beyond her passing. From what I gather, the Quorum has you to blame for finally putting her to rest yet again."

"The iPad would not have stayed hidden forever." I shrug. "So much for 'immortality.' From what I could tell, the planting of new memories in the twins had its limitations. I didn't know Salem or Tatyana as well as I knew Carl, but I knew them well enough to suspect they weren't who they said they were."

"The initial research on Dr. Wollstonecraft's memory modification was so promising that it made us hopeful. And when the technique was applied to the twins, our monitoring showed that the memories were in fact taking root in the fertile synapses provided by their young robust minds.

But unfortunately, we could never emulate Dr. Wollstonecraft's success."

"It didn't work, thanks to a little thing called free will." I'm proof of this, although I'd never let him know that.

He shrugs his own acquiescence. "Perhaps. In any event, we made the decision to shelve the dream of immortality. Still, it made a convincing dog-and-pony show as we moved to our Plan B: sell our methodology to those who are willing to try anything to recruit new members: the myriad of terrorist cells that pock the earth." He laughs. "Welles insisted he could enhance Dr. Wollstonecraft's memory modification techniques so that when the moment came for a united front, a key memory planted deep within the recesses of each soldier would have turned them against their leaders, into a united Quorum army spanning the world."

"It didn't matter what ideology motivated any individual group," I reason, "as long as anarchy was created."

"Yes! You understand now!" He nods at me, his star pupil. "The cells' leaders never realized that they'd be training their armies to march, lockstep, in *our* war."

"Did you truly believe Welles was up to the task?" I ask.

"I guess we'll never know. More than a third of our test subjects—the kidnapped covert field agents—resisted the process. They were exterminated. But there are enough who showed progress for us to at least pretend we'd created our own army of super soldiers, all of whom were once loyal to their own countries." Eric shrugs. "The research being done by Dr. Brooks would have brought the body to its optimum physical level. Dr. Welles showed us how to resurrect the injured, sick, and dying. Linked with Dr. Wollstonecraft's memory research—or so we thought—we should have created the perfect soldier: strong, regenerative, and unwavering in his or her commitment to the cause." He shrugs. "Instead, when the planted memories were in conflict with their own thoughts and beliefs, it created anger and agitation that could not be controlled." He smiles. "So you see, my dear, by exterminating these mutants, you did the Quorum a favor. We thank you to no end."

"You act as if you're still a part of it."

Eric looks at me as if he's seeing me for the very first time. "My pet, one never quits the Quorum."

I rise with a smile. "You forget. I did."

Eric's laughter follows me out the door.

ERIC IS RIGHT ABOUT ONE THING: THE WIND. GEORGE AND I have a stomach-churning helicopter takeoff from the butte.

I'm still thinking about the project's failure when we land in Salt Lake City, where Acme's plane waits on the tarmac.

"Go on, let me hear you say it," George teases me. "'Home, Jeeves.'"

I laugh. "You took the words out of my…no, wait! Would you mind if we took a detour?"

"If we get caught, will you face the wrath of Ryan?"

"He'll appreciate why I did it, so yes. Besides, it will only take a couple of hours. See if you can get clearance into Oakland."

He does, and we're on our way: to find the missing link.

Shelley Wollstonecraft is surprised to see me, as she should be. As to be expected, she is even more surprised that Evan isn't with me. Still, she ushers me into her office.

"He wrote me to apologize for being the cause of the malware." She laughs. "It happens so often—even here at the university, with all of our tech security measures—that he really shouldn't feel guilty. It wasn't his fault. It's just that this was a particularly virulent strain. I wanted him to be aware of it, for the safety of his own computer, or other emails he may have been sending out."

"Evan truly didn't have any idea what was sent with the file. Thank you again, for not holding it against him." I hesitate before adding, "In fact, it was a Trojan virus, sent with the approval of POTUS and Director of Intelligence Barnham."

She sits, stunned. "How do you know this?"

"My company is a consultant to several security agencies in the U.S. government, including DARPA. The president assigned it the task of plugging a leak on the research of Operation Hercules. Evan's appointment was to have given us an opportunity to access your cell phone's photo archive. It didn't work out that way."

"Because I didn't have the phone with me," she reasons.

"Yes, exactly. But then, when you encouraged him to send you his memory research, we saw our way back into your photo archive, which we assumed was synced with your computer and some cloud archive."

She nods.

"Dr. Wollstonecraft, I'm not proud that we used an unsuspecting teenager's budding relationship with you to do it. That being said, you know better than most what is at stake here. It's why I'm being honest with you."

"I realize that." Shelley shrugs. "I also realize you could have found a myriad of other ways to access my phone."

I look down at the ground. "I wish we had."

She sighs. "I presume you're here because I was cleared of any wrongdoing."

"Yes. But another scientist was implicated: Norbert Welles."

"Ah. So, he acquiesced to Graffias International?"

I look closely at her. "Graffias approached you too?"

"Yes. The contact, Heinried Müller, came with a very generous offer—much too generous for what he claimed he really wanted, which was a license for commercial use of the research—after we were released from our contract with the government, of course. When I didn't accept it, he thought threats would work better. I quit hearing from him when he finally got what he wanted." She smiles slyly. "Only, he didn't, really."

"What do you mean?"

"Müller's full court press put me on edge. Then one night, after I'd gone home, I came back here to my office to pick up a student's research paper I'd forgotten. As I opened the door, I sensed a presence. It wasn't a person, but something that looked like a tiny insect. It was flying around my desk. My entrance startled it. First, it froze. A moment later it flew toward the ceiling and hovered there. Only then did I realize it was a drone." She shakes her head in wonderment. "It was looking at the latest results of an Operation Hercules test subject! After that, I hid all the research. When it came time to write my white paper, I deliberately left out important techniques used in the gathering of the project's true findings. I knew that when the time came for the military's actual implementation with live subjects, I'd be assigned to lead it anyway. At that point, all of these techniques would be put back in play."

"As of now, the operation has been aborted," I reply. "You'll probably get notice of this later this week."

"Maybe it's for the best. The idea of a super soldier is too tantalizing to the wrong people, for all the worst reasons." She shrugs.

"So, mind modification actually works," I murmur.

"Donna—may I call you that?—frankly, it depends on the individual. In some people, it is innate to their nature that they are bad. In others, no matter the temptations presented, they will always do the right thing. Evan's paper was right about that."

"I'd like to keep our conversation private. I hope you'll feel the same way," I implore.

She nods. "Yes, of course, certainly."

"Shelley, I know I shouldn't ask, but…does Evan have a chance to get into Berkeley?" I wince in preparation of the answer I'm afraid to hear.

"I can't make any promises. Like every other applicant, his will have to run the gauntlet of the admissions team"— she smiles—"but he certainly has my vote. We like to give a leg-up to those who are less financially advantaged."

Yikes. "Um…does that mean no?" For now, having his trust fund restored has worked against him again. He may have money, but academia sees it as tainted funds.

She looks at me strangely. "In Evan's case? Hardly! Should the selection committee see his potential as I do, I'll do what I can to line him up with a job here on campus, to help him offset his expenses."

Well, what do you know?

I'll let Evan choose the time to tell Shelley he doesn't need the job, but is honored to join Cal's student body.

My bet is it'll happen sometime next March—on the very same day he gets his acceptance letter in the mail.

And knowing Evan, he'll probably offer to fund a few scholarships too.

18

Rest in Peace

The nicest prayer you can give a dearly departed is to say, "Rest in Peace."

On the other hand, saying it to someone still living may be construed as a threat.

Should you want to follow through on it, consider this: whereas they'll end up pushing up daisies, chances are you'll end up in an orange jumpsuit doing life in the hoosegow.

Is it worth it? Of course not! Instead, wait until they die of natural causes.

Or, if you get antsy, figure out a reason to incite someone else to do the dirty deed instead.

I'VE BEEN HOME FROM BERKELEY LESS THAN A FULL DAY, AND already I can tell that things have gone back to normal.

That is, normal for the Craigs.

Trisha is no longer afraid of ghosts. But she's asked if she can remodel her room. We sit together on the couch, comparing paint samples with fabric swatches she's chosen. It'll be our last mother-daughter summer project before school starts up again. Sometimes, as parents, we tend to forget just how resilient our children can be.

Aunt Phyllis didn't disappoint, and indeed fainted from the shock of seeing me alive. When she came to, her tight hug and tears of joy were punctuated with the declaration, "Donna Craig, you'll be the death of me! Oh, well, I should have known you'd come back to haunt me."

Mary is in full-flirt mode—with Evan, even if he hasn't yet realized it. Jean-Pierre is only a means to an end.

Beside us, Jeff sits, playing video games: fantasy sports. He now abhors games with senseless violence.

Jack and Evan, on the other side of our sectional sofa, are working on their computers. Jack is writing up our mission summary, whereas Evan is tackling his college applications and essays. He's stoked, now that his trust fund has been released to him. I haven't told Evan about my conversation with Shelley. Despite her assurance that she's his ace in the hole at Berkeley, fate may lead him in a different direction. Part of humanity is having free will.

Jeff pipes up, "Hey, when does Jean-Pierre leave for San Francisco?"

"Not until tomorrow," I reply.

I'm proud of our French expat. He's purchased a used car in order to drive around the country. I hope he loves what he sees and has many wonderful experiences.

Evan perks up. "He's leaving—*tomorrow*? Good riddance! I'll start counting down the minutes."

"FYI: The more you act jealous, the more Mary likes it," Jeff counsels him.

Jack folds down the screen of his laptop. "Since I'm not going to get any work done here while you do your lovesick schoolboy routine, let me weigh in with my own two cents."

Aunt Phyllis snorts, "Oh, now, this ought to be good!"

"There will be no heckling from the peanut gallery," he warns. "Evan, Mary has very strong feelings for you, and you for her. When you started your college application process, subliminally you started the inevitable process of moving away emotionally, from her. Her way to keep close —and to gain closure—was to help you in the application process. When Jean-Pierre showed up, it gave her a reason to accept your distance, and to create distance of her own."

"Well, well, well! Listen to Dr. Jack Freud," I murmur. "Someone deserves his own radio call-in show."

Jack pulls me down into his lap. Putting a hand over my mouth and continues, "You are at a crossroads, my boy. Man up and let her know how you feel or let her go. So, which will it be?"

To Jack's dismay, Evan isn't listening. Instead, he stares out the window.

Jack turns to find the target of his stare:

Mary, and Jean-Pierre, of course—

And Mary's friend, Wendy.

The girls are giggling at some joke Jean-Pierre is making.

Evan scowls. "So, now he's coming on to her best friend? Who the heck does he think he—"

Before he can finish his sentence, the back door opens. The girls come in, still laughing. Jean-Pierre brings up the rear.

Evan is still scowling when he stands up. "Mary, we need to talk."

"I know, I know, Evan—I promised to read over your essays. Please don't be mad at me! I swear I'll get to them tonight. Besides, you need a break. I'm treating everyone to the movies." She raises a brow suggestively. "A double date, with Wendy and Jean-Pierre."

"But I don't like Wendy! I—"

Wendy chokes down a gasp. "What?...You *don't like me*? Why? What did I ever do to you, Evan Martin?"

"I didn't mean 'I don't like you.' I meant, I don't like you in *that* way—like I'd ever choose you as a girlfriend."

Evan looks from Jack to me to Jack again. In unison, we shake our heads. Nope, sorry. He got himself into this, so he can get himself out of it.

Wendy sticks out her tongue at him. "Good, because I don't like you either. But I do like Jean-Pierre, so thank you very much, Evan Martin, for making me look like a loser." She punches him in the arm. "And F-Y-I: I merely tolerate you because Mary thinks you hung the moon—*OUCH!*"

Mary has elbowed her friend in the side.

At least Evan is smiling. He grabs Mary's arm and takes her out back.

"*Oh, mon Dieu,*" Jean-Pierre murmurs.

"*Rentre chez toi, connard!*" Trisha declares proudly.

Jean-Pierre's eyes grow large before he bursts out laughing.

Jeff smacks his forehead with his palm. He grabs his little sister by the arm. As he drags her upstairs with him, Trisha pleas plaintively, "Why? What did I say?"

"Don't worry about it," Jeff shouts. "We'll get a great view of Mary and Evan from your window."

Maybe not. Evan and Mary are smart enough to walk as far as the playhouse to have their argument.

"I'm out of here," Wendy mutters.

Jean-Pierre smiles wistfully at her. "May I come with you? I don't want to be—how do you American say, *'la troisième roulette'*?...Ah yes, 'third wheel'!"

Wendy sighs dramatically. "I know what you mean. The two of them should get a room."

It's not until Jack and I turn to stare at her that she realizes what she's just said. She claps her hand over her mouth.

"Perhaps we can go to the beach?" Jean-Pierre suggests with a sly grin.

It's enough for Wendy to forget her faux pas. She bats her eyes at him. "Sure, why not?" She grabs her purse with one hand while she wraps the other around his waist. "I'll take you to El Piedra...Oh, wait! You don't mind the fact that it's a nude beach, do you?"

Jack smothers a grin as Jean-Pierre shakes his head innocently.

As for me, I'm still fixating on Wendy's revelation that my daughter and our ward should quote-unquote get a room—

And, apparently, it looks as if they've done exactly that, since they're now *in* the playhouse.

I'm just about to go there myself when Jack's cell phone rings. The way his smile disappears, I know it has to be Ryan. I know I'm right because he holds up a finger to warn me to wait. "Wait...what did you say? ...Where? ...When? ...We'll meet you at the office as soon as we can get there."

He turns to me. Sadness darkens his eyes.

"Jack…what is it?"

Instead of saying anything, he walks toward me. I am enveloped in his arms. When he sighs, I want to cry even though I don't know why.

Will my heart break when he tells me?

"They found Carl," he murmurs. "The real one. Where we left him—off Vancouver Island. Donna, We need to meet Ryan at Acme."

I drop to the floor.

It's not me who runs out to the playhouse to round up Evan and Mary, but Jack.

They follow him back toward the house. Their faces are grave, but their hands are linked in solidarity.

When she spots me, Mary runs to hug me. She then tucks my hair behind my ear, as if soothing me is the only thing important right now.

This is wrong. I should be comforting her and Jeff and Trisha.

But she isn't the one in shock—not yet, anyway.

I rise and take a deep breath. The sooner I'm done with the fresh hell awaiting me at the office, the sooner I can come home—

Hopefully, before my children's memories rise in a midst of sadness—the mere ghosts of another place, another time, another reality.

Another father.

~

RYAN IS WAITING AT THE FRONT DOOR. THE GRAY UNDER HIS eyes is etched in a patchwork of tiny wrinkles. His hand moves across his bald pate—an old habit from when there were once silver strands among the gold. I seem to remember a few of the silver. The gold strands were long before my time.

"This way," he says simply. He starts down the hall.

He has always been a man of few words. On the other hand, Jack, who has no problem spouting opinions, pithy *bon mots*, or lascivious innuendos, drove us to the office in complete silence.

I was too nervous to ask questions. I am trying to be calm. For the past couple of years, I've presumed my ex-husband is long dead. Instead, I may find him standing in front of me in shackles before heading off to some extraordinary rendition black site.

What will he say to me? What will I say to him? Somehow, "You bastard! I told you they'd finally catch up to you," doesn't seem fitting.

I guess I could say: "I've moved on. I hope you have too."

I can only hope he'd respond: "I had—until they brought me here."

And then there's the issue of our children. What do I tell them—or not? What will he demand of them?

Does he have a right to ask anything?

I may not have to worry. He may be gagged, after all.

Knowing what he thinks of me, one can only wish.

We stop in front of the door of Acme's lab.

Odd.

Oh.

No.

ALL THAT IS LEFT OF CARL IS A SLIVER OF A JAWBONE. IT HOLDS a solitary tooth. A tag notes it as NUMBER 30 MOLAR.

I hope my children don't ask for details, since, from the look of things, this is all I have.

"Where was it found?" Jack asks.

"It washed up on a beach near Neah Bay, Washington. It's located in the far northwest corner of Olympic Peninsula. A couple of hikers found it. They thought it was human, and gave it to a local sheriff. He remembered the explosion during the Lark conference, and that there had been a missing body."

"How do we really know it's him?" Even to my ears, my voice sounds puny…barely a whisper.

"Ideally, you'll give us permission to take this tooth from the jaw," replies Dawn Mortimer, one of Acme's forensic scientists.

"Why do you need it?" Jack asks. "Why not just use the jaw bone itself?"

"Believe it or not, teeth provide the best source of DNA for forensic analysis. Unlike a corpse's skin, bones, or organs, which are exposed to the elements, they are the last part of a corpse to decompose. Remember, dental pulp has its own coat of armor: first enamel, and then dentin."

Definitive proof, once and for all.

I owe that to myself, and my children. "Go for it."

She takes a pair of pliers and struggles with the tooth

before it gives way from the jaw. "There are several steps to DNA fingerprinting. Now that the tooth is extracted, I'll break it open in order to remove the pulp from the tooth. We'll then isolate the DNA for analysis. As you know, Acme keeps samples of its operatives' blood, which I'll use for comparison. It should take an hour."

Jack nods. "We'll be on the roof."

He neglects to add that Ryan will be joining us with a bottle of Crown Royal and three tumblers.

That's okay. She'll realize it soon enough when she smells it on my breath.

She has kind eyes behind her glasses. It's got to be hard straddling the world between the living and the dead.

I have a different dilemma, since I'm the one who usually puts them six feet under.

Note to self: If you want to make the body harder to identify, take along a set of pliers. That way, if you find your-self with a free hour after an extermination, you can ensure the corpse will end up in a pauper's grave and won't come back to haunt you.

Up there, Acme has a garden with a view of the ocean. Up there, the Acme family has celebrated weddings, births, and funerals.

Up there, for a moment we forget we are agents of death while we celebrate life.

Our version of a memorial service for Carl is a drinking game.

"Worst thing Carl ever did?" Ryan tosses out there. "Let

me start: What about the time he killed all of the witnesses you found that could have sent him away for life?"

"Or when he left Donna to take the rap for Jonah Breck's death," Jack answers.

"Nope. It was when he tried to blow up a stadium of kids," I declare.

"You win," Jack and Ryan say in unison as they gulp down what's left in their glasses.

Other questions have included:

Carl's worst kill. (Hands down, it was the mother of his unborn child: Jack's first wife, Valentina. Again, I win.)

Carl's worst comment. (Despite the fact that there were too many to count, the winning answer was, "Maybe you should put your head between your legs. Better yet, put it between mine. That'll make us both feel much better." To me, of course.)

Carl's worst act of vengeance. (Leaving me drugged, naked, and sunburned on a beach so that the SEAL Team 6 DevGro could find me—along with a suitcase filled with cash, making it appear as if I helped him plan his escape from Guantanamo Bay.)

You get the picture. I've won every round.

Lucky me. It's left me stone cold sober.

Ryan's phone buzzes. We are being summoned for the results.

I down my drink in one gulp and take a deep breath. I guess I'm ready.

❦

Dawn nods. "Yes, it's Carl Stone."

I am both elated and saddened.

I want to cry, and I want to laugh.

Most of all, I want to be held by Jack.

He must have this desire too because he nods politely, takes my hand, and starts for the door. Ryan stops him in order to hand him something: a small vial holding Carl's ashen remains.

It's late afternoon. We are at the beach.

The sun slants low enough that the surf glistens as the waves roll in and out. We stand at the water's edge, staring at the gauzy haze sitting over the horizon.

Jack hands me the jar of dusty gray powder—supposedly what is left of Carl, but I know better.

Carl is in Jeff's profile and his laugh. He is in Mary's deep green eyes and her will to survive at all costs. Trisha's smile is Carl's, and so is her sense of determination.

I think of the last time I saw Carl as his loving innocent wife: on the day Trisha was born. At the time, I reveled in the presumption that our future together was rock-solid; that we would share the rest of our lives together—

And our love would last as long as one of us still breathed.

I am that one.

I can't remember when I stopped loving Carl. It's been too long ago.

I can't remember the day I first realized I loved Jack. It now seems like forever.

The wind goes still. I open the jar and fling its contents out to sea, knowing full well it will wash back my way.

Memories do that, too.

Carl will never leave me alone.

At least I have Jack to protect me from his ghost.

We turn from my past and walk toward our future.

—THE END—

Next Up for Donna!

The Housewife Assassin's Terrorist TV Guide

(Book 14)

Housewife assassin Donna Stone must be more than just ready for her close-up if she's to infiltrate a television reality show in order to stop the broadcast of a live terrorist act.

Other Books by Josie Brown

The True Hollywood Lies Series

Hollywood Hunk

Hollywood Whore

The Totlandia Series

The Onesies - Book 1 (Fall)

The Onesies - Book 2 (Winter)

The Onesies - Book 3 (Spring)

The Onesies - Book 4 (Summer)

The Twosies - Book 5 (Fall)

The Twosies – Book 6 (Winter)

The Twosies - Book 7 (Spring)

The Twosies - Book 8 (Summer)

More Josie Brown Novels

The Candidate

Secret Lives of Husbands and Wives

The Baby Planner

How to Reach Josie

To write Josie, go to:
mailfromjosie@gmail.com

To find out more about Josie, or to get on her eLetter list for
book launch announcements, go to her website:
www.JosieBrown.com

You can also find her at:

www.AuthorProvocateur.com

twitter.com/JosieBrownCA

facebook.com/josiebrownauthor

pinterest.com/josiebrownca

instagram.com/josiebrownnovels

www.ingramcontent.com/pod-product-compliance
Lightning Source LLC
Chambersburg PA
CBHW071738190726
48292CB00003B/799